NOT THE

HEIR

NOT

THE

HEIR

HUDSON WARM

Copyright © 2020 by Hudson Warm

Editor: Margaret Morris, The Indie Editor

Cover Designer: Stefanie Saw, Seventh Star Art

Formatting: Enchanted Ink Publishing

ISBN: 978-1-7354098-0-1

Library of Congress Number: 2020916546

Printed in the United States of America

LEARN MORE ABOUT HUDSON AT
WWW.HUDSONWARM.COM

The Legend

rederick turned the shattered stone corner before halting his horse. Crushed remnants littered the ground and screeches of despair sounded in the distance. An archer appeared in Frederick's peripheral as his horse's hooves dislodged loose stones.

"Tobias!" he shouted, eyes darting between the enemy and his friend. "An archer is approaching, they're—"

A feathered wooden arrow flew straight by Frederick, puncturing his partner's heart before he could say another word. His warning had done nothing. Tobias let out a piercing screech, but it didn't last long.

"Tobi!" Frederick turned to face him, but it was too late. Tobias tumbled off his steed and choked on the blood that trickled from his parted lips. Everything happened so fast. Too fast.

Tobias lay in the rubble, bathing in a growing pool of crimson. The gore drenched his pale body and spread to the hooves of his horse. But before he'd embarked on the dangerous quest, Frederick had been prepared. Death was unavoidable. If that was the price he'd have to pay for a chance at the key—the key that would make any ordinary subject king—it was worth all the bloodshed.

He knew that almost every subject set out to find King

Philip's key, and nobody could. Silverkeep was in a state of chaos: lifeless bodies appeared at every turn; the hierarchy was in ruins, and Philip's son was hardly fit to rule. The kingdom had descended into anarchy after the great king's death.

Frederick couldn't save Tobi, but he could save himself. Besides, with Tobias's death, if he were to find the key, he wouldn't have to share the royalty. So he snarled at the man who'd killed his best friend and made a sharp left turn before he could be shot, too.

Frederick, like any other subject, pictured what the key could look like—gray and purple, gilded in amethyst. He liked to envision the colors of Silverkeep, but he hadn't any clue of its actual appearance, where it was, or whether it was even real. All the subjects relied on the great king's last words, the words he'd muttered on his deathbed: "*My power has been compiled, stored in a hidden key. Whoever has the virtue and intelligence to find it must take the throne, for he who can do so much will be the most fit to rule, with everything I have and more.*" King Philip's dying wish had been written down in books, etched in every subject's mind, and told far and wide.

But Frederick wouldn't find the key. In fact, nobody would—not for a while, anyway. The subject would give up a few months later, preferring failure over the callous death many subjects had suffered. Frederick Turner wrote a book detailing his journey—a book that would remain in the royal Silverkeep library for centuries to come.

And heirs remained those of the bloodline.

King Philip's last words were never forgotten but became more fable than truth. The mysterious tale was passed on through generations. Philip was remembered with great honor and respect, but the people began to assume that he'd been in another place when he'd spoken his final thoughts—a fantasy. That perhaps he wasn't thinking straight as he neared his death. And over centuries of seeking and no finding, the Legend of the Key became just that—a legend—and nothing more.

I

CENTURIES LATER . . .

ashed vegetables sat on Basil's china plate. It was the same nightly fare, but a different color and form. He stared in contempt, forking around the puree.

"Basil," the queen spat, "What's wrong with you? For goodness' sake, eat already." But he was used to his mother's rebukes.

"*Eat already,*" Basil mocked, exaggerating her facial expressions and pitchy tone. His eighteenth birthday was approaching, but the prince had the taste buds of an infant. The castle's eclectic cuisine seldom seemed to appease him.

Splat. As he prepared his mouth for the insipid paste, a beige glop hit Basil's cheek. Caught off guard, he shifted his glance to Regis V. Basil's brother chuckled from across the mahogany table, but it was hardly playful. The urge to seek revenge on his twin was impossible to resist. Basil spooned a bit of the mysterious mush and closed one eye to aim.

"Boys!" the queen yelled, punching her fork to the table. "I am appalled." She looked to her husband for support. "Regis, your help?"

"Yes, boys, listen to——" The king turned mute, choking on his words. He couldn't speak or even move, and his ivory skin began to pale. *Ping.* His spoon chimed as it collided with the marble floor. This had never happened before.

"Regis!" Bridget screamed. Her husband's name seemed to be the only word she could manage as she repeated it over and over.

His face turned purple as he attempted concise gasps for air. Hadwin Timbers, a stubby, gray-bearded man and the advisor to the king, could usually offer a helping hand, but even he was unsure.

The twins and Regis V's fiancée exchanged nervous glances, unsure of what to do. Clearly, the king and queen were incapable of controlling the situation. Basil's mother was bred to wear finery and be waited upon, and his father was . . . falling out of his chair and onto the ground. "Doctor! Doctor!" the adolescent brothers cried in unison. They watched the cooking servants sprint toward the chamber of medics.

Within moments, doctors circled the king, inserting needles and experimenting with their abundant tools. Basil watched from his seat at the dinner table, mouth fallen open. Regis's eyes bulged from his sockets while Basil was his antithesis, his lids rapidly blinking. Bridget finally stood from her velvet seat and scurried to her husband's side. Tears soaked her cheeks, and her whole body contracted.

Indistinct murmurs spread throughout the small bunch of medics. All at once, they looked up at Bridget with sorry eyes. Regis IV no longer had a heartbeat, and his body lay sprawled on the floor, tinted purple. "Your Majesty, he is . . ." The lead doctor didn't want to break the news. But Basil knew.

He's dead.

"No! Impossible, he can't be . . . he can't . . ." Bridget rested her head on Regis IV's stomach and filled the room with muffled cries. Tears and running eye makeup dampened Regis's tunic. The end of his life meant the end to her world.

Hadwin stroked her back uncomfortably, clearly attempting to remain within the fine line that existed between comforting Bridget and making an inappropriate pass at her. He, too, was speechless, but he was not the sort of man who would make the king's death about him. So Hadwin visibly held in his tears as he moved his hand from Bridget's back to touch his own gray wisps.

Father is . . . gone.

Basil's shoulders quaked, and his lips quivered. The boy never cried, but this was an exception. He walked toward his brother; perhaps their hate could be forgotten just this once because of the circumstance. But as he turned to Regis V, the heir to the throne, Basil saw a sly, fleeting smile stretch across his face. In a matter of milliseconds, it was replaced with tears. Basil knew, though, that it wasn't his imagination.

The dust had settled when the lead doctor approached the teenagers. Bridget, Regis IV, and most of the doctors were still in the dining room, but the twins and Lydia Rose had relocated to the solar.

"A pulmonary embolism," the doctor said. But Basil didn't understand how such a thing could slip past the finest minds in medicine; his father's health had been monitored so closely. "There was blood clotting wedged in the lungs, which blocked the flow of blood. You see, this raised the pressure, working the heart so hard that his body simply couldn't keep up. There was no way to anticipate it. I'm so sorry, Your Royal Highnesses."

Basil struggled to keep his composure. Tears spilled from his eyes as he nodded to the doctor. But Lydia Rose and Regis V didn't seem very distraught.

"We should've tracked his physical activity—the lack of it was the root of the sudden embolism."

"That's all right. I trust you did your best." Regis V was oddly forgiving.

Lydia sat on his lap as Regis stroked her blond tresses. From the adjacent velvet sofa, Basil heard them whisper blissfully back and forth, but the words were inaudible.

Father is gone. How are you just fine?

Basil's jaw clenched, emphasizing his piercing bone structure, so sharp, it could have cut like a knife.

The lifeless body of Regis Avington IV lay in a gilded open casket. Embraced in soft velvet, he looked comfortable, a satisfied smile on his face. The king died far too young, but his life had been fulfilling; Regis IV experienced love, luxury, and power—more than most men ever did.

"Regis Avington the fourth was not only an excellent leader, but also a loving father. He should have ruled for many more years, advancing his reforms and maintaining order in Silverkeep. I am honored to carry out his name and legacy though it's an impossible task," Regis V announced to the subjects as he stood behind a silver podium. Tears began to escape his eyelids, but there was a glimmer of excitement behind his sorrowful facade; becoming king was nothing to cry about.

Because it hadn't been anticipated, Basil's brother barely

had time to prepare for his reign. At only seventeen years of age, he had been expecting to enjoy much more time as a prince, admiring his father's duties from afar. He'd barely scratched the surface of ancient texts and ruling codes.

Basil Avington struggled to stare at his brother with anything more than envy and hatred. He fought against the urge to bare his teeth. His brother spoke of the death with a tone as if it were any other trivial matter.

"He will always watch us from above," Regis V added, his voice bellowing through the clustered auditorium. Dusk was an unusual time for a funeral, but the ceremony was last minute. Silverkeep's subjects were eager to attend and see the king's body one last time in the open casket, but only a small percentage of Silverkeep could fit.

If things were different, Basil would have been the one behind the podium, alerting the royal subjects. But because of the seven minutes separating the twins' births, Regis V took the throne, his father's name, and the respect of the kingdom.

Basil knew the queen couldn't bear to speak; the death was too fresh. Not only was her husband dead, it wouldn't be long before her son held more power than she did. Regis V had an ego large enough to distribute among the land, and it would only expand when he took the throne.

After Regis concluded his speech, Hadwin embraced him beside the podium. "I-I will be t-taking the throne temporarily until the f-fifth Regis is of age," he stammered. Hadwin Timbers wasn't good with public speaking; his only experience was behind the scenes, advising the king and helping him make decisions. However, Regis V still had a few weeks before he turned eighteen—the legal age to commence his rule. The meticulous Hadwin was the first person the royal family could think of; he knew almost everything the king did. Hadwin came from a long line of advisors that had helped restore order after the chaos of post-Philip Silverkeep. The man dined with the royals, spent leisure time with the royals—he might as well have been part of the family. But of course, blood ran thicker, so once Regis V turned eighteen, he would become king.

And then there was Basil, often neglected by his own family, viewed as the unlucky prince. The twins had the same muscular build and porcelain face, taking Bridget's straight nose and chiseled bone structure and Regis IV's pouty lips. Their only distinguishing characteristic was eye color, but soon it would be the crown. Regis V's eyes were a sunken brown, while Basil's resembled shiny emeralds, possessing a closeted jealousy that Regis lacked. Looking at the two asleep side by side, the brothers would look the same. But a situation like this hadn't occurred since they were children; the two were always squabbling, seldom content with each other.

There was a lot Basil wanted to say at his father's funeral, but who would grant the chance to the lousy prince when there was only so much time to spare? Bridget decided to let her elder son speak for the whole of it. The seven minutes that separated the births of Regis V and Basil Avington were everything—to the boys and to the kingdom.

The claps of the royal subjects resounded through the auditorium. Basil was thankful for the three weeks before Regis V would turn eighteen; it postponed the exclamations and "All hail the kings" for just a bit longer. Basil knew that when the time came, Regis V would take advantage of the power he had over his seven-minutes-younger twin.

The orchestra played the original Silverkeep symphony, a song that was, in Basil's opinion, much too jolly; incongruous with the occasion. It had been Regis IV's favorite, though.

"And now, I will be honoring my father by reading aloud his original poem. He often read it to me, but never had the chance to share it with the kingdom," Regis V announced. "He would want his noble subjects to hear it." Basil felt a sting of jealousy yet again; Regis IV had never shared the words with *him*.

"My heart and soul is Silverkeep,
never leading ye astray.
As I sit atop my throne, I work hard
each passing day.
My heart and soul is Silverkeep, as
the rivers ebb and flow
My royal subjects feel my love, and
they shall always know
That my heart and soul is Silverkeep,
so reach out my friend.
I won't abandon the throne until my
life has reached its end."

Regis V's tone shifted when he read the last line aloud; his father had written about the end of his life as if it had been so distant, yet it had come abruptly.

"And now, we shall silently pray for the dedicated father, the virtuous king, the loyal husband—Regis Avington the fourth—to live a blessed eternity," he added. There was a moment of reverent silence, and rather than mourning his father's death, Basil found himself enjoying the short time during which he didn't have to listen to Regis V's maddening voice. In this moment, everyone was equal, even the subjects—just praying for the great king's afterlife.

Their relationship was blurry—the two brothers naturally shared an eternal bond; it was impossible for *only* hate to stand between them. But they didn't quite get along—at least not these past few years.

"Your prayers are greatly appreciated, my fellow subjects. And worry not, for you are in good hands!"

The people of Silverkeep filed out of the royal auditorium, tears lining some of their cheeks. Regis Avington IV had been a great king, often recognized as the best since Philip. He was sincere and dignified, at least in the eyes of his subjects.

Once the chandeliered auditorium was empty save for the

royal family, they shared a few words. "Thank you, Regis. Your father would be proud," Bridget said before kissing her elder son on the forehead.

"I appreciate that, Mother." He bowed his head solemnly.

Bridget had tried to keep her composure in front of the subjects, but now that they were gone, she let out abundant tears. Her dark hair was curled tightly into a bun, but she removed her tiara and let the waves go.

"He would be excited for you to have it," she said between hiccups, gesturing to the king's crown. Not one glance was thrown Basil's way.

Regis IV's body was pale, his lips slightly parted. Bridget's hands trembled as they neared the face of her lifeless husband. Her fingertips lingered on his plump lips as she trailed his features and stubble, her long brunette locks draping over her shoulders to tickle his chin. She seemed resistant to move her hands to his crown, but she had to. The diadem was heavy, but she managed to pick it up off his head. Regis IV looked different without his crown—he was like any other commoner.

Regis V extended his arms, reaching for the crown. Lydia Rose stood, excited to be queen, by his side. But Bridget pulled it back. "Not yet, Regis. You must wait until the coronation. Until then, Hadwin is in charge," she said, passing it to Hadwin.

But he flinched. "I can't wear that."

"Very well, but take good care of it for Regis."

Hadwin nodded. He was too modest to accept something so grand—likely the only one who would refuse such an offer. "I will, Your Majesty." His courtesy was ironic, considering he was in power, even if it was only temporary.

Basil glanced at Regis V happily standing with Lydia Rose. He stole everything from him, even his first love. The most baffling part of Basil's envy was that he kept it to himself. Not once did he ever state or imply how he felt. But he was brooding on it in this moment, and for that reason, he had to exit the room.

Silently, Basil slipped through the back entrance of the auditorium and escaped into the empty corridor.

Noticing her son's absence moments after his exit, Bridget yelled, "Basil!" as if this wasn't what she needed; her loss was enough.

But he didn't respond. In fact, Basil didn't care; he began to walk faster through the halls when he heard his mother's distant call.

Everything that Basil used to admire in the castle corridors got on his nerves. The paintings of previous kings with the same, ancient crown atop their made-up faces, illustrated by the finest artists of Silverkeep, especially bothered him; he would never be one. In a century or two, his selfish older twin would be on that wall, remembered with great respect. Sure, people might know Basil's name, but his relation to Regis V was all he'd be remembered for.

After Bridget called his name once, she didn't care enough to follow up. Hadwin, on the other hand, wouldn't let him off the hook. The prince slowed his pace when he heard footsteps and turned around to find Hadwin emerging from the shadows.

"What is this behavior, Basil?" he scolded. Hadwin held the crown sturdily in both his hands, careful not to drop it.

Basil shrugged, unsure of what to say.

"Your Royal Highness, Regis the fourth is dead. Would he want to be remembered with this . . . immaturity? This truly isn't about *you* or your *place* in this family."

Nobody understood Basil, not even the wisest man in the castle. Hadwin would never speak to Regis V that way; he would call him *Majesty* instead of *Highness* and would never dare say he was immature. But Hadwin was the king for the time being, more powerful than Basil would ever be.

Basil didn't want to be seen as weak, so he refused to admit his jealousy of Regis V. He'd take *immature* over *envious* any day. "You're right," he responded. "My apologies, Hadwin."

"No, I'm sorry. He was *your* father." At Basil's blank gaze,

Hadwin said, "But that's not what's rattling you, now, is it?"

Basil nodded his head, hiding his deeper pain, and lied to Hadwin's face. "Of course it is. People grieve differently."

"Well then, Basil, return to the auditorium. Your mother needs all the support she can get." But Basil knew that was a bunch of nonsense; Bridget barely bothered to acknowledge her younger son, let alone 'need his support.'

"Very well." Basil took a few deep breaths and turned directions.

After a few moments of synchronized footsteps, Hadwin said, "We all admire the sacrifices you've made for the good of the kingdom."

"Thank you," Basil answered. But both of them knew it wasn't his choice. If he had the option, he would still be with Lydia Rose. However, it had been impossible to refuse a command from his father.

Basil couldn't reflect on their relationship without being filled with fury. Day by day, he was forced to watch Lydia Rose stand beside Regis V. It was almost as if she'd forgotten Basil existed. Even if she was doing it to protect them both from more pain, it hurt all the same.

If he ever were to vocalize his agony, Basil would be called *petty* or *immature* by Bridget, Regis V, or his father. Now his father was gone, and there was one less person to scold him, but it didn't feel good, not at all.

Regis V would get anything he wanted simply because of those seven minutes. *Seven* damn minutes. Things hadn't always been awful, though. There was a time—ages ago—when the twins were inseparable. But growing up, as they were forced to face the harsh realities of the world, their bond was strained to the point of snapping. Still, there were rare instances in which the brothers got along. *Rare* instances.

Basil and Hadwin walked back to the auditorium. When they entered, Bridget didn't even acknowledge Basil's presence. She sat atop her throne, biting her fingernails. Red splotches covered her face, but they slowly faded as if she'd resolved to be strong for Silverkeep.

"Hadwin," she said, her voice broken yet solemn. "Though it will only be a few weeks, a lot can happen in a short time span."

"Of course, Your Majesty."

"Well, I will handle the duty of public speaking for the time being. The choices, laws, declarations—just do what Regis would have. And lead the council meetings," she added, her effort to keep her voice from breaking obvious.

"Of course, Your Majesty," Hadwin repeated.

Bridget turned her gaze to Regis V. "Good. Regis, you must never leave his side for these next few weeks. You have much to learn. Observe him."

"Yes, Mother."

Basil was neglected yet again. He would have to get used to the treatment; soon Regis V would be king. And Lydia Rose would be queen, ruling by his side.

Basil wasn't sure of his feelings toward Lydia Rose. Hatred? Sorrow? Love? He didn't find it fair that, after everything, she'd become queen while he remained a mere prince. She must've felt at least a bit of guilt, flaunting her happiness with Regis in Basil's face. But no matter how upset he was with the situation and how she handled it, there were still feelings, at least on his side. He couldn't simply stop thinking about her on demand; he'd tried that and failed. And her constant presence didn't make it easier.

"You should learn also, Lydia Rose. Watch closely," Bridget said.

Lydia Rose nodded in obedience. "Gladly, Your Majesty."

It was as if Basil were invisible—he might as well have walked to his chamber; the conversation would be the same, excluding him altogether.

"Well, you are dismissed. My sons and Lydia, to your chambers," Bridget ordered. "Hadwin, it's best you get comfortable on your new throne."

Basil allowed Lydia Rose and his brother to leave first, solely to avoid walking with them. However, Bridget seemed to want the room and would not tolerate even that small slice of delay. "Basil, I said to the chambers."

He nodded and turned out of the auditorium. Basil plodded in his brother's shadow—literally—and watched him giggle with Lydia Rose. The bottom of her black funeral dress trailed behind, ending only inches in front of Basil's feet. Regis and Lydia were excited about becoming king and queen even though Regis IV had just died. They fumbled with each other's hands before disappearing around the corner.

Basil was glad he didn't have to look at them anymore as he entered his bedroom. He let his body flop onto the bed. Sure, his room was grand and beautiful, but what did it matter if he shared it with only himself? He'd been proud of his riches when they satisfied Lydia Rose. Now, no degree of wealth would cure Basil's loneliness.

His room wasn't far from his twin's. Through the walls, his ears were often cursed with the sounds of Lydia Rose and Regis together. In this event, he would exit his room and head to a place far enough away to find silence. But when it was night, and he had to stay in his sleeping chamber, Basil would call in the orchestra to play him a loud lullaby, shielding the noises with sonatas and trills of violin and cello.

This night was tolerable; the castle was silent. Unfortunately, the quiet allowed Basil's mind to wander. What would the rest of his life entail now that adulthood was approaching—now that Regis IV was dead? Would he simply watch his brother thrive while he was tossed aside? It wasn't fair; nothing made Regis V more qualified than him. But of course, nothing was fair. And Basil was too smart to give up so easily.

ONE YEAR PRIOR

Basil first set his eyes on Lydia Rose during the dinner celebration of the union of kingdoms when Silverkeep was hosting. Authorities from the kingdoms of Lundbridge, Glardosia, Thuzebet, and Nilahar gathered at Silverkeep's castle that night.

She was wearing an emerald-green dress that brought out her eyes—the same eyes Basil had. Seeing the feature they shared, he was sure she was his destiny. She turned back to the table, showing only her wavy blond hair, and Basil needed more than that fleeting glimpse.

At the time, Basil's life was perfect. He was a privileged boy who lived in luxury. There was no need to think about his place in the family, his brother . . . anything bad. Their eyes met, and Basil's stomach flipped. He stood from his seat and made his way toward her table—the Lundbridge seating.

"Hello . . . Your Majesty of Lundbridge," Basil greeted the eldest man at the table, incredibly embarrassed that he didn't know the king's name.

"Derek, Derek Searle the second. And this is my daughter, Lydia Rose," he said. The man's blond hair reached his shoulders.

Basil smiled and reached out his hand. "Basil Avington, Prince of Silverkeep." As they shook hands, it was apparent in Derek's eyes that he was curious whether Basil was an heir, but it would have been impolite to ask.

Basil turned his gaze to Lydia Rose. "I'm pleased to meet you," he said, his etiquette lessons in mind. Basil wasn't used to talking to royalty from other kingdoms, much less royalty he was so attracted to.

"The pleasure's all mine," she said.

Basil bent down to kiss her hand, making Lydia's cheeks blush.

"Would you like to go on a walk?" he asked.

Derek encouraged his daughter to accompany Basil, and she agreed without objection; she was happy to.

As they strolled through the halls that Basil knew so well, the princess took in each and every corner slowly. Her perspective was interesting to Basil—so unknowing and naive. They spent the rest of the celebration walking together, sharing stories of the kingdoms, confiding in each other. He spoke about his innermost feelings, including his envy of Regis V. Lydia told him about her mother's death and the difficulties of growing up without one. Basil wasn't used to being understood, and he loved the feeling.

After the celebration, they wrote to each other, saying in their letters words they'd never admit to anybody else. After the one evening they'd spent together, they missed each other so much that Basil brought up the matter with his father. For once, Regis IV was happy for him. It wasn't much later that Derek visited the castle of Silverkeep with his daughter.

The two were too young to marry, but the kings agreed to let Lydia Rose live in the castle of Silverkeep until they could. Basil and Lydia Rose were overjoyed at the chance to spend every day together, especially after months of communicating only through letters.

At the time, Basil was sixteen. The times he spent with Lydia Rose were the happiest months of his life. He studied, dined, and slept beside her. On the weekends, the two would adventure on horseback and compete in archery. Everything in

Basil's life was perfect. In fact, he was all right remaining prince for all of his life so long as he had his love by his side.

But Regis V saw his happiness and wanted it for himself. Basil noticed his brother's eyes lingering on Lydia Rose's facial expressions, noticed him laughing at her jokes . . . being *extra* kind. Basil had almost a year of happiness before Regis V stole her, everything.

Ominous clouds gathered in the sky, and Derek was back in Silverkeep for the first time since he'd dropped off Lydia Rose. Basil assumed he was there to visit, but his conflicted expression in the throne room said otherwise. He stood before Regis IV, the two conversing.

Basil had come to ask his father a simple question regarding the next ceremony. He'd been getting along with Regis IV; they'd recently bonded on a horseback outing—a rare occurrence. But today, Basil was greeted with two sorry expressions.

"Ah, the timing. Well, here he is," Regis IV said, looking to Derek before Basil could get any words out. "Son, it has come to Derek's attention that you are not the heir to the throne. You see, this would not be the future he wishes for his daughter."

"I'm not sure what you mean."

Derek clarified, "Lydia Rose must be Queen," with emphasis.

Regis IV nodded and said, "That would mean that Lydia Rose must be wed to the heir." Basil began to understand where he was going and cringed. "The fifth Regis."

The room spun around Basil. Baffled by the cruelty, he said, "But, Lydia Rose and I are in *love*. Regis doesn't even know her, he doesn't—"

"Affairs of the heart don't matter in the eyes of the king-dom. I'm glad you understand," his father said. But he *didn't* understand. He never would.

Soon, Lydia was brought into the throne room, and her father explained the situation. She was in tears, and Basil couldn't understand how she ever forgave her father. Lydia Rose let her father embrace her and wipe away her teardrops. Basil didn't want to admit to himself that perhaps Lydia Rose agreed this was best.

"They look the same, dear," Derek whispered to Lydia in an effort to comfort her.

And that day, Basil stormed out of the room, seething with spite toward his family and a cruel realization about the unjust world that would never fade.

II

adwin proved himself to be worthy of the throne. After all, even during Regis IV's reign, he'd often handled matters behind the scenes. If it were based on merit, Hadwin could have had the position for life as long as public speaking wasn't involved. Regis V followed his every move, day and night. He began to annoy Hadwin with his pestering questions and firm viewpoints.

When it came to decision-making, Hadwin had far more experience than his young counterpart. There was a request for a new military protection law, and the two could not agree. Regis seemed to forget that he was there to *watch*.

In his abundant spare time, Basil would listen in on their conversations from the doorway of the throne room.

"They want a higher budget on artillery," Hadwin said one day. "We can definitely spare this expense. So, when a choice like this comes along, remember that these requests are important. Do not neglect them, you see——"

"Why would we give them more money? They have so much already. We should spend that extra on something important, like that dress Lydia Rose wants for the coronation," Regis V answered, sniffing obnoxiously.

Basil could see that it took everything Hadwin had not to roll his eyes. "She can still get the dress, Regis. There's plenty to go around."

And this is the man—the boy—to be king?

Hadwin's coronation was nothing more than his few words at the funeral. However, Regis V's began weeks in advance of the official ceremony. Dinner parties and dancing balls celebrated the commence of his rule. Basil regarded these activities as absurd and seldom took part. He'd only attend the events at which his presence was demanded.

Basil did *not* have fun at the second dinner party, especially when it consisted of watching his mother ramble on about her better son. It was similar to the union dinners, when the five kingdoms would come together to symbolize unity and peace. These types of events were difficult for Basil; they reminded him of the first time he'd met Lydia Rose. But as he watched her on this night, her eyes said she wasn't thinking about their past.

An array of circular tables filled the second royal dining hall. This room was nearly four times the size of the Avingtons' normal dining room, full of ornate grandeur. In the middle of each marble table stood a charming centerpiece: gold-tipped flowers crawling out of vases. Looking around, Basil admired the diversity of the royals. Complexions darkened the farther each kingdom was to the south, Thuzebet the farthest.

Derek was back in Silverkeep, and he spent the evening

chatting with his daughter and Regis. He ended up seated at the Silverkeep table, not the Lundbridge one. Though Basil watched it all before his eyes, it was as if the poor prince wasn't there. Besides a quick handshake, Derek barely spoke to him. And Basil was reminded just how superficial the system seemed to be.

Basil's seat was in direct view of an annoyingly happy Regis V and Lydia Rose. Fingers intertwined, their eyes danced as they seemed to share some private joke.

Is that spark in her eyes genuine?

The room probably cost more than an average subject's lifelong earnings. Diamond chandeliers lined the ceiling, and imagery was painted along the walls. The chairs were gilded, yet comfortable; a velvet cushion sat atop each one.

Before the dinner began, Bridget stood to share a few words with the guests. She wore a light blue dress, subtle and modest. Though the death of Regis IV was still very fresh, Basil noticed the bit of excitement stirring up inside of Bridget for her son. She would still remain queen, but there would be another one, too. She could handle everything to do with intelligence, while Lydia Rose would be the symbol of Silverkeep's beauty.

"Thank you, all the great kingdoms, for joining Silverkeep on this special night," she said. Basil didn't understand what was so special about it; events like this had occurred consecutively for the past week. He sipped his champagne.

"We have mourned the death of Regis Avington the fourth, but the new beginnings that come with this have not been celebrated enough. We will always remember the great king in our hearts. In a few weeks, Regis the fifth will take his position." Her words sent a chill down Basil's spine. The boy gulped down the rest of his chalice to distract himself. "But first, I would like to acknowledge the fine work of Hadwin Timbers these past few days as regent." Applause reverberated through the dining hall, and when Bridget gestured with a pinch of the hands, the crowd was silent again.

Bridget continued, "So, please raise your glasses for the success of Silverkeep as well as all of your fine kingdoms. The fifth Regis will be a great king! And of course, there will be more on that, but for now, I won't suspend your hunger any longer. My fine servants will be bringing filet de boeuf to each of your tables."

Bridget knew that the other kingdoms weren't very concerned with the succession; they were simply there for a dinner party. Each kingdom had its own matters to worry about.

Basil was surprised when he tasted the beef filet; it was nearly too delicious. He suspected the fine meal would pair well with his champagne, but his chalice was finished. Basil refilled the sparkling wine without further thought. It was difficult for him to eat like a proper prince, but he resisted the desire to scarf down the filet.

"Lydia Rose, I'm envious. Do they feed you like this every day?" Derek asked.

Lydia laughed. "It's quite good, isn't it?"

"The chefs are masters," Bridget said. "Hadwin actually helped a few years ago, coming up with an extravagant process to select the perfect cooks."

"Well, I might have to move in," Derek said, running his finger along the rim of his chalice. "There's an empty spot, isn't there?"

Though it was only a lousy attempt at humor, Bridget's expression turned stern. Her lips pursed, and she looked back down at her plate, spurning the gourmet dish. Basil could practically hear her wondering how somebody dared turn her husband's death into a laughing matter. "Excuse me," she said before throwing her napkin on the chair and exiting the room.

Basil knew how such a statement would affect his mother, and for that reason, was interested. He guzzled some more champagne and thought about how he and his mother could have a secret nemesis in common.

It was never a good idea to get into an argument with a monarch of another kingdom; a conflict of interest could quickly turn into a potential war. Bridget was smart enough to know that Derek's ignorance wasn't a reasonable cause for wasted lives.

When she left the dining hall, the entire room watched as her heels clinked against the floor. Basil understood that his mother didn't want to change her public image, or put a new headline in the papers—"Queen Exits Her Own Banquet in a Fit of Rage"—so she took a minute in the hallway to gather herself.

It wasn't long after her exit that Hadwin followed.

"Ooh," Basil murmured, laughing. Regis V shot him a filthy glare. Basil refilled his champagne a third time . . . or was it the fourth? Well, it seemed he'd lost count. But he liked the way the room would spin—the way his sense of balance would vanish. He could barely talk without slurring his words, but it hardly mattered; nobody wished to hear his voice.

A few minutes later, Hadwin and Bridget entered the dining hall in silence, and the entire room hushed. People liked to assume things when they weren't sure, thus, rumors were always spreading.

"I needed some fresh air. My apologies!" Bridget announced, wearing her calm facade.

When she sat back down at the table, Derek forced himself to apologize. "That was uncalled for, I'm sorry, Your Majesty."

"I appreciate that."

And the squabble was over before it could start because Bridget had experience dealing with situations like this one.

The rest of the dinner was fabulous. The filet was followed by a small salad and then little pastries. Basil couldn't stop drinking champagne or eating, even when he thought he was full. There were so many different desserts; he felt guilty to miss one.

Everyone was invited to sleep over in the various guest rooms of the castle, but only some did. Lundbridge was the farthest kingdom north of Silverkeep, so Derek decided to stay. Bridget gave him the smallest guest room out of sheer pettiness. Of course, even this room was quite grand.

After the representatives from surrounding kingdoms were dismissed, the Silverkeep royals were the last left in the dining hall. The family was small; Basil had never even known his grandparents. Bridget was fatigued, so she went straight to her chamber. Basil did pity his mother; she would have to lie in her empty bed again that night, nobody by her side.

Hadwin left soon after her, leaving only the twins and Lydia Rose in the dining hall. They shared awkward eye contact, and Basil brought his champagne with him to the hallways, sipping it little by little as he reeled to his chamber, lost in a drunken stupor. He lost count of how much he'd consumed that night.

Regis V and Lydia followed close behind. They were whispering to each other, but Basil could hear. "*King Regis Avington the fifth.* It sounds perfect. I'll be even better than my father," Regis said.

The buzz was getting to Basil, and he started to wobble. He could hardly walk in a straight line.

"Queen Lydia Rose. How regal!" Lydia responded with a giggle.

"You'll be the most beautiful queen." Basil was sure that his brother was gazing at her beauty as he said it.

"And you, the most handsome king."

Basil was utterly disgusted with their conversation. He ignored the fact that Lydia Rose was calling him handsome (because the twins were identical) and thought only about how his brother compared himself to Regis IV.

The last straw was when he heard their lips, smacking messily against each other's. Surely, they knew Basil was in front of them. Was their public affection purposeful? To bother him?

Basil began to put a pep in his drunken step, but it didn't work out very well. He found himself leaning on the walls, and he certainly didn't want to appear weak in front of his brother and Lydia.

After a derisive chuckle, Regis V called out, "Brother? Are you all right?"

Basil's intoxicated voice was slow. "Shut up, Regis. Don't act like you give a—"

"Basil! What did you do? How much did you drink?"

At this point, he laughed. It was funny how clueless Regis pretended to be. "What did *I* do? Brother . . . oh, brother."

It was the first speaking interaction the twins had had since Regis IV's death. As children, they used to be best friends, always playing together, switching spots for fun to see whether anyone noticed. They would paint each other and, when they got older, practice fencing. But as soon as their youth expired, everything changed. The boys began to see the world for what it was—superficial and unfair. These things were positives in Regis's eyes but negatives in Basil's. When Regis stole Lydia Rose, Basil promised himself that Regis V deserved none of his respect.

Basil knew that Regis V hadn't *chosen* to be king. He hadn't *chosen* to have a twin who was seven minutes younger than he was. The occurrences had happened as they did, and nothing could've been done to stop them. However, even if he *hadn't* chosen to steal his brother's first love, he welcomed the opportunity with open arms. Regis never stood up for Basil.

"My goodness, how much champagne did you *have?*" Lydia joined in.

Basil shrugged.

"Go get a good night's sleep, brother. Remember, we have a celebratory breakfast tomorrow. Be there at nine o'clock sharp."

Basil didn't see a point in calling the meals celebratory when they happened every day, but he was too lazy to say so.

"You're not my father, for goodness' sake," he said, goaded by his brother's arrogance.

"I know that, Basil. I'm simply your older brother, just trying to help you," Regis V responded, pity in his tone. Just hearing his voice was enough to make Basil's skin crawl.

"You're not going to replace Father, Regis! Get over yourself." Basil intended to yell, but it came out as a soft disconnect of words. "And it was seven minutes. We're *twins*, Regis."

"Twins, but I still get the throne. And you don't." Regis V let out a cackle, almost evil.

Basil's muscles tensed, and his fists clenched. He was embarrassed to be seen as he was in front of Lydia Rose: disheveled, angry, and drunk. It didn't stop him from throwing a punch. *Thwack.* Basil watched his fist collide with his brother's cheek in slow motion, sending an epic rush of adrenaline through his veins.

"You're not better than me," was all Basil's intoxicated mind could string together. Regis's cheek had looked so juicy, too perfectly plump to let be. Obviously in pain, Regis let his head drop to the side, covering the red handprint with his own palm.

"He's intoxicated—he doesn't mean it, Regis. Don't do anything," Lydia Rose advised.

Regis nodded. "I know. I'm not stupid."

"I wasn't saying you were—I was just saying . . ." Lydia's voice faded as Basil sauntered to his room before he could say or do anything else he'd regret.

The best and possibly only good thing about Basil's wealth was his four-poster bed, complete with a canopy and white drapes. The sheets were so comfortable that it was difficult for him to lie in bed *without* dozing off. But this night was different, and for some reason, he couldn't put his onslaught of thoughts to rest.

Everything spiraled around in his brain at a greater pace because of all the alcohol in his system. He hadn't suspected champagne would make him like this. Basil thought back to the punch and questioned himself. The most baffling part was that he felt no remorse; his actions were justified—at least to his belief.

There were so few weeks left before Regis V would become king. Basil hated thinking about it, but eventually, he'd have to. He'd have to watch his father's crown be placed atop his brother's unworthy head.

Minutes of tossing and turning passed, and then hours. He turned around every so often to check the ticking clock, and soon it was half past two. Basil furrowed his brows; he'd thought alcohol would help one fall into slumber. He felt almost completely sobered up and stood from his bed.

Perhaps a stroll along the palace halls would soothe him; it would be a change of scenery. His vision slowly coming into focus, Basil reached for the torch by his bedside and made for the door. The halls were dark, but his small torch lit up the night. Everything looked more beautiful this way, illuminated by the flame. He approached a vacant silver corner and let his body slide to the floor. It was peculiar that, on this night, he got more comfort from a marbled floor than a soft bed. Basil enjoyed sitting there and just forgetting.

But he couldn't when he began to hear footsteps nearing. They were soft but concise as if she was scared. Without even seeing her face, Basil knew who it was. She turned the corner, clad in a plush nightgown, and was startled by his presence.

"Basil?" she asked, unsure.

His torch illuminated his features. "What are you doing? We're supposed to be in chambers."

"I could ask you the same question."

"Fair enough, but I asked first."

Lydia Rose sighed and seemed to debate what to say. "I'm restless."

"Me, too." There was an awkward tension between the two ex-lovers. Lydia stood in place as if daring to move would cause harm. "So why didn't you discuss it with Regis V?" Basil said his brother's name in disgust, and to his surprise, she laughed. "He would be upset if he saw his queen with . . . yours truly," he added.

"Oh, hush. I didn't know you would be here," Lydia responded. "Earlier tonight, that was quite a punch."

Basil was surprised she wasn't scolding him or taking Regis's side. Of course, the two had been in rooms together since their relationship was halted, but they never had true conversations. Everything felt more intimate past midnight. "I wasn't in my right mind. But don't get me wrong—I certainly don't regret it."

Lydia Rose let herself sink down the wall across from Basil—the first movement she'd managed. For the sake of his gentlemanly standards, he stood up, knowing it was against every rule for them to be there together, alone. To his surprise, she opposed it. "Basil, it's all right."

What's all right?

Basil returned to the corner and slid down the wall, this time next to Lydia. For this split second in time, it felt as if things had never changed. They were in the same corridor they'd strolled through the night they met.

What I'd do to go back.

He cherished the moment, refusing to acknowledge the truth.

The minutes passed, and the conversation between them flowed freely. They spoke of Regis IV's death and how she missed Lundbridge. Lydia Rose said those were things she would never speak about with Regis V. And then reality hit Basil.

"Are you happy?" he asked.

She hesitated. "I have to be." But Basil knew that her constant giggles and such couldn't be fake. Perhaps she was saying so out of courtesy.

Basil swallowed. "Do you miss me?"

She looks uncomfortable. Are my questions too provocative?

Though Lydia Rose wouldn't have dared say so aloud, she closed her eyes and nodded once, slowly. The question had evoked something in her, causing her eyes to water when they opened.

Basil knew it was wrong, but it was three in the morning; surely nobody could be lurking about the halls at that hour. He turned to face her and slipped his hand in her hair. She looked different without makeup, but beautiful nonetheless.

Should I just . . .

His face neared hers, and he felt a tug at his hand just as fast. She pulled her hair from his grip and stood up. "I can't," Lydia whispered before scurrying off.

"Wait, Lyd—" But she was off, and Basil wouldn't raise his voice above a whisper; he didn't want to wake the palace.

He was alone yet again, left to stare at the dark walls. Basil had absolutely no idea how she truly felt; Lydia had always been a good actress. Then again, the happiness she felt with *Regis* could have been the real act.

Eventually, Basil headed back to his chamber, but he never fell asleep. The rest of his night was spent staring at the artwork on his ceiling. It felt like an eternity before morning finally came.

He was out of bed before the crack of dawn, unusually punctual. Basil got dressed straight away and headed to breakfast. He was much earlier than the nine o'clock that Regis had mentioned. The dining room was the most naked he'd ever seen it. Basil watched as the servants arranged the tables and chairs and smiled at him. He could smell the cooking of omelettes . . . hear the pans sizzling.

Basil took a seat at the head of the table for fun; nobody of the royal family was there to tell him otherwise. He enjoyed watching the servants at work; as terrible as it was, they made him feel better about his place. The sun rose through the curtains and lit up the room.

Time passed more quickly when the sun was up. "Good morning, brother," Regis V greeted as he entered the dining hall. "How was your sleep?"

Basil was careful to keep his eyes away from Lydia. "Terrible, actually."

It wasn't until Regis turned to face the buffet that Basil saw the red irritation on Regis's cheek. A shiver ran down his spine; the moment the queen found out, he'd be in deep trouble.

Regis noticed Basil's nervous expression and said, "Don't worry. It doesn't hurt."

But that didn't matter. The mark was still there, and Basil started to regret last night's decision. Still, he kept a strong guard. "I wasn't worried."

Bridget and Hadwin entered promptly at nine in full regal attire. An embellished tunic draped across Hadwin's shoulders, and Bridget wore a gray flowy dress. "Greetings, children. Hungry?" she asked.

"The selection looks delicious," Lydia Rose answered. Her voice sent an abashed tingle to Basil's throat. He shouldn't have tried anything last night. And if Regis were to find out what he'd tried—no, she wouldn't tell him.

"It really does," said Regis. With his words, Bridget's gaze moved to his face . . . and to his red punch-mark.

She let out a gasp. "Oh, dearie. What happened? Is this from *Basil?*" She cast a condescending glare of disgust at her younger twin, the first acknowledgment she'd given him in days.

Basil opened his mouth to retort something about Regis's words triggering him, but there was another voice before he could. "No, Mother. I don't know how it got there. I must have—I don't know—collided with the dresser."

The response surprised Basil, but he was thankful. Why would Regis do such a thing? "All right, Regis. Don't let it happen again—you shan't present yourself like that in front of Silverkeep at the coronation."

He nodded and threw a smile at Basil. He could've perceived it wrongly, but Basil thought the gesture might've been genuine.

After breakfast, Basil lingered in the dining hall, putting off his daily studies. A few minutes after the meal was over, only he and Regis were left in the room.

"Aren't you supposed to be following Hadwin?" Basil asked.

Ignoring his question, Regis V responded, "Do you have anything to say to me?"

Basil forced a mumbled, "Thank you" under his breath.

"I could've told Mother, you know. Should I have?"

"No, Regis. I appreciate that you didn't." Basil's gratitude brought a delighted smile to Regis V's face, which pained Basil. Regis must have known that it would be hard for Basil to give up. "Thank you for your forgiveness," he added reluctantly.

"Who said anything about forgiveness, brother?" Regis V snickered.

"Pardon?"

Regis's eyes narrowed. "I protected you from Mother. But it was only so I could deal with you myself."

Of course he wouldn't forgive and forget; Basil knew Regis wasn't like that. "What do you want from me, Regis? You have *everything*."

"Vengeance. To set this straight. The only thing I'm sure of is that using my hands would be . . . improper." Regis paused and made deadly eye contact with his brother. "Don't you think?"

Basil stood from his chair and made for the dining room door. He didn't want to be around Regis any longer.

"Perhaps swords would be more adequate!" Regis called out to Basil as he left.

III

eathered pen in hand, Basil flawlessly solved the next trigonometry problem. His royalty didn't exempt him from mathematics. If anything, it added a load of pressure; he needed to be intelligent to serve as an "example." Yet, while *he* was hard at work, Regis V's only duty was to watch Hadwin.

Though Regis was to be king, in all seriousness, the position was largely symbolic. His advisors, like Hadwin, would be doing much of the work. Most of his reign would consist of "yes" and "no". Basil knew that his own duties would entail many tiresome tasks. He'd have to speak to Silverkeep's schools and organize events. Bridget loved these types of things, but Basil couldn't dislike them more.

Trigonometry was an easy subject for Basil. It was more difficult for him to channel his creative side, like art. Once he finished the work for his favorite subject, it was time for the dreaded painting. Basil didn't want to leave his office. Unfortunately, the still life was on the other side of the palace. He neatly arranged his papers and reluctantly exited the capacious room, only one of many such offices in the castle.

The servants always set up weekly still lifes for the twins to complete. They ranged from bowls of fruit to nude models. Painting was Basil's least favorite activity. Still, he had to get it over with.

When he arrived at the setup, Basil was pleased to be alone. The paintbrush lay in the curve of the wooden easel, and a palette was already set up with paints. A trencher with cheese sat in the space before him. He questioned whether or not it was edible but decided against finding out.

Basil always skipped the sketching step and went straight for the paint. He knew it wasn't wise; he also didn't care. His paintings seldom resembled art—more like accidental smudging. Basil's mind kept sidetracking, and he thought about what the cheese might taste like, what type it was.

He thought back to his art lessons and remembered the strokes they'd learned—sgraffito, smooth strokes, dotting. He always thought the last one was interesting but wondered who had time for that. He questioned why anyone would spend hours painting little specks when they could be doing . . . anything else.

If one didn't see the setup, one wouldn't recognize the random brush strokes on Basil's canvas. They looked like a bunch of scribbles. Nevertheless, Basil was glad to be finished with his project. He left it to sit on the easel and stared at the white paint covering his hands. He went in search of a servant and requested he draw a bath with lavender oil and mineral salts. Basil went back inside to wash off his hands and didn't breathe through his nose, avoiding the acrid reek of oil paint. After, he headed to his chamber, excited for his splendid bath—some time to mull over . . . everything.

The rest of the day consisted of normal activity: reading and physical exercise. Basil took advantage of the sunlight and rode Prancer for a bit. Horseback was an area in which he shined, especially when he paired it with archery. When he sat atop Prancer, shooting arrows, Basil was . . . regal.

The acres of land surrounding the forest were abundant, and Basil always took advantage of the space they had. "Hey li'l horsey," he'd tell Prancer, tugging on his reins. And he'd gallop through the endless trees. Nature had always piqued Basil's interest—too bad there wasn't much of it in his life.

Basil had dressed in full armor, by command of Bridget, just in case anything were to happen. Stallions could be unpredictable.

When he had nobody else, Prancer was always there for him, silently understanding whatever Basil had to say.

After riding, Basil took a moment to catch his breath. He walked Prancer back, stroking his golden mane, and picked the arrows from the targets that were, like most other days, entirely bull's-eyes.

"Oh, Prancer. Lucky little horse. You don't need to do anything. You don't need to worry about—" Basil realized how strange he was to have been talking to a horse. In response, Prancer simply groaned, his classic and only noise.

Back in his chamber, getting changed into normal clothes, Basil heard Bridget's voice.

"Basil!" she called from the hallway. Her footsteps were impatient. "Report to the solar."

"Okay, Mother," he said, wondering what could be so urgent. Whenever Bridget spoke like that, Basil inferred he was in trouble.

When he reached the solar, Regis V was already seated on the baroque sofa, an evil smirk plastered on his face. These days, it seemed that look had become his trademark. Basil missed the innocent smile that used to be the norm. Neither of them had managed *that* smile in a long time—too long. Bridget stood in front of the fireplace, her arms crossed. "Turn around, Basil," she said.

He shifted his gaze to find his cheese painting next to Regis's.

"What is *that?*" Bridget spat, biting her thumbnail. "Is painting a joke to you?"

Regis V chuckled in his peripheral vision. "Of course not, it's just . . . abstract."

Bridget shook her head. "Look at your brother's." Sure enough, Regis V's painting was perfect—the shadows, texture, and details were all there.

I'll never be Regis, and I don't want to be. There are things I can do that he can't, too. You're just too busy to notice them.

But of course, he couldn't say such a thing. "I'm sorry, Mother. I'll redo it."

Bridget removed her fingernails from her mouth. "You must. Have you completely forgotten that your works will be displayed at the next benefit?"

Basil truly hadn't remembered the upcoming art showcase, but he didn't admit it. "I'm sorry. I was busy today. I rode Prancer for a while and did some archery," he tried.

"Your tomfoolery mustn't come before the castle duties. Look at these two paintings side by side," she said. "I wouldn't even believe you two are twins—this juxtaposition—there's such a gap between your skill levels. Or is it just effort?"

Basil felt defeated. Even if he did have a valid argument, it wouldn't matter; the queen always won. "It's not tomfoolery,

Mother. I'm sure if Regis were to do the same, you'd admire him for it."

"Excuse me?" Bridget's eyes narrowed, puzzled at his response; Basil never talked back to her.

"Forget it." Basil wanted to leave but knew it wasn't a good idea. Instead, he took a seat on the couch, the furthest seat possible from his brother.

There was a quiet moment before Bridget spoke. "I hate it—how you two are always at odds."

Regis furrowed his brows. "At odds? What do you mean?" he asked. "We're each other's best friend."

Basil almost laughed at the irony of the statement. He didn't understand why everything had to be so serious all the time. He was never able to enjoy himself.

"You better be. Because you're going to have each other forever."

As much as Basil wanted to dismiss it, he knew there was truth in her words. Things could get lonely in the castle, and they were each other's only friend. The twins made quick eye contact—it was hostile more than anything.

"All right, Basil. Visit the library. Read something worthwhile to educate yourself about painting, perhaps." Basil interpreted that as his mother trying to get rid of him, but he gladly complied.

It had been a few weeks since Basil last visited the library. He wasn't opposed to it. He loved reading the ancient texts of kings and philosophers before his era. Of course, he wouldn't be spending his time there studying painting or *anything* to do with art.

Instead, as he crept through the bronze entryway, Basil got lost in the limitless stacks of literature, glad to be alone. Each book's spine was painted metallic for show. Basil walked beneath the engraved arcs. Fleurs-de-lis and regal symbols adorned every inch. The crackling fireplace and its scent comforted Basil.

The books were arranged in chronological order, the first ones being Philip's original teachings. They were considered the most coveted literature in all of Silverkeep, with only one remaining copy of each. All of his books were in mint condition despite their many centuries sitting in the royal library.

Basil practically knew his first few teachings cover to cover. Back when he and Regis V were young, their parents would read the books as bedtime stories. Today, he wanted to read something he wasn't familiar with, or at least hadn't seen for a while.

The Legend of the Key was the first book to catch his eye. Its spine was textured fabric embroidered with faces and abstract detailing. Unlike most other tales, there were several copies of Philip's last words.

Basil vaguely recalled hearing about the key from his father, but he never dove deep into the legend; it had never seemed relevant. But these were the types of things he found particularly interesting, and he had time on his hands.

Basil struggled to remove the book from its shelf, where it was tightly packed into its spot. Sure, there was lots of space, but there were even more books.

A mahogany table stood beneath one of the bronze arcs, and Basil almost sprinted to it as the book was heavier than he'd expected. *The Legend of the Key* thumped as it met the table. When he dropped it, particles of dust released into the air, causing Basil to cough.

A drawing of Philip's face illustrated the heavy book's front cover. After seeing so many paintings of Silverkeep's first king, he was never sure which ones truly looked like him. In this particular image, Philip was drawn with long gray hair, fair skin, and green eyes. They were the exact color of Basil's. Philip's reign was centuries ago, but Basil was related to him. He found comfort in their matching irises.

Though the library was accessible to anyone in the castle, for some reason, Basil felt mischievous as he flipped the cover open.

The text that filled the pages was an ancient font—difficult to read, but legible if he focused. Each line was spaced tightly. But the first page had only a quote on it.

> *My power has been compiled, stored in a hidden key. Whoever has the virtue and intelligence to find it must take the throne, for he who can do so much will be the most fit to rule, with everything I have and more.*

Beneath the quotation was Philip Avington's name in cursive.

Basil wasn't sure why Philip's name hadn't been passed on. Perhaps a generation skipped a male descendant, and a nephew ruled. Basil learned about history, but his studies didn't cover every generation of the past few centuries. Teachers deemed other subjects more "important"—like painting. If it were up to Basil, the system would be different.

He found himself reading the quotation aloud, emphasizing each word and pretending he was someone important.

Philip Avington was a well-respected king—perhaps the most beloved man in history. Basil doubted his words were anything but the truth. But then why, centuries later, was the key still missing, hidden somewhere?

The book was written by Philip's followers, and therefore, wasn't as popular as his own works. But Basil was curious why all of Silverkeep hadn't picked it up. Hoping to understand the whole story, he flipped the first few pages, absorbing each word faster than those in any of his textbooks. In an interesting reiteration of what he already knew, the book discussed how and why Philip was recognized as the most successful, valiant leader to date. Before him, Silverkeep was a mere disarray of tribes, linked only by their name. But the great king was able to make it something more—something beautiful. After him, though, the chaos was back. His son couldn't rule for his life, and many subjects were searching and fighting for the key. Silverkeep gradually became whole again—but it took time, funds, and the Timbers family. Centuries later, war and violence were nearly unheard of.

After reading the words he already knew, Basil decided to skip to the next segment; he was eager to learn something new. It was titled *The Journey of Frederick Turner: Searching for the Key*. Basil didn't want to miss a word.

> *To my dear friend Tobias, an unfortunate casualty of my foolish endeavor.*

He flipped past the dedication page and became engrossed in the subject matter.

> *If one thinks finding the key is an easy task, one is sorely mistaken. I understand the appeal—the temptation of becoming king. Nevertheless, my journey shall be a lesson to you. A spoiler: I never found it. Quite honestly, I'm not sure it's possible to locate something when your only clue is a dead man's last words.*

> *I planned it all out but rushed myself as I didn't want anybody to beat me to it. Every notable location of Silverkeep was circled on my map, and I followed a specific path. The woodland was first.*

The story went on, and Basil devoured a thick stack of pages in one sitting. Dinner was probably soon, but he wasn't keeping track of time. Though there were more segments, recounting other subjects' journeys, he knew they would all end the same—a hopeless subject—if they were even alive to tell the tale. If their stories had ended differently, Basil wouldn't possess the royalty he did. It should've angered him that random subjects had tried to take away his family's power, but it evoked something else entirely.

In a sense, it was inspiring. He struggled to wedge the book back in its bronze shelf. Basil brushed his hands over all the books' spines, trying to find another about the Legend of the Key—one that was more recent. The book he'd just read was from centuries ago, dating only a bit after Philip's death.

He found another that piqued his interest. It was from a decade ago, called *Thinking of Philip*. This book was lighter, allowing Basil to carry it with ease.

He skimmed the foreword and chapters, but what interested him was the last part. The title read *Is King Philip's Key Real?*

Basil was surprised to feel his heart plummet when he continued to read.

> *No. Every inch of Silverkeep has been searched one time or another in the past century. It has been declared by many authoritative figures that the renowned Legend of the Key is spurious. That is not to say that King Philip didn't mention it, because he very well might have. However, as virtuous and intelligent as Phillip was, a dying man may have fabricated his words. He was weary and feeble, and it was centuries ago.*

Basil flipped back to the cover to find the author. What did L.J. Manor know, anyway? Anyone could've written some words and called it the truth. Basil refused to accept that the key was fake, even though it had nothing to do with him.

So, he rummaged through the shelves in an effort to find something hopeful. When such a thing was proven impossible, Basil became sweaty and red—and the fireplace didn't help. He'd wasted too much time in the library, searching for something that wasn't there.

He threw down every book that taught the key wasn't real and stomped on them. The castle had managed to keep the editions pristine for centuries, but it took only moments for them to be destroyed—to reverse the hard work.

He tore out the pages without regret. The illustrations of Philip became distorted with every jump and the papers tattered. It wasn't only the key that worked him up, but everything he'd had to keep inside, building up like bubbles in a saucepan, desperately wanting to evaporate. Regis IV's death, Regis V, Lydia Rose, Bridget . . . destruction was the only way for Basil to channel his rage, even if it wasn't the best solution.

Basil tried to keep his voice down; he didn't want anyone to join him in the library. "Damn you, L.J. Manor," he whispered with exasperation. The author was innocent, simply stating his opinion, but Basil didn't like it. Quite frankly, there was no explanation for Basil's hatred. The bile had accumulated as he read each book, each one defeating any hope that was stirring up inside.

Basil wasn't used to being opposed by anyone who wasn't the royal family; he held power over the subjects. Even if they didn't like him, the subjects would keep it to themselves. Reading the books made him feel as if someone were yelling at him.

After seeing ripped out pages and broken covers, tattered and torn on the floor, Basil collapsed. All the energy was drained out of him, and he allowed his breath to steady.

Oh no, what have I done?

He knew that when Bridget had a chance to see what he'd done, his actions would reap consequences, but that wasn't the first thing on his mind. He still had to know if the key was real; he didn't like being unsure.

But Basil knew he couldn't leave the disassembled litera-ture sprawled across the floor, so he reluctantly began to fix the books. Though his actions were irreversible, he was able to fake it quite well by stuffing the out-of-order pages between the golden covers and placing them carefully on the shelves. The next time someone picked up a book regarding the Legend of the Key in hopes of reading it, they'd be disappointed. But he wasn't thinking about anyone besides himself. He never did.

Basil was surprised by his unusual curiosity concerning the key. And the swarming thoughts refused to go away.

IV

asil stared down the cheese plate in contempt, but his mouth still watered at the sight. He must have truly been hungry; even the bits of mold hardly repulsed him. Of course, he'd exclude the green splotches in his painting.

The palette sat as he'd left it, and a fresh canvas stood on the easel. Basil groaned and forced himself to focus on the task at hand, but with every charcoal stroke, he thought about the key—whether it was real, where it could be.

Forget about it, Basil.

His new sketch impressed even himself, but his skills still paled in comparison to Regis's. Besides, his mind was somewhere else.

Why do I care so much about the stupid key?

The charcoal stained his hands, but he didn't bother to wash them. Just as he prepared to paint, Basil heard three precise knocks at the doorway.

"Who is it?" he asked.

There was no answer, but Basil felt an unwelcome presence loom over his shoulder. He could tell it was Regis V without turning around.

"What a shame it is that you must redo your painting. I liked the abstract one," he said. Regis was supposed to be following Hadwin.

Basil didn't understand what Regis was doing—most likely, playing some type of game. "I'm trying to focus," Basil responded, his eyes glued to his work. "Please leave me be."

Regis squealed. "Oh, brother. You don't truly think dry brush strokes will suffice, do you?"

"Please, Regis, just go."

"You need help. I'm here to give it to you," he said. "I'm being genuine, truly."

Basil would take anything over having to paint, but he wouldn't give up his pride—especially not to Regis. "I'm okay, but thank you."

Without warning, Regis snatched the paintbrush out of Basil's hands and chuckled. He'd been laughing so much lately. Both of the twins had experienced Regis IV's death, but it meant different things for each of them.

"Just let me help you," Regis insisted. "I'm good at this."

Basil shook his head. "It'll look like yours. I need to develop my own style." It was nonsense but had a better chance at getting Regis to leave than mere yelling would.

"We'll work together," Regis compromised.

Basil rolled his eyes. As much as he hated his brother at the moment, his help would be useful. Gradually, as they painted, Regis began to take over, and Basil allowed it to happen. He moved to sit in another chair, observing Regis at work. He hated his brother's perfection—how flawlessly he was able to execute brush strokes and shadows.

Regis noticed Basil's intent stares, and said, "Don't worry, brother. You'll get there someday."

Basil tried to ignore the backhanded statement, but it bothered him. "Get where, Regis? To be stuck up and selfish with an ego the size of—"

"I'm *helping* you. Did you forget about what I said?" Regis V asked aggressively, his jaw clenched. He clearly had the urge to attack though he restrained himself.

Basil wasn't scared of his twin. "I'm afraid so."

"About how you won't get away with punching your *king*? About playing together, but with swords," Regis clarified. It was baffling that just moments before, Regis had posed as a kind brother, helping Basil with his duties. He'd turned cold in the blink of an eye.

"You're not king!" Basil yelled.

Regis V smiled. "Yet."

"You'll be a terrible one."

With that, Regis smeared the paintbrush across the entire piece, ruining the work they'd both spent time on. Basil gasped. "So that's why you wanted to 'help.' I get it now."

"I wasn't planning on ruining the art—I liked it, too—but your words angered me. Do not forget that once I have the crown, I'm in charge. That means you better play nice."

"Or *what*, Regis?"

He shrugged and paused for a moment. "I'm hoping it won't come to that."

Basil was sure his brother's words were exaggerated; he wanted to scare him. All the same, it perplexed Basil that Regis would threaten him. "Tell me, what were you referring to after breakfast yesterday?" Basil asked, sourly punctuating every word.

"What, about the swords?" When Basil nodded, he said, "I was just thinking about how we haven't had a sword fight in a while. Recreational, of course."

"Now?" Basil asked.

"No, I didn't have a specific time in mind."

"Then let's go." Finishing the painting was barely a concern. His brushstrokes would wait.

Regis looked pleased. "Fair enough."

The last time the two had sword-fought recreationally was long enough ago to escape Basil's memory. He hadn't worked on the craft for months. He'd decided it wasn't as important as horseback riding and archery. But his lack of practice put Regis at an unfair advantage; Basil's brother could frequently be found outside, a sword in hand.

Though sword fights required safety spotters, the two of them didn't alert anyone of what they were about to do. Servants would be pesky, watching, commentating, trying to protect and whatnot. They also decided against the usual armor; it would be too much of a hassle.

Basil and Regis had trouble choosing their swords; everything was usually brought to them by servants. Since they wanted their match to remain a secret, they would have to set everything up on their own.

The sword closet was grand, holding more weapons than countable. But one stood out: their father's. He'd never gotten into actual fights; he'd used it for leisure. Basil naturally selected a bland silver sword that blended in with the rest. But he cringed when Regis V reached for their father's sword.

"How old do you think it is?" Regis asked.

"I don't know, but you shouldn't be using it."

Regis smirked. "Why? It's passed down from king to king."

"You're not king yet."

"Oh, well," he said with a shrug. "I should break it in."

It just gave Basil all the more motive and rage to beat him. But it would be difficult when all he had was a scrawny silver sword.

The boys stood in the closet for a little while, feeling the weaponry come alive. Regis rotated "his" sword, admiring it from all angles. He lightly tapped the blade with his index finger and, once satisfied, gripped the bejeweled hilt and held the sword tip-down. "Let's go."

The twins exited the closet and took the least serviced passages to the field.

The afternoon sunlight forced Basil to squint, and before he could say anything, Regis indicated the beginning of the match with a swoosh. It was unnecessarily close to Basil's stomach.

"Woah," Basil reacted, unprepared.

"We're not children anymore, Basil," Regis V said.

Both of them stood at long point, their swords held straight out from their chests, before Basil made the first move. He thrust the sword over Regis's shoulder, but Regis deflected the hit.

Basil retreated, maintaining the same stance. His eyes were glued to Regis's bejeweled weapon as his brother stood en garde, his eyes narrowing. Basil went for another slice—the blades screeched against each other in midair. "Ambitious," Regis yelled. Basil was too focused to think about talking.

Neither of them was used to the knee-deep blooming spring grass and flowers. This time, Regis leapt toward him, his sword inches from Basil's head. The blade of Regis's sword gleamed in the sunlight.

Basil was sweaty and exasperated as the thrusts and retreats went on, the intensity growing. What had started as a recreational match soon felt deadly. One look in Regis V's eyes made that clear.

The clicks and clatters of the blades colliding became quicker, and Basil used all his reflexes. But after a while, it was too difficult to stay on point. He put all his remaining energy into lunging toward Regis and pivoting away, careful not to stumble into the tall grass.

His vision went blurry when Regis V had him where he wanted him—the sharp tip of his sword pointed directly at Basil's groin.

"The femoral artery is the most lethal point on the body."

Regis was whispering, but his voice boomed. A string of spittle dripped from his mouth and down his chin. For a moment, the vigor in his eyes said Regis planned on *hurting* him.

But Basil used his wit to distract Regis. He stomped his left foot on the ground, remembering a sword-fighting technique from years ago.

The appel—it never fails to distract the opponent.

With his unexpected tactic, Regis flinched. Basil took advantage of his brother's time free of intuition and escaped the trap. "You weren't really going to do it, were you?" Basil asked.

Now it was Regis's turn to ignore him. His eyes were peeled for Basil's next move. Basil had a sudden unthinkable idea, which he pushed away just as fast. If they carried the fight until death, Basil had a chance at being king. But he was smart enough to know that such a thing would poison him with lifelong guilt. Besides, no matter how deep down and far away, there was good inside Regis—Basil had seen it before.

How nice it would be to see his brother's head roll across the field, detached from his body, but after the initial sense of accomplishment, he'd regret it. Instead of being overwhelmed with thoughts, he let his body and reflexes think for him.

At this point, the fight was dangerous. Basil slashed Regis's shoulder, leaving a crack of open, bloodied skin. If anything, the move just angered Regis.

"Settle down, brother. It's only recreation," Regis said. But they both knew it was so much more than that. The sound of silver screeching became louder, and Basil wanted silence.

When all his energy was used up, Regis began to take the upper hand. His swipes were fast and purposeful. Eventually, it became too much for Basil, and he welcomed the pain that surrendering entailed. His knees gave out, and Basil felt his body drop to the ground. He found comfort in a grassy patch.

As his body collapsed, Regis stayed alert. He sliced Basil's bicep just before snatching his sword. Basil was finished, but Regis wasn't. He kneeled to be level with his brother. His left arm looped around Basil's neck, holding both their swords.

"Please, Regis. Please, don't. Don't do anything . . ." Basil's voice trailed off as the ground became his bed. His eyes shut and found peace.

"Damn you, Basil. I can't hurt you if you're asleep." But Basil hardly heard his brother; he was already passed out.

Basil woke up around a half an hour after the fight, overcome with malaise. A metallic reek wafted through the air, like iron.

Blood.

He was sinking in a pool of his own red fluids, nauseous and lightheaded. The grass beside him, too, was drenched. He spotted the site of the blood loss and put pressure on his arm with the other hand. Slowly, he recalled the previous events.

Regis had left him there, alone, swordless, and bleeding. Basil very well could have bled out if not for waking up. Regis probably wished that were the case.

As Basil's sight became more and more fuzzy, he realized his need for help was urgent. "Someone!" he called out. But nobody could hear; the boys had picked an abandoned location on purpose. Basil clambered to his feet. The walk back to the castle seemed impossible, even though it had only taken minutes on the way there.

As he approached the castle, servants became visible. Basil didn't know any of their names, but yelled, "Help! Please!" With his words, the servants rushed toward him. One tore off a scrap of his tunic to wrap Basil's wound.

"Is it Basil or Regis?" One whispered to the other.

The other replied, "Basil—he's got green eyes." Everything was fuzzy, and Basil could barely distinguish their faces.

But the servants soon laid him down on a bed, helping him

sip nectar while half asleep. A dressing tightly enclosed his wound, cutting off his circulation so it wouldn't fester. By dinnertime, the medical servants had nursed him back to health.

When he was escorted back to his chamber by a kind old woman, concerned faces looked his way. All that remained of the fight was a wound on his right arm, but it was covered.

"What happened, Your Highness?" the woman asked.

Basil wasn't sure whether telling a servant was a good idea; they all talked to each other . . . and the outside world. Soon, everyone would know about the drama between Basil and Regis and could turn it into something more. "I'm not sure, exactly," Basil lied.

The old servant didn't ask more questions; it would be considered impertinent. "All right, well, I hope you feel better."

The lady dropped Basil off in his chamber, and he plopped down onto his sheets. He let himself lie there for a bit until he saw the sun set through the windows. The sight reminded Basil that it was dinnertime. He quickly changed into appropriate clothing and checked himself out in the mirror. His hair stuck up from all angles, and his body looked frail. His own reflection repulsed him, and he did whatever he could to his matted tangles with a comb.

Luckily, that night's dinner was only with the immediate family. Still, his disapproving mother and annoying brother were the last people he wanted as company. Basil sighed and knew he had to go downstairs.

When Basil walked into the dining hall, he was greeted by stares of distaste, the strongest being Bridget's. His glance shifted to Regis, and Basil saw the reason. Regis had stitches in his shoulder. Basil knew that he'd cut his brother but didn't think it was that bad.

"Basil Avington," Bridget said. Her voice sounded dangerous. "This is unacceptable."

"What do you mean? I did nothing wrong," Basil retorted.

Bridget's arms were crossed. "Nothing wrong? Your brother needed stitches."

"So? Look at my arm! He cut me, too."

Bridget paid no attention to her son's words. "He's three weeks away from being proclaimed king, Basil. He can't have stitches at the coronation."

"Why? His body will be covered in some extravagant robe." He stretched out the word *extravagant*.

Hadwin, Lydia, and Regis all watched the two speak. "It doesn't matter. Do you not recall what I said? You two are *brothers*, not enemies! First the punch, now this . . ."

He glared in Regis's direction and saw a slight grin on his face. But when Bridget turned to Regis, it quickly faded and was masked with a false expression of agony.

Off of Basil's silence, the queen continued. "How did this even happen? Did you attack him?"

Basil no longer cared about the foolish spotter rules. He wanted his mother to see the truth for what it was.

"It was a sword fight," Basil admitted.

Bridget gasped. "Are you serious? Why would you request such a thing? You know it's not—"

"It was his idea."

The queen swallowed and looked to Regis. "Is this true?"

Regis didn't respond. Instead, he shrieked in pain, distracting his mother. It worked to make her feel pity instead of anger. All the evidence in the world wouldn't make Bridget believe the younger twin.

"Okay, Mother. Just favor him like you always do," Basil said.

Bridget's brows furrowed. "Excuse me?"

"You don't even bother to *pretend* you love us the same. It's ridiculous."

Basil expected her to say *something*, but she stayed silent. The queen had never been a liar. She finally managed, "This is a tough time for the family, Basil. My husband—your father—died days ago. Please be thoughtful."

Bridget wasn't lying; she was mourning a loss very close to her heart. Of course, Basil couldn't object to that, though it didn't change the way she treated her son.

The topic was silently resolved, but Basil didn't forget. The kitchen staff served a cheese platter on a trencher, and it reminded Basil of the painting. Would Bridget care that Regis destroyed the piece of art? Would she even *believe* it?

Over the course of dinner, Hadwin explained some choices he'd made and lied that Regis had been a great help. The coronation was nearing, and everyone seemed to be excited—everyone but Basil.

Lydia Rose's cheeks blushed every time the topic was brought up (which was frequently), and a sly grin would stick to Regis's face. Basil couldn't help but wonder what the kingdom would turn into once his arrogant, swine of a brother took power. Regis IV had done amazing things for Silverkeep, and Basil was sure Regis V would mess it all up.

After dinner was concluded, Basil left without being excused. He didn't even stay for dessert. If he didn't *have* to be with his family, he'd rather spend his time doing something useful like sleeping.

That night, Bridget didn't call after him to come back. Nobody did. They let him go. Were they finally beginning to pity the neglected prince?

Basil curled up beneath his sheets and did something he hadn't since childhood—he cried. Basil had never cried for Lydia Rose. He'd only teared up for his father's death. But he bawled for some inexplicable and complex reason.

It was in part due to the searing pain in his bicep, but mostly because of his family . . . and things that swirled in the back of his head—the reason he'd been so curious about the key in the library . . . the reason he still was. There had been a spark of hope all along though he hadn't wanted to admit the truth to himself; it was a sacrilege. And that was the reason he'd destroyed each book that deemed the task impossible.

The idea of escaping the castle didn't seem too bad to Basil—appealing, even. He couldn't live the rest of his life like this, treated like nothing. He wanted to get away from his family, and he longed to become king. If he killed Regis V, it would subtract the satisfaction altogether; Regis wouldn't have to watch his brother win. Of course, there were other, less important reasons why murder wasn't the solution. But besides killing his brother, there was only one way to acquire the crown.

The idea of ruling Silverkeep was enough to halt Basil's shedding of tears. Instead of sulking, he plotted a devious idea. It made the abstract and out-of-reach crown closer to his fingertips. It allowed him to imagine beating the heir to the throne and taking his first love back. But it also entailed leaving the only place he'd ever known.

An imaginary clock ticked in his mind, urging Basil to take some sort of action. Once the coronation occurred, Regis's spot on the throne would be set in stone.

The legend might be fake, but it wasn't as if Basil had urgent duties.

He would have to find King Philip's key.

V

lumber was absent that night. Basil lay on his side, facing the black iron pills that sat atop his nightstand. The servants had brought them to his chamber after the sword fight; Basil needed to make up for the lost blood. He stared at them, refusing to swallow one. Hopefully, his body would heal on its own.

The night was still young, too early for the impetuous boy to take action. Servants were likely still lurking about the corridors, working. Basil had forgotten that it was earlier than he was normally in bed; he'd left halfway through dinner.

Basil questioned himself, but the doubts were overshadowed by the possibilities—the possibilities that had driven everyone mad centuries ago.

Am I crazy?

Most definitely.

The chance the key existed were slim to none, but that small spark of hope was enough. Nothing could be worse than having to watch Regis become king.

Usually, Basil preferred to sleep on his right side. Tonight, it pained him too much. He unwrapped the dressing and allowed his scar to air out. The wound was worse than he'd thought; his arm was deeply carved into. The sight was revolting, and he decided to look the other direction, hence his continuous glare at the iron pills. Soon, blood began to erupt from the cut again, and he probably should've rewrapped it, but he didn't know how to go about such a thing.

The sky was pitch black when the castle silenced. It was late, and most of the palace must have been asleep. Hesitantly, Basil uncovered the blood-stained sheets that embraced his body and stretched out of bed. He was reluctant to cover his arm, but he had to. Basil did the best he could with the dressing while looking away.

Basil lit the candles on his silver nightstand and began to deliberate. It wasn't something he did a lot; most of the time, his actions weren't very well thought through at all. But if he was about to embark on a risky journey, a plan would be necessary. However, as he contemplated, Basil realized he knew nothing—besides what he'd read in literature—about the outside world.

He felt alive amongst the sleeping castle. Basil's feet developed a quiet rhythm as they paced around the corners of his room. The idea of leaving everything behind, even if it was only temporary, was almost as nerve-racking as it was exciting. Once he was to leave, Basil wouldn't be gone for good, but he was sure his family would not be pleased with him upon his return. If he were to find the key, he'd be in charge of all of them. And most importantly, he'd have more power than his brother.

Basil looked disheveled and fatigued, but the twinkle of hope in his eyes was enough to steal the upper hand. He let his body fill with the power that comes with ambition because, for once, however small, he had a chance.

Now far past everybody's bedtime, not even a whisper

was audible to Basil. He hoped that no restless servants or royal family members would be wandering about the halls and crossed his fingers that Lydia Rose wouldn't be awake as she had been the previous night.

Basil clutched a flickering torch—the only light source. He focused on his footsteps, making sure his tiptoeing was quiet in his brown shoes. He'd dressed in a normal day outfit and hoped it would be fitting for his journey. He held a small drawstring bag over his shoulder. Basil had no idea whether the quest would be days or weeks. Any longer than that, and it would be pointless—once Regis was crowned, he would be king. At this point Basil had but a fortnight to find the key.

He'd considered what he'd need on his journey. Food would be necessary; even if he was able to get it along the way, Basil didn't want starvation in the question—better safe than sorry.

Regis IV had done revolutionary things with his reign, the first being kindness to servants. In the past, they would slave away in the night hours, cooking, and cleaning the palace to perfection. Now, they were allowed to sleep a fair number of hours. Basil was thankful for his father's choices (in this particular instance).

The kitchen welcomed Basil with the thick, delicious aroma of boiling cinnamon; the chefs always let the sweet smell fill up the castle overnight. The flames were protected, of course, but they burned through the night hours. When everyone woke up, the fresh cinnamon scent was the mark of a new day's beginning. The smell was much stronger, though, as Basil stood before the evaporating pot.

He searched the kitchen for something that would keep. Artisanal breads and jams lined the pantry. They would be a reliable solution. Basil selected the best ones based on smell and texture. He shoved them in the drawstring bag—there was barely room for a few loaves. Basil narrowed down his decision to one loaf. He was the only one in the family to prefer pumpernickel.

Bread alone wouldn't be enough to appease him, especially being accustomed to the daily delicious meals prepared by the chefs. He looked around the room in search of something more filling. A slab of beef caught his eye. The steaks were raw, but Basil took them anyway; he needed something to accompany the bread. He hoped it wouldn't come to needing raw meat, but he wasn't sure what life was like outside the castle walls. He'd seen Silverkeep through a lens his entire life, concealed in his own royal bubble.

He was cramming the meat into his drawstring when he realized he'd need water on his journey, too. He recalled science lessons in which he'd learned that humans could barely last three days without hydration. Basil had no idea where to get water; quite frankly, servants had always done the dirty work for him and his family.

Basil seized a cup from a lumber kitchen shelf and silently crept outside. It took him quite a bit of time to locate the castle well. He was glad he'd given himself extra hours by leaving in the middle of the night. With each action, Basil didn't think about what he was doing. He only focused on carrying on with his preparation.

Once he reached the well, he bent down, clay cup in hand. Basil had no idea how such a process was supposed to work, but he tried his best. When the cup was filled to the brim with cold and clear water, he tossed it in the drawstring. It added weight on his back, which would make it difficult for him to maintain a fast pace. However, he couldn't neglect his need for water.

Basil stood by the well, hauling the drawstring bag over his shoulder, when his teeth began to chatter uncontrollably. He wasn't used to the physical discomfort; he'd always been dressed in capes and wool vests to stay warm. Though it was spring, the nights were still freezing. He should've brought another layer, but it would just add to the overwhelming weight he had to carry.

After he had food and water, Basil was ready to go. In fact, he almost set off into the abyss before realizing he'd left a necessity in the castle—something to protect himself with in the case of an emergency.

He was reluctant to enter the palace again, but he turned back toward his "home." The cold wind prickled Basil's face, forming goosebumps on the surface of his limbs. He crept in through a windowpane, already cracked open, and landed in the throne room. It was unlike the castle staff to leave the window open, but it helped Basil all the same.

This atmosphere used to be special to him. He'd look up to the throne and watch his father sit, making important decisions. But now it seemed foreign—as if it weren't supposed to be there. He was about to embark on an entire, dangerous journey, all for the mere possibility of being able to sit on that very throne.

The sword closet was only a few rooms away, so he basked in the potential glory of the throne for a moment longer. Torch in hand, he took a seat in the foreign chair. If anyone had witnessed it, he'd have been in trouble. As he sat down, Basil felt as if he were sitting on a cloud—soft and welcoming. He sank into the velvet and reclined against the back. His arms went straight to the armrests, his posture regal. It was dark, but he could see his reflection in a shiny window across the room. Only certain features were illuminated with the flames of the torch.

If not for a crownless head, it was Basil's dream to be sitting just as he was. He lost his train of thought, overtaken with the glory that sitting there brought him. He needed to get on with his priorities. The next and final thing he had to do was select a sword.

He walked like a king to the weaponry closet. Basil's head was up high, but each footstep was quiet; he didn't want to wake anyone up. Once he arrived, he wasn't sure which sword to choose. It was the same room that he and Regis had been in yesterday. Basil found it odd that the silver door was unlocked—perhaps because the throne room was rarely occupied by anyone but the king. There was still a bit of blood on the blades of both their swords.

When Basil had awoken with no sword, he hadn't known where it went. Regis had put them away. Usually, servants cleaned them after a fight, but as they'd brought none . . .

Basil couldn't decide which sword to choose; there were so many options. But one jumped out at him: the one in the front, the one Regis had neglected to return to its correct position. It was the sword passed down from generation to generation, only in the hands of the kings. Regis had used the same one just the day before. The blood covering its tip was the same blood that escaped Basil's shoulder.

The hilt felt so right, and Basil's fingers slid perfectly into its grip. He picked up the sword and slipped it through the pocket of his day pants. He felt regal as the bejeweled bottom peeked out from his pants—as if the weapon had been made for him.

Basil said one last goodbye to the only home he'd ever known before going on his way. He inhaled the smell of cinnamon and admired the fine artwork on the ceiling. "I'll be back," Basil whispered to nobody but the dark air . . . and the throne, on which he left a lingering glance.

He whisked through the endless corridors to the front entrance and left the castle without a hesitant bone in his body because it wasn't a question of right or wrong. Basil knew that he shouldn't leave, but the decision was made. And he was convinced it would all be worth it in the end.

Although nobody had been able to find the key for centuries, Basil had a gut feeling that he was somehow different . . . that *he* would be the exception. The hairs on his arms stuck up from the dropping temperatures, but he didn't let it distract him. He was unsure of where to go or what to do. He'd only ever been outside the palace property for horseback outings. Even then, Basil hadn't paid attention to anything but Prancer.

Prancer.

If he wanted to get anywhere, his horse would be essential.

After taking Prancer from the most lavish of stables, Basil rode and rode until the castle was a tiny smudge in his field of view. Trees and woodland surrounded Basil for *hours;* the castle was purposely isolated for safety precautions.

His muscles were fatigued, and Basil wasn't used to the feeling. Every move felt like a fight for survival. Every hour felt like a year. But he would find comfort in thinking about the potential outcome of his journey. When he imagined himself on the throne, he didn't feel like collapsing anymore.

The scenery remained the same for hours of his ride; it felt as if he was going nowhere. However, Basil was miles away from the castle by the crack of dawn. It was impossible for him to turn back—especially because he wouldn't know how to navigate.

By morning, Basil could barely keep his eyes open, but he forced himself to. Prancer never slept—how did he do it? When Basil heard muffled whispers, he convinced himself he was hearing things due to his lack of sleep. It wasn't until silhouettes and shadows began to loom in the distance that he finally believed he had a chance at some company.

People—finally.

"Hello?" Basil called out, stopping Prancer. His voice was tired. The forest before him was different from the woodland he'd been walking through; the trees were flourishing, and greenery surrounded him from all angles. Unfamiliar flowers and blooming plants began at an immediate point of entry.

The morning sun seeped through the branches, illuminating a bright and promising path ahead. Finally, it felt as if Basil was getting somewhere. Just seeing people—anyone at all—was a relief. After trudging through endless bare-branched nature,

Basil was thrilled to be greeted with evergreen. Reaching this place was a small victory. It had a certain *life*—one he didn't experience regularly.

The group of silhouettes he'd just seen disappeared behind a tree, and the whispers stopped. "Hello?" Basil said again. He was more hopeful than scared.

And suddenly, from the tree trunk emerged the most beautiful woman he'd ever seen. Nay—the most beautiful *creature*. Her ears were *pointy*, and she possessed a foreign type of light. Black locks trailed all the way down to her feet, and the air around her glistened. The creature's body was clad only in bark, petals, and leaves, her skin a deep umber. The natural materials were put together in an alluring way.

She nodded and smiled but didn't say anything.

"Hello, um . . . do you know anything about a key? King Philip's, specifically?" Basil asked, his voice hopeful.

The female chuckled. It started as a small hiccup but grew into a guffaw. She stood there, slapping her knee and showing her teeth. Tears started to fall from her eyes, stemming from her aggressive laughter.

"What? What's so funny?" Basil's cheeks flushed in embarrassment at the feeling of an inside joke that only he wasn't privy to.

She continued to laugh, the sound growing violent and hostile. He'd never heard such a noise come from somebody.

"Excuse me, um . . ." Basil tried to speak over her, but she didn't respond. The female either didn't hear or didn't care for courtesy. The feeling of being ignored wasn't new.

When the laugh became more and more boisterous, the only way to stop her was with force. Basil needed to talk to someone, even if it was solely to keep him sane. He slowly reached into his pocket and unsheathed the kings' sword.

"Speak to me!" he bellowed, surprising himself with his own harshness.

Basil didn't plan on hurting the creature, but he wanted her attention. As he stood en garde, her laughs came to an abrupt halt. She still didn't speak, but her expression became stern. Her eyes turned to slits and stared directly into Basil's, and she gritted her teeth.

The foreign female looked lethal, and her face made up for the absence of words. It seemed she was mustering up the strength to do something dangerous. And suddenly, Basil's sword was rendered useless as he stood before her. He tried to do something, but his body was paralyzed. He couldn't move his hands or swipe the blade. Even Prancer froze, and a gold hue appeared around both their bodies.

Is this my fatigue talking?

All at once, Basil plummeted off the side of Prancer and smashed onto the ground, his sword falling beside him. He clutched the legs of his steed with all his might, but his grasp wasn't quite tight enough. Basil didn't know what happened or how, but he felt himself collapse. He couldn't speak or yell for help, and the last sound he heard was his drawstring hitting the dirt. Darkness lined the edges of his vision, and the world turned blurry . . . black . . . absent.

VI

asil's eyelids were heavy, but he forced them open. To his right was a tree stump, rotting from time. He lay on his side—his left side—because his wound from Regis still throbbed. But his entire body ached, and he wasn't sure why. The fatigue alone couldn't have been enough to evoke that type of pain, and neither could sleeping in a funky way.

Gradually, the world around him came into focus. Basil could barely see the top of the trees that towered over him, and the nature around him was incredibly foreign.

What's going on?

A wave of remembrance washed over him, and the last thing he recalled was that stunning creature, staring at him viciously.

Where am I?

Birds' chirps and natural swooshes of leaves filled Basil's ears, and he allowed himself to lie there in the place so unknown. He wanted to get up, but his body needed rest.

"I was wondering when you'd wake up," a female whispered, kneeling on his right side. Her voice was like honey, sweet and continuous. She had an accent that was foreign to Basil.

After flinching, he let out a gasp; he'd been unaware he had company. Slowly, he sat up onto his knees and turned to face her. Long red hair. Sparing freckles amid her ivory cheeks. Clear blue eyes—like the sky at dawn.

She's beautiful.

"Wait a second—who are you? And how long have I been here—asleep?" Basil said it in the kindest voice he could manage, fighting the urge to scream.

When he reached behind him, all he felt were leaves. He looked to his sides and in front of him . . . nothing. The drawstring bag holding water and food was gone. Prancer was nowhere to be found. The kings' prized sword—bejeweled with the finest stones—had vanished, as well.

The creature didn't answer with her name. Instead, she stood and sauntered gracefully away. "Wait!" Basil called out to her lengthy red locks of hair, cascading down her back.

But the stranger left after he got only a fleeting look at her face, and Basil was alone again, lost in the vast Silverkeep. He wanted her to come back.

Basil grabbed a twig in front of him and snapped it into pieces to occupy himself. With each tear, he groaned as if he were struggling, even though it was an easy task.

Soon, the ground beneath him was littered with one-inch fragments of sticks. They formed a circle enclosing Basil's body.

Footsteps became audible in the distance, worrying Basil; this forest had not been kind to him thus far. The first creature he'd met had viciously put him into some kind of slumber, and the second creature up and left his side.

But she was back. And in her hands were a certain type of leaves. They weren't like the crusty ones sprinkled around the trees. Instead, these ones were brightly colored and beautiful.

Basil wanted to ask about their purpose, but he didn't want to seem naive. He'd learned quickly that questions weren't the best idea with the inhabitants of this eerie forest.

She, too, was dressed only in nature's materials. She ran her fingers through her luscious red hair after placing the leaves on the ground. After, the female tucked her hair behind an ear—

Pointy, like the other's.

She cocked her head downward, signaling for Basil to take the leaves. Nobody in this forest seemed to talk very much. Unsure of what she was getting at, Basil wrinkled his brow. The creature raised her eyebrows and tilted her chin down again. This time, she used her hands to gesture to the leaves, as well.

The female seemed annoyed when Basil didn't take her cue, and she stomped over to his side. She picked up one of the vibrant leaves and placed it on Basil's forehead. He flinched for the second time in minutes.

"What are you doing?"

"Shh," she whispered. The placement of leaves gave off a peculiar sensation, but he enjoyed it. As her fingers brushed his head, Basil noticed they weren't normal; her fingernails weren't *nails* at all. Instead, they were green, like small versions of the leaves she placed on him. The throbbing pain in his body slowly receded.

The female began to unbutton Basil's day clothes. "What are you—? Stop!" But again, she hushed him in response. There he lay—butt naked—and she acted as if everything were normal. Out of instinct, his hand darted to cover his crotch.

She tossed aside all his clothes and covered his entire body with the red, yellow, and green leaves until no inch of skin was visible. *Is this some twisted dream?* Once the leaves were all over him, they began to glow. The familiar golden hue lit up the space around his body and lingered in the air for a few moments. Basil had never been more confused.

"What's happening?"

Yet again, she urged him to be quiet by placing her finger over her mouth.

When the questionable glowing stopped, Basil's body felt strengthened. He looked to his right arm, and the wound on his bicep was gone. Not even a scar remained. The pain he'd woken up with was gone, too.

"Welcome to Golden Grove," she said, a bright shimmer in her eyes.

"Where's my horse? And my sword? And my water and food?" he spat.

The creature shrugged. "Nice to meet you, too."

"Where's my stuff? I need it! And what happened?" Basil's muscles naturally tightened. "I don't know where I am, what I'm—"

"You're all right," she cut him off. "There's water and food here." As he looked up at her, Basil lost his train of thought. All he could think about were her luscious red locks . . . her pointed nose . . .

She reached out her arm, offering it to Basil to shake, but he spurned the offer. He had never seen such a hand; leaves as fingernails seemed unusual. Basil didn't want to touch it, so he ignored her.

"Where am I?"

The female opened her mouth to speak, but she stopped when a distant noise grew louder and louder. It was the hooves of horses, galloping across the woodland. And with the harras of horses were voices—familiar voices.

"Where do you think that lousy prince could be?" One of the distant servants called out, just in earshot.

There were three of them, and Basil assumed they'd been tasked with the mission of finding him. Guilt stirred up inside.

"I haven't a clue."

The three came nearer, and it was all too quick for Basil to understand. The creature grabbed his hand with hers and pulled Basil behind a wide tree. "Stay silent," she whispered. The simple touch of her hand made Basil tingle.

"There are shadows in the clearing!" The voices were loud enough to be close by.

The creature pulled Basil farther behind the tree, removing his shadow. The two of them were uncomfortably piled atop each other—Basil and the beautiful stranger. By the time the other two servants looked for the shadows, they were gone.

"Never mind," one said, annoyed. "Let's keep going."

Basil was stunned they were doing all that for him. He'd been convinced his family couldn't care less if he left the castle. For a split second, he considered revealing himself to the searchers and allowing them to take him back; the past day had driven him insane, and he'd had no luck concerning the key. After all, why would *he* find it if it'd been impossible to find for centuries?

Once the sound of the horses was inaudible, Basil and the creature emerged from the tree trunk. They sat on two adjacent stumps.

"Sorry, they don't know my kind. I'm not sure what they would do if they found me," she said. "But I wonder who they were looking for."

Your kind?

"Hmm," Basil said, attempting nonchalance. He didn't wish to reveal his identity just yet.

There was a dead silence, but the female broke through it. "Why did you hold a sword to Haldi?"

"Who's Haldi?"

The creature rolled her eyes. "The nymph you held a sword to."

"Oh," Basil said, evading her question. "Wait—did you say *nymph*?"

"Of course," she said as if it were no big deal. "Oh my . . . have you never been to the forest?" Her voice inflected at the end.

Basil didn't want to seem stupid again, but he reluctantly admitted to his lack of experience. "Is there something wrong with that?"

"Not if you're an ogsue," she said.

He furrowed his brows, clueless. "A what-now?"

"The creatures of the rocks. It's an expression used to portray that one is not well acquainted with the world. Or if somebody's uncultured. Because, quite literally, ogsues—"

"Live under rocks?" Basil finished her sentence, half joking.

But she nodded and spoke seriously. "Exactly."

"Well, no. I haven't been to a forest. In fact, I've barely left my own property."

"Then you must live in a *castle*. It would drive me insane to be concealed in a small work of wood and stone."

Little does she know . . .

"What's your name?" Basil asked in an effort to avoid the subject.

"Scarlett," she answered.

"Scarlett. That's nice. Scarlett what?"

"Just Scarlett," she said. "And you?"

"Basil. Basil Avington," he admitted. He didn't want to lie to her, even if she was just a stranger.

"Avington? Like the royals?" the nymph asked. Basil smiled, but it didn't meet his eyes. He didn't like that his only identification was his bloodline. "Oh my—you *are* a royal, aren't you? You're who they're looking for."

"Maybe." But he knew the secret was out.

"Why would you ever leave? Why are you here, Your Majesty?" she questioned him, her voice rapid.

He didn't want to admit his overly ambitious plan; he knew it would sound out of reach to anyone normal. Or anyone not normal. Merely anyone at all. Basil settled with, "I needed a break from the castle." It wasn't a total lie, but not the full truth, either; he didn't want to receive the same reaction as the first time. "And if you address me like that again, I just might—"

"A break from the *castle*?" she repeated as if she wasn't sure she'd heard him correctly. He nodded, and Scarlett said, "Interesting. And all right, I won't call you that."

To Basil's surprise, she didn't begin to act differently, and he was happy about it. He hated the fake treatment he'd always received from everybody solely based on his royalty.

"Ambrosia would hate you, you know."

"Who?" Basil's confusion was only growing.

"Ambrosia. She loathes all royals, because . . ." But Scarlett didn't finish her sentence.

Utterly lost, he had no idea who Ambrosia was, how the leaves had taken all his pain away, and how nymphs were suddenly real—he'd only ever learned about them in his Greek mythology tutoring sessions. But it was nice to have somebody to talk to, even if she was a mythical being.

"What were you saying earlier? Golden something?"

"Golden Grove?" Scarlett offered, finger-combing her flaming-red hair.

"Yeah, what is it?"

She raised both arms in the air. "This place. My home. It used to be called something different, but when Ambrosia took over . . . when Ambrosia took over, she changed the name to Golden Grove. She wanted to spite Silverkeep as much as she could."

"And gold is the polar opposite of silver." Basil was catching on.

"Exactly. She hates everything to do with Silverkeep."

Basil understood the feeling of hating the royals. The empathy was ironic; he *was* one. But he was curious why she felt this way. "What was it called before she changed the name?"

"I can't say—speaking of it is forbidden, now."

"Fair enough." But Basil thought such a demand was odd.

Basil never would've imagined himself sitting beside a nymph. There was another silence between them, this time a cozy one. Their comfort in the quiet signified some sort of connection—the first step to a friendship?

"How did that nymph Heidi freeze me? She stared at me, and suddenly, I couldn't move."

Scarlett smirked. "*Hal*di. And, I don't know—we're not supposed to impose enchantment on outsiders. But you were holding a sword to her, so what did you expect?"

"*How*, not why," Basil said.

"It was her desire, and she hadn't used up her daily enchantment. Put the two together, and there you have it."

Basil's eyebrows raised. "What do you mean, *enchantment?*"

"I know. It was difficult for even me to understand at first. But she gives us all a daily allowance of magic, refilled each morning. Ambrosia came and just . . ."

Basil noticed a pattern. Whenever Scarlett mentioned this *Ambrosia* woman, she'd stop mid-sentence, and her eyes would turn sad.

"What?"

"Golden Grove is . . . magical. In every sense of the word. Believe it or don't," Scarlett said matter-of-factly.

Basil struggled to wrap his head around everything he'd just learned. For seventeen—almost eighteen—years, he'd been trapped in the grand palace. One day after deciding to leave, he'd suddenly been exposed to this entirely new world?

He didn't want to think about the enchantment and magic because he knew they were things he couldn't possibly understand. But he wanted to learn more about Scarlett. She was a mystical and stunning creature.

Basil had never seen such red hair; everyone in the Avington bloodline was either blond or brunette. Even at the outings he'd taken to villages of Silverkeep, the hair of redhead subjects didn't possess the fire that Scarlett's did.

"Well, Scarlett, are you going to tell me about you?" Basil asked, surprised by his own curiosity.

She giggled. "What about me?"

"I don't know. What you like? Your story? Your family?" Scarlett's smile faded with the last question. "I'm sorry—I . . . I didn't mean to pry."

"You're okay," she said, shaking her head as if to rid herself of nostalgia. "Well, I like doing *this*."

"Doing wha—" Before Basil could finish talking, Scarlett jumped up. She leapt onto the tree beside them. Her body embraced the trunk, and she crawled up. Gradually, she made her way to the top and sat atop a twiggy branch. Basil had to tilt his head all the way back to see her; the top of the tree was tens of yards in the sky.

It baffled Basil that her entire body mass didn't snap the branch. "That doesn't look sturdy," he said.

"It doesn't matter. I'm using the magic."

A gape of the jaws was all he could manage. His eyes widened in disbelief. "What else can it do?"

"Well, for us nymphs and satyrs it's nothing special. It just enhances natural abilities—jumping, holding the breath underwater, you know. Ambrosia's powers are far stronger. I've heard she can't die, and she has healing abilities, too—not that she would ever purposefully heal someone—but she doesn't tell us much."

Basil nodded, taking it in. "Well, what *can't* she do?"

"Resurrect, revive, I don't know." She shrugged.

"Where does it come from? I have so many—"

"I'm going to use up my daily enchantment if I stay here any longer," Scarlett interrupted before jumping from the branch. She fell a moderate distance, but found a way to make it graceful.

"If you have all this *enchantment*, why would you use it to climb trees?" He'd never thought magic could be possible, but she'd just proven it. He couldn't dismiss what had occurred before his eyes.

She thought for a moment. "What else would I use it for? It's not like there are monsters to fight or places to fly."

Basil wondered what the purpose of the magic was if all it did was embellish nymphs' leisure activities, but he didn't say so, worried it would have been perceived as offensive. "Would you teach me?"

Scarlett chuckled. "Not just anyone can do it."

"What makes you think I'm *just anyone*?" he asked, wry humor in his tone.

"All right." She gestured to the tree trunk. "Try."

Basil closed his eyes and gave himself a running start. He squinted and sprinted for the tree trunk. When he reached it, he jumped and wrapped his limbs around the bark. Sure enough, he fell backward just as fast. The sharp ground knocked his nape.

"Ouch," he groaned, reaching the palm of his hand to the back of his twisted neck. "You're right."

"I know. But worry not—you just need magic," Scarlett suggested.

Basil shook his head and refused the hope she tried to instill. "No way am I doing that again," he said with a grunt, his neck stuck. Basil was still dressed only in the bright leaves that clung to his skin. Soon, the pain in his nape was gone, and the leaves enclosing the affected area glowed.

"That could've been bad, if not for the scouns," Scarlett muttered in concern.

"Scouns?"

"The healing leaves I put on you. They're one of the only good ways Ambrosia uses the enchantment," Scarlett said. "Anyway, I'll summon the enchantment upon you. But only for a moment—my daily allowance will run out if I do it for too long."

Basil was unsure of the "enchantment" she spoke of, but he blindly agreed. "Fine. And what do I do?" Something about Scarlett made Basil give in.

"Just jump. It should work."

Scarlett's eyes focused intently on the tree, and she whispered some gibberish. The look in her eyes was the same one Haldi had given him when he'd held the sword to her. Perhaps it signaled the summoning of magic.

"Go!" she yelled after producing a golden hue around the tree.

On her command, Basil leapt onto the trunk just as Scarlett had before. He was able to become one with it flawlessly, and he climbed upward as if it were a rock wall. He looked down as if he were on top of the world.

Scarlett smiled up at him, but her expression changed when the golden hue began to weaken. "Basil! Jump down," she ordered.

He did so just in time, moments before the magic would've faded. If he'd plummeted to the ground of sticks and stones, he'd have been injured. Even though he could have been healed with scouns, no initial pain was ideal.

Once he was back on the ground, Scarlett said, "I would've come up with you, but it's hard enough to control the magic for one person."

Basil nodded. Even if the key wasn't yet in the picture, he was glad to have a new friend. But it would be dangerous to forget that his mission was time sensitive.

VII

asil had fallen asleep on a bed of leaves. Slices of wood created a frame containing bunches of soft leaves—more a nest than a bed. After a bit of getting used to, it was actually quite comfortable.

The previous night, Scarlett had shown Basil how they never went hungry; her leafy fingernails were edible, and they would grow back in moments. At first, Basil was repulsed, but when his hunger took over, he realized the ability was interesting more than anything.

Naturally, Basil slept far past a normal waking hour; his energy had been sapped in the days before. He learned he'd only been asleep a few hours after Haldi had imposed the enchantment on him, but he still didn't know why she had (besides the fact that he was holding a sword to her).

Despite the welcoming and homey vibe it radiated, Golden Grove was vast. There were many different parts to it, and Scarlett had decided to bring Basil to an abandoned section. Ambrosia would spare a royal no mercy, so Scarlett hoped she wouldn't see him. When he did wake up, Basil found Scarlett watching him. She'd been admiring him as he slept. He should've found it creepy; instead, it made his heart tingle in a way that was unfamiliar but warm. Scarlett tried to look away before being caught staring at him, but Basil noticed right away.

"I was just making you some clothing," she said, twigs and leaves in hand. Two wooden cups of water sat beside the stump on which she sat.

Basil's sight was still adjusting; he'd just awoken. "What are you doing?"

"I just told you, I'm making—"

"No," Basil snapped. "Seriously, *what* are you doing?"

"I don't know, I . . . I want to help you. You're a human—you won't know the first thing about living here without guidance."

"I'm not *living* here. And I have clothes," he said. She was getting the wrong idea—Basil needed the key and only the key. The fresh day redirected his perspective. He shouldn't have asked questions the day before—shouldn't have welcomed her company. "They're right here, behind . . ."

Scarlett didn't say anything. She just watched him search for his things that didn't seem to be there. Once he realized they were gone, Scarlett said, "I had to get rid of your clothes. They might give away your royalty, and that isn't something you'd want Ambrosia to know. Besides, you should blend in with the rest of us."

"But I don't want to wear whatever that is you're making," he whined. The last part was nothing more than a mumble; he didn't want to offend Scarlett.

"Would you rather be dressed in *scouns* forever?"

Basil looked down at his body and realized he was still covered in the healing leaves. "First of all, I want my clothes back. And second, not *forever*. I'm leaving today, in a few hours. Once I search around here, I'm leaving with or without the . . ." Basil remembered he didn't want to mention the key to Scarlett, so he made up some nonsense on a whim. "With or without . . . the sword that I brought here."

Scarlett managed a bitter smile and nodded her head. "If you want to be killed by Ambrosia, be my guest."

"Killed?" Basil's eyes widened.

"She's done it before," she said, visibly biting the insides of her freckled cheeks. But she changed the subject before Basil could ponder the possibilities or ask any questions. "Anyway, you're going to need these. Just trust me." Scarlett held up a finished pair of "pants," and Basil struggled to refrain from laughter. He almost preferred the body consciousness of scouns, feeling like a sculpture with leaves strategically placed for modesty. The "clothing" looked odd, like a string of leaves that would be found draped across the walls of the castle solar on Christmas day.

Scarlett could read his expression well. "I know. I know. Honestly, I've never made them for a male before. But they'll look better on."

As funny as Basil found the forest attire, he'd rather look like a moron than die. If her words were true, it would be a worthy trade-off. So he took the binded leaves from Scarlett and walked behind a tree out of Scarlett's sight. The scouns were difficult to remove, but once he got the hang of it, Basil was able to peel them off.

The pants fit like a glove, and Scarlett was right; they did look better on. The outfit would take some getting used to, but it was all right.

"Here, the shirt," Scarlett called out to him and tossed over a top. "Oops!" Her aim wasn't very good, and they could both hear the leaves hit Basil. Luckily, the "shirt" held together.

Without a mirror, Basil had no idea how stupid he looked. It was all right, because his perception of normal was different from everyone's in Golden Grove.

When Basil emerged from the tree, Scarlett smiled. "Wow," she said, "Not too shabby."

Basil's cheeks warmed in embarrassment; he felt uncomfortable—physically and mentally. All he'd wanted was to get the key and bring it to the castle. Instead, he'd entered an enchanted forest—the kind in children's storybooks.

Basil began to question whether his awkward leaf ensemble was necessary, but Scarlett felt strongly about it. If only he'd been born seven minutes earlier, he wouldn't have had to leave home, he wouldn't have had to embark on this strange journey, and he wouldn't have had to be dressed head-to-toe in bark and leaves.

"What's wrong, *Prince* Basil?" Scarlett teased as he approached the stump on which she sat.

"I just want to go home, or to wherever is next. This all sucks." He may have sounded like an infant, but there was no other way to put it.

"You've only been here a day." She frowned. "Give Golden Grove a chance."

"I need to get out of here—I can hear the clock ticking in my head. I need to find . . . I just . . . this place is freaky and weird and . . ." Basil stopped talking after he realized his words were offensive. She needn't have known he felt off-kilter.

Scarlett became self-conscious, and she untucked her hair, covering her pointy ears. She then bunched her hands into fists to hide her leaf-like fingernails. "Well, then, you should go."

Basil didn't want to look into her eyes. Though the two were barely more than strangers, he felt something odd every time their pupils met. Seeing her ashamed and upset could have hindered Basil's journey. "Farewell," he said, his eyes glued to the ground. Basil questioned the point in dressing himself in forest attire if he was only going to leave.

He began to walk, forcing himself to look straight ahead. But he didn't know how to navigate through Golden Grove. And Scarlett likely knew he'd be back any moment. Basil could barely fit through the lines of trees and sharp nature. He didn't want to falter his ego, but he turned back toward Scarlett after barely making it a few steps.

A grin spread across her face. "Hmm," she said. "I thought you were leaving."

And suddenly, thoughts of the key vanished.

"Me, too." He had a serious look on his face, but something about Scarlett made him forget his pride. They both started laughing for reasons neither of them knew.

"Come along," she said, standing from the stump.

"Where are we going?" Basil sipped on the tepid water Scarlett had prepared, quenching his thirst.

She shrugged. "I assume you don't want to be a stranger to Golden Grove, am I wrong?" Basil shrugged. "I'll need to show you the way around."

He allowed his feet to follow Scarlett, and Basil stopped thinking and started *doing*. She made him that way, but he didn't understand why.

Scarlett exclaimed, "The stream! You might like it."

"Stream? Like with rocks?"

"*Like with rocks*," Scarlett mocked him in a low, masculine voice. "Follow me."

Basil did as she advised. Even though his intention was finding the key, it could have been in an unusual spot. Perhaps the key was hidden in the rocks or submerged underwater. Chances were, it wasn't even in Golden Grove, but there was still a chance.

He had difficulty keeping up with Scarlett; she was sprinting though it presented itself as an effortless stroll. Basil wasn't able to admire the imagery as much as he would've liked, but he could see blurry weeping willows and sequoias in passing. Silhouettes of other creatures were visible, but he wasn't in one place long enough to focus on a single being.

By the time they reached the stream, Basil's hands were on his knees, and his breath was heavy, his face red and damp.

Scarlett, on the other hand, looked energized. Not a drip of sweat clung to her body. She didn't point out his flaws perhaps for the sake of courtesy. In Golden Grove, success on *horseback* likely counted for nothing.

"Look," Scarlett said.

Basil's head was curled into his chest, and his heavy sullen breaths were only intensifying. "I'm so tired. I can't—"

"The water's refreshing. It will help."

To satisfy Scarlett, Basil lifted his head to come face-to-face with the most beautiful body of water he'd ever seen—and one of the only, to be honest. The small waves glinted with fresh rays of sunlight. Blossoming on the surface were flowers, unrecognizable to Basil.

His jaw dropped. "I'll admit, this place is—"

"It's nothing." Scarlett swatted her hands. Such a declaration was easy for *her* to make.

"The only water I've ever been in is my pool. It's royal and luxurious, sure, but not comparable to this." Just looking at the stream took away the fatigue that had a hold on his body.

"I guarantee you'll like it even better under."

"What are we supposed to wear?" Basil asked.

"The clothes we're wearing," Scarlett clarified as if it were obvious. "They're not just any leaves. This is Golden Grove— get used to the abnormal."

Basil didn't see how the leafy articles of clothing wouldn't disassemble, but Scarlett hadn't proven herself a liar. "All right," Basil agreed as Scarlett jumped in. He followed close behind her, and sure enough, the leaves remained intact.

The freezing waters startled Basil, and goosebumps rose on his limbs. "Cold. It's. So. Cold." He convulsed, helpless, teeth chattering.

Yet again, Scarlett was well adjusted to the temperature right away. She didn't hesitate to submerge her body beneath the crystal-clear stream. To Basil, it didn't seem safe; they were surrounded by rocks, and occasionally, fish would brush parts of his body and peck at his skin. Unrecognizable mysteries of nature lined the sandy bottom.

But once Basil's body met equilibrium with the temperature, it wasn't so bad. The light waves were comforting, and the whole setting was much more entertaining than the castle pool. Gilded rims and water laboriously filled by servants were nothing more than unnecessary luxuries. It was similar to his bed in a sense, extravagant solely for comfort. Piles of leaves had proven just fine for slumber the past night.

Scarlett's red hair spread out on the surface of the water, revealing its voluminous length. The water darkened it slightly but didn't wane the fiery quality the tresses possessed.

"What?" Scarlett asked as her head bobbed up from beneath the water. Basil had barely realized his unwavering, awestruck gaze. He blinked rapidly and shook his head.

Why am I so awkward?

"Uh, nothing. Nothing at all."

I'm not usually this awkward.

Scarlett's cheeks turned a rosy color, and she giggled, revealing her somewhat uneven teeth. They were perfect—everything about her was perfect.

Stop it. She's a stranger . . . a nymph . . . a creature.

To avoid further discomfort, he sank down into the stream. The water imposed another cold sensation when it brushed across his face for the first time.

Since Lydia, Basil had deemed it impossible to be attracted to anyone but her; he'd always believed that his heart was reserved for one person. He also believed that one person was Lydia Rose. And his stubbornness refused to think that, perhaps, the truth wasn't always black and white. He didn't acknowledge the plethora of shades of gray, cluttered messily in between.

When he couldn't hold his breath any longer, Basil emerged from the waters. Before he could catch his breath, Scarlett asked, "What's life like in the castle?"

Basil's "normal" was so far out of reach to every subject. It was a difficult idea for him to comprehend. "It's all right. A little lonely, sometimes," he admitted.

"Lonely? Don't you have a whole big family to keep you company? And servants? And books? And whatever it is you—"

"You wouldn't understand the feeling. You're constantly surrounded by nymphs and nature and . . ." Basil realized he didn't know Golden Grove very well.

"Trust me, I know. I understand loneliness all right." Her grim expression implied she was keeping something from Basil, but he hardly caught on. "Who lives there, anyway? I know Bridget and whatever Regis number they're up to—" She stopped as if she'd just remembered something, and her tone shifted to one of consolation. "I forgot. I'm so sorry about your father. Are you mourning?"

Basil grumbled. "How do you know?"

"King dies, it's common knowledge, Basil. People do come through the forest—we just hide from them. And we hear them gossip."

The one thing—well, *one* of the many things—Basil despised about royalty was that every family matter was public knowledge. Scarlett knew about his father's passing before he was able to mention it. "It's all right." He could have droned on about Regis IV and V, but he didn't want to think about death. "Why didn't you hide from *me*?"

Scarlett giggled. "You seemed harmless."

There was a pregnant pause. But he didn't understand what she meant by asking whether he was mourning; he would always be mourning.

"I know how it feels—the loss, I mean."

He hated it when people did that—pretended they were struggling; it wasn't about her.

"Truly," she said, "I've been there." Scarlett must've read his twisted expression. "Well, who lives with you, anyway?" she asked in an effort to change the subject.

"Mother, Hadwin, my brother," he gagged having to think about Regis V. "Lydia Rose, chef Ma—"

"Who's that?" she asked as if recognizing the feeling that pronouncing Lydia's name evoked in Basil.

"Who? Chef Marius?"

"Lydia Rose."

"Oh." For some reason, he was reluctant to discuss Lydia in front of Scarlett. "It's a long story."

"I didn't ask for the story. Only who she is."

"Of course." Basil was overthinking her request. "My brother's, my brother's um . . . she'll be Queen soon." He couldn't bring himself to speak of her relationship with Regis, but the disgusted look on his face revealed enough to Scarlett.

"Why is that so . . ."—she lingered on *so*, struggling to find the right words—"displeasing to you?"

"Because she used to be mine," Basil admitted, spitting the words out like venom. "And then he took her from me like everything else. He took her, that lousy, stuck-up, half-witted brazen arse with the inverse ratio of brain to mouth."

Scarlett stared at him, possibly in awe of the insults he could recall off the top of his head. "So you don't like your brother," she assumed, holding back giggles.

"Doesn't take a genius."

"All right." Her voice inflected. "And this Lydia Rose—you love her?"

Basil felt awkward admitting his innermost feelings to someone he'd met the day before; he shrugged.

A sympathetic frown appeared on Scarlett's face "I'm sorry," she said. Her words were sincere, surprising Basil; feeling pity for a royal wasn't something most were capable of.

He splashed Scarlett playfully, speckling her face with water to accompany her freckles. "So what about you? Who do you live with?"

"Well, we all live together, surrounded by different nymphs

every day. But I'm closest with my siblings, Batellia and Phobos."

"Those are some interesting names," Basil said. "How old
are they?"

"Batellia's only four. She's a cute little one, my half-sister.
And Phobos is fourteen. We're only two years apart."

Basil hadn't thought about her age before, but sixteen didn't
stray from his estimate. He was curious about her family and
half-sibling, but Basil knew better than anyone that nobody
enjoyed talking about those matters. Or maybe it was just him.

"So, you like your siblings." It was easy for Basil to infer
from the way her voice grew excited as she spoke of them.

She laughed as if feeling otherwise was unheard of. "We
have our days, but of course I like them. I love them. And even
though you don't *like* your brother, you love him, too."

"You don't know my family."

"You're right," she said. Basil was surprised and slightly
disappointed that she settled for his response; he liked the way
she became passionate during their healthy banter.

They stared at each other quietly, and Basil felt a foreign
emotion that he couldn't put a finger on.

Distracting both Basil and Scarlett from the intimate eye
contact, a stampede of distant hooves cut through the silence.
Then there were voices, similar to the day before. However,
unlike the previous time, the sounds were abundant; there were
clearly more than three servants. "Hide!" Scarlett yelled in a
whisper.

This time, they were both aware of who the searches
were looking for. Basil was surprised his family cared about
him enough to send out so many servants. Then, of course, it
couldn't have taken them much time and effort. All they had to
do was say a few words to some servants.

"Basil Avington?" one of them called, his voice weary as if
he'd been repeating the name for days. Basil felt a tinge of guilt
as he watched them through the trees, noticing their fatigue.

The servants were dressed in purple and gray tunics, the colors of Silverkeep.

They were close enough for Basil to make out their silhouettes, but he couldn't see any faces. Scarlett submerged her body beneath the water to hide from the searchers, but a slight splash sounded in doing so. "Basil," she whispered, "come under."

"A sound!" another servant exclaimed.

Basil's heart raced.

"It was only a rippling of waves, sire."

It wasn't just any servant, but the commanding official; no other servant was regarded as 'sire.' "There's no harm in checking. We must be sure."

Great.

Basil puffed his cheeks and silently dove beneath the surface. Below, he found Scarlett smiling. Her mouth was open, and water flowed freely in and out of it. Careful not to make noise as he kept himself from floating to the surface, Basil furrowed his brows. In response, she opened her mouth wide and then smiled. Scarlett could breathe underwater. He'd forgotten.

The servants' voices were wavy and muffled from underwater, but Basil could make out the words they uttered.

"It came from the stream," one of them said. Just as the claim was pronounced, Basil ran out of breath. He pointed to his cheeks to signal to Scarlett that he had to breathe no matter how risky it might be. At this point, the searchers were hanging over the stream. It was a miracle they hadn't already identified Basil or Scarlett.

Scarlett rapidly shook her head and placed a finger in the air as if to say "one moment." Basil could have remained there just a few seconds longer if he'd had to, but any longer than moments, and he would've lost his breath. He already felt faint and nauseous. But if they found him, everything that'd hardly started would end.

Scarlett narrowed her eyes and lifted her hands, and he

assumed she was summoning the enchantment. It was a new day, which meant Scarlett's powers were refueled.

Basil looked down to find his limbs outlined in a golden hue, and at once, his breath became natural. He didn't need to puff his cheeks out, and he didn't long to gasp for air. Basil smiled at the second sacrifice Scarlett had made for him. It wasn't anything significant, but he appreciated the small favors; he wasn't used to feeling protected.

Close by, Basil could hear one of the servants jump off a saddle. He trudged toward the stream. The servant's arms plunged into the water and cupped some into his hands for drinking.

"Wow," the servant muttered to himself as if remarkably refreshed.

"Come on, Dixon," the commanding officer yelled from his horse. "We haven't got all day."

"Yes, sire. It appears the stream is empty of persons," the servant said without a second glance. He hadn't even looked, but Basil and Scarlett were relieved by his negligence, and they sighed in unison.

"All right. Let's divide and conquer from here on out." Irked grunts spread throughout the crowd of servants, but soon, the group was far out of earshot, and Scarlett and Basil could finally get some air. The gold hue around Basil faded as Scarlett retracted it, and although Basil was able to temporarily breathe underwater, he needed the crisp air.

"How did you do that?" Basil asked, gulping the fresh air and releasing his breath.

Scarlett looked around as she thought up a response. "We nymphs, we're one with nature. Your solace may be money, but mine is . . . a tree. We protect the forest, and the forest protects us."

Two days ago, Basil would never have believed such a thing, but he knew it was the truth. "And you used some of your daily allowance on me?"

"Of course," she said.

"Why? Why do I deserve it?"

"I wouldn't want to lose the only human—friend—I've ever had," she admitted, the word *friend* coming out as a question. "And, don't flatter yourself—my power is refilled daily. It is for all of us."

"Right," Basil said and paused before speaking again. "What were we talking ab—oh, right, siblings."

"Yes," she said. "Would you like to meet them?"

Off her excitement, Basil agreed. "That would be nice."

"Perfect. We'll dine with them tonight," she said with a bright grin.

But he couldn't merely fly by the seat of his pants; he was on a *mission*, and he needed Philip's key, which he seemed to have forgotten about these past few hours. But he supposed food was necessary, and dining with company wouldn't be the worst thing.

"So you told me about your siblings—what about your parents?" Basil asked.

Scarlett swallowed. "My mother is a kind nymph who does her duties. Now, do you see the flowers around us?" Her voice was rushed.

Basil noticed how Scarlett glossed over the subject with avoidance, not even bringing up her father, but he didn't push it. "Yes, they're beautiful."

"Pick one."

"All right, uh . . . that one." Basil pointed to a flower to Scarlett's left with purple petals and an orange center.

"Uclina," she said. "My favorite. You have good taste." Scarlett swam to the flower and tucked her fingers around its stem. "Smell it." She brought it beneath Basil's nose, the petals tickling the hairs above his mouth.

As he inhaled through his nose, Basil took in the fresh aroma of the uclina. The flower was everything perfumes aspired to be but failed to execute. It was the smell of new beginnings—a pleasant scent that could send him into slumber or jerk him awake. No words could describe the sensation it evoked in him, so he remained silent.

"It's yours," Scarlett offered.

Basil grinned as he reached for the blossom and took it from her grip. "I will treasure it." And he tucked the petals into his leafy blouse.

The shrinking space between them was dangerous. "Why are you here?" Scarlett asked.

"I told you—I was sick of the castle. I needed to get away."

She shook her head in denial. "I'm not stupid, Basil. A prince wouldn't just run off for no reason. I just can't think of a plausible motive. Why are you *really* here?" It was fair for anyone to question a royal leaving the luxurious palace to join a forest of misfits.

Basil didn't want to admit his ambition; even he knew the task was nearly impossible. But he'd rather admit the embarrassing truth than tell a lie. "King Philip's key," he mumbled.

"King what's what?" Scarlett asked, unable to identify his blurry words.

"Philip's key," he clarified, his voice rising. An unexpected reaction appeared on Scarlett's face. "I know it's impossible, I just—"

Her lips pursed. "You won't find the key, Basil. Don't waste your time." Her tone was jarring.

"That's why I didn't want to tell you," Basil said. "Everyone believes it's a myth nowadays, but King Philip wouldn't lie. I know it."

"I didn't say he lied. But you're not going to find it, Basil. Save yourself while you can."

"What do you mean? I—"

"Basil! Don't try and find the key. It will hurt you!" yelled Scarlett. Basil hadn't yet heard her speak that way.

"I shouldn't have said anything. I should've just kept to myself. I'm sorry, Scarlett," he said as she emerged from the stream. As the water surrounded her, Basil saw Scarlett in a different light. She stood tall and beautiful, and her blue eyes fired with rage.

"You don't understand what you're getting yourself into," Scarlett insisted. Before Basil could say another word, she pivoted away from him and scurried out of the stream.

"Wait! Scarlett!" But it was no use; she was gone.

He'd only get clarity if he followed her. As fond of the stream as he was, she was more important. As he quickly climbed from the waters, the cold air felt extra freezing. It emphasized the tiny drops of stream water and erected the hairs on his arms.

The only place he knew in Golden Grove was his bed of leaves, but even that was difficult to find through the twists and tangles of the enchanted forest.

After some time, he was able to retrace his footsteps and find the bed of leaves he'd slept in the night before. Basil found Scarlett leaning against the trunk of a tree, her cheeks tearstained and blotchy. "What's the matter?" Basil asked as her tristesse became visible.

"Oh, hi." She laughed ironically, wiping away the excess tears, embarrassed to be found as she was.

Basil went to sit beside her, and Scarlett scooched over to make room. "It's okay if you don't want to talk about it," he said. In any way he could, Basil wanted to be unlike his brother. If he were Regis, he'd have forced Scarlett to speak of the matter whatever it might be.

"Thank you," Scarlett whispered. To Basil's surprise, her head fell to rest on his shoulder. Scarlett's red tresses draped over Basil's body, falling onto his arms and legs. In this brief moment, Basil wasn't thinking about Lydia Rose as he usually did when he was around a female. He wasn't in the past or the future, but the present—for the first time in a while.

Basil knew that Scarlett was battling a sorrow of her own, and he didn't want to push her to reveal something she wasn't comfortable with. The silent time they shared allowed Basil to think. But he didn't think about home or the key. Instead, he pondered the wonders of Golden Grove—the magic, the nymphs. What were men called? How did scouns work?

Time passed quickly like that, Scarlett's head comfortable on his broad shoulder. Her eyes fluttered shut, and Basil watched her gracefully nap. He'd lost track of time simply watching her.

Meanwhile, the sky slowly became darker. He didn't want to disturb her beautiful peace, but his stomach growled. As gently as possible, Basil tapped her. Scarlett's legs jerked awake, and out of instinct, she slapped Basil.

"Ouch," he said, covering his cheek.

Scarlett's eyes widened in recognition. "I'm so sorry, I forgot. I must have fallen asleep. I didn't mean to—would you like some scouns?"

"No, it's all right. It doesn't hurt too bad," Basil lied. "I was just going to say it might be dinner time."

"Ah, yes! Let me get Phobos and Batellia." Scarlett's body shot up. "You should like them. They're . . . gregarious," she said before sprinting away.

Alone under the tree, Basil wondered about his family. Now that Scarlett wasn't here, his mind wandered into places he'd rather it not go. But it was uncontrollable. He assumed nobody knew what he was up to; it would take a fool to search for something that wasn't believed to exist, and Basil wasn't known to be dull-witted. But Scarlett's peculiar, disingenuous reaction had led him to believe that perhaps she knew something about the key that Basil didn't.

In a few moments, Scarlett returned, her two younger siblings holding either hand. Scarlett had promised not to tell them he was a royal. Though she trusted her siblings, it was better to be cautious. And if Ambrosia knew . . .

"I'll go gather the meal. Why don't you introduce yourselves," Scarlett said before grabbing a basket that hung from a nearby oak tree and scurrying off. Basil felt awkward in the company of two strangers though that's all *Scarlett* was to him a day before—what she still was.

"Phobos," the boy greeted, holding out a hand. His legs were horse-like and hairy, and small horns were attached to the top of his head. "It's a pleasure to meet you."

Basil was freaked out by Phobos's physicality, but he reached out his arm to be polite. "Nice to meet you, too," he said, his hand trembling.

"Have you never seen a satyr?" Phobos asked. It clicked for Basil; he'd learned that satyrs were the male equivalent and brothers to nymphs throughout his mythology studies. "Batellia, introduce yourself."

But opposing Phobos's request, the young auburn-haired nymph hid behind the hairy left leg of her brother and grabbed on in fear.

"Come on now, have some manners," Phobos advised, tugging her arms off his lower limb.

"It's all right," Basil said. A four-year-old refusing to introduce herself didn't offend him.

The young nymph pointed a leaf-tipped finger at Basil. "He threatened Haldi! And we're not supposed to talk to him! Ambrosia said so!"

Basil swallowed, and his face reddened. As little as he knew about Golden Grove, he gathered this couldn't be good.

VIII

asil was left alone to dine with Scarlett, but it didn't bother him. After Batellia's remark, Phobos had thought it'd be best for them to leave. Scarlett was disappointed to find Basil alone when she returned with a full basket of food, but she was put at further unease when Basil explained her sister's accusation. Even if Ambrosia didn't know Basil was a royal, there was still a human in the forest: someone who didn't belong.

But they were able to share an intimate meal together. The last night, they'd eaten only what fell from the branches of certain trees and Scarlett's leafy fingernails. The fruits had appeased Basil enough to fulfill his hunger, but they weren't anything delicious. Tonight, Scarlett held a basket full of meat and bread.

"That looks oddly similar to the contents of my lost drawstring," Basil said as Scarlett came into the clearing.

Scarlett giggled. "I wonder why."

Clearly, it was the food from the royal kitchen, but Basil

wondered how she'd acquired it. "Did you steal my food when I slept?"

She didn't say yes or no. "Back then, I didn't know you. I was hesitant to trust a stranger."

"Back then? You mean, yesterday?"

"The passage of time is different here," Scarlett said, providing no further clarification.

"Okay." But Basil wasn't sure he believed her. "Well, I assume it's dinnertime."

Because of Batellia's and Phobos's exit, the food would be too much for both of them. But Basil was hungry after straying from his royal eating habits. In the castle, Basil scarfed down three meals daily. Each one filled him up to the perfect degree of satisfaction.

"As do I. Hungry?" Scarlett said, dumping the basket onto a wooden table. It was unsteady and crooked, and Basil assumed it was made from trees, quite possibly the ones that used to stand atop the lone stumps.

Basil looked at the beef in contempt as he realized it was borderline rotting. It produced a putrid odor, and its color was slightly off. "Are we going to eat it like that?" he asked with a gag.

"I'm a nymph, not a lunatic!" Scarlett laughed as she stood and wandered off. At this point, Basil didn't bother to ask where she was going. But a few moments later, she came back with a few logs. Basil knew nothing about life beyond the castle and looked at her with curious eyes. "Fire," she clarified, rolling her eyes at Basil's ignorance.

"Of course." He'd never seen flames produced like this; his only experience with fire was the solar and library fireplaces. "But won't it still be gross?"

"Nope. The high temperatures should fix everything." But Basil's stare of disgust didn't fade. Scarlett ignored him and carried on. "You should be glad I have some daily enchantment left. Otherwise, we'd have to slave away, rubbing the logs at each other until they produced a flame."

"Lucky us," Basil muttered sarcastically, causing Scarlett to roll her eyes.

Once Scarlett conjured her enchantment to produce the fire, the flames grew tall and fierce, emanating warmth. "It's my specialty," she said, staring at the crackling blaze in awe.

Scarlett did remind him of fire: her hair, her compassion, her *literal* fire-making skills.

Sticks were abundantly distributed on the ground, and Basil picked one up. "You're getting the hang of it." Scarlett grinned. "Now just poke it through the—"

"Yeah, I know. I'm a prince, not an idiot!" he said, imitating her prior remark, along with its precise tone.

The two held the slabs of beef above the fire, and slowly, the poignant smell diminished. Crackling flames illuminated Scarlett's features. Her pointy ears that had initially disturbed Basil seemed to frame her face beautifully. He stared with soft intent, and any thoughts of Lydia Rose disappeared.

Basil suddenly became aware of his every move. The simple suspension of his arm above the hearth sparked unease. He didn't want to feel as he did, physically and mentally. Scarlett's eyes never seemed to close. The two stayed like that, their visions intertwined, as they hovered the meat above the blaze.

Time stopped in that moment as if the world had frozen. And his mission was no longer his largest concern. He cared about Scarlett, the nymph he'd barely known for two days.

But the special moment was interrupted when the fire got the best of the meat. Orange flames surrounded Basil's slab. He flinched when he noticed, which wasn't for a while. Unsure of how to deal with fire, Basil dropped his stick to the dirty ground. If it were any other two starving friends, dropping half their food supply would be no laughing matter. But Scarlett and Basil couldn't help themselves. After she bent down to blow out the flames, they got lost in a shared laughter. Basil felt the most liberty he'd felt in his lifetime. Nobody was there to yell at him, and Scarlett was laughing *with* him, not *at* him. Regis V would have done the latter.

Dirt, pebbles, and woodchips crusted the combusted beef. "Yummy," he said, glancing at his mistake. Scarlett continued to hold her stick above the fire, maintaining a perfect distance.

"We're nearly always herbivores—I'm surprised I haven't made the same mistake."

Once her slab was cooked to a *T*, she pulled the stick away from the fire and released it atop the wooden table. Basil frowned. "I'll just starve, I guess."

"Oh, stop it," Scarlett said, chopping the meat with her bare hands. The slab glowed with enchantment and split into two equal pieces. "Cutting is hard work. I'd rather take a short-cut if I can."

Though Basil was beginning to feel an odd something for Scarlett, he was never one to impress. With his hands and mouth, he gobbled down the entire piece before Scarlett took her second bite. She let out a burst of giggles.

"I was hungry!" Basil said, mouth full of chewed-up chunks.

Yet again, Scarlett held no judgment over him. She grinned. "I'm glad you're appeased." Bridget would've told Basil to act like the man he would soon become, or to excuse himself and return when he was prepared to be mature.

He watched as she gracefully ate. Her face melted with the delicious taste.

"Have you never had meat before?"

"Not *never*," she said. "Okay, maybe never."

"How do you like it?"

But her delighted expression was a response in itself.

One couldn't tell the meat was once spoiled; the tempera-ture subtracted all the decay. When not a morsel remained on the table in front of her, she turned to Basil. Dusk was ap-proaching, and the sun would soon disappear behind the pines.

Basil had expected his journey to entail nobody other than

himself, but just two days in, he'd made a friend—or . . . a relationship he wasn't sure how to describe.

He admired her every feature—the way her hair fell messily around her shoulders and the freckles that spotted the bridge of her nose, spreading out as they reached her cheeks.

Their eyes locked, and Basil fell into a trance. He'd never seen Scarlett so serious.

Perhaps because I've known her but a few days.

As her smile faded, it revealed a conflicted expression. She felt something, too—Basil knew it.

The wooden bench was comfortable for neither of them, but their shared gaze made them careless. Scarlett's lips naturally parted, and Basil inched closer to her, each tiny movement building a foreign anticipation. He could almost taste her breath.

He wanted to say something, but his mind went blank. Even if he was acting up based on the circumstance, the emotions he felt were raw and natural. Moreover, he needed a release. He'd almost forgotten Lydia Rose's face as he was lost in Scarlett's. His hand found the hair he'd so desperately wanted to touch. Its texture was special—a bit rough. He didn't make it happen; it just did. Scarlett didn't object. Instead, she leaned closer into Basil. The act provided him with the validation he was hoping for—that their playful joking was flirtatious, not her mere personality.

The thought of kissing Scarlett didn't daunt Basil—it tempted him. Allured him. Their breathing quickened, and Basil could hear his heartbeat through his ears. It was the only noise aside from the crackling flames. No blinking. The two had only each other—no rules, no pesky twin. But he was scared to kiss her. Simply put, his fear of rejection hindered his choice.

Lucky for him, Scarlett had no such fright. She could sense his nerves from his flushed skin and placed her hand on his shoulder. Slowly, she leaned into him, parting her lips. Basil had never felt such a thing, and as it went on, he allowed himself to enjoy the moment beside the glowing embers—a moment he would never forget. The pestering thoughts swirling around his head diminished as she reached her hand into Basil's scalp. The kiss was nothing like Lydia Rose; it was aggressive and raw. Assertive—not a light, lingering touch. But Basil realized he liked it. Better?

Surely, it was too soon. She was a stranger; they barely knew each other. But they'd shared every recent moment, divulged their innermost thoughts.

Scarlett's hair was tangled up in his arms, and he reached for her waist. Sweat drenched him. Their lips remained together as his moistened hands explored her leaf-covered back. It was dark, and the forest was quiet. Basil had never felt so free. And every haunting thought regarding the key evaporated.

The kiss was dangerous, pulling him into a state of mind he didn't have time for.

It felt immoral; he knew nothing about her. Had she kissed another before? A satyr?

He didn't want to get ahead of himself, but the feelings the kiss evoked were so much more than those from Lydia Rose, yet they'd only known each other for two days. They were strangers. But their tongues overlapped.

After Scarlett pulled away, Basil realized that time had barely passed, but it felt like slow motion. Tasting her somehow made Basil tired. The beds of leaves weren't far from the table, and together they found them without words. Though there were two "beds," the night was cold, and they needed each other to warm up.

Basil was pleased when Scarlett tucked herself into his bed. "Goodnight," she said, a flutter of excitement in her voice.

"Sweet dreams." Basil planted his lips on her forehead.

They lay, tangled in each other's arms, beneath the twinkling stars. Basil's fingers rested behind her pointed ear, his other hand on the small of her back. The bed was big, yet the extra space lingered on either side rather than between them. Scarlett fell into immediate slumber—it wasn't so easy for Basil.

He lay awake, thinking about everything he'd forgotten when he'd been lost in Scarlett. It was dangerous. Now that dawn had turned to dusk in the blink of an eye, Basil was reminded of the quick passage of time. If every day was like this, Regis V's coronation would happen before Basil knew it. When he did return to the castle, he'd be recognized as the greatest fool. He'd refuse to admit the purpose for his journey, but leaving the palace at all would be looked down upon. The key had to be his top priority. Finding it wasn't a choice, but a necessity.

But as time passed, he let slumber take him. His body was fatigued and unused to the lifestyle of Golden Grove.

Basil woke up alone, his open arms empty. Scarlett was no longer embracing his body, so he figured she must have gone to her own bed. But when he looked to the second bed of leaves, it seemed that wasn't the case.

"Scarlett?" he called out, a soft yell. Drowsy, he paced their immediate surroundings in search of the nymph. "Are you playing hide and seek with me?" But there was no response.

Rejection. Scarlett had merely wanted to be *kind* the night before, offering herself to Basil. Or worse, it was solely because of his royalty. And now, she wanted to leave before she had to break it to him. But parts of it didn't add up; she was the one who'd made him the clothes and implied he should stay here forever . . . who'd leaned in for the kiss . . . who'd crawled into his bed before falling asleep.

Perhaps he was overthinking, and she'd woken up early to

gather some berries for breakfast, or she was dipping in the stream.

But Basil reminded himself that Scarlett wasn't his grandest issue. He wanted—needed—to find the key. Perhaps Scarlett's leave was the best thing that could have happened to him. He hadn't worked on locating the key for two days too long. Still, the chances were slim . . . near impossible.

He wandered aimlessly around Golden Grove, visiting the spots with which he hadn't yet familiarized himself—maybe the key would be there. Basil found a large cluster of stones and a campfire with benches surrounding the hearth. He barely found use in dismantling the pile of rocks; it was a grain of sand in the scope of Silverkeep. But he did it, anyway.

The weight of the rocks surprised Basil, and he tossed them to the side, one by one. His veins popped out of his skin with each lift. If no other outcome resulted, it would be his exercise for the day—something he'd forgotten about. Perhaps that was the reason his body felt odd.

Each stone felt pointless as the same thing was revealed beneath each one: another rock. There was no shining key or glaring clue. Basil was stupid to think there would be. He no longer found purpose in destroying the neat cluster, so he stopped. And he failed to fix the mess he'd left behind. It would be a waste of time.

Finding the key felt impossible, and he began to doubt whether such a thing existed. But overthrowing Regis V was his grandest desire, and the key would let him do it. It might've been for the wrong reasons, but he didn't care. The kingdom would adore him if he was able to rule like Philip. However, doubting and questioning wouldn't propel him further on his journey.

He was different from the rest of the hopeless and destitute travelers that had longed for the key centuries ago; he *believed*. The others had nothing better to do than search, but Basil did.

He *had* places to be and a kingdom to assist. It was a choice. A calling.

Basil's day was filled with exaggerated sighs and complaints. No matter where he looked or what he did, he felt as though he was flogging a dead horse—nothing would come of his search. But something kept him there—something told Basil not to leave, not yet.

The thoughts circulated from one pole to another. There would be a moment of hope, but when he remembered his reality, the dread would come rushing back.

Basil searched in every nook and cranny, hoping for something more than blank space, but the answer never arrived.

This was the essence of his day—hoping and regretting. Though he knew the key was probably not in Golden Grove, something drove him to stay. He made of it what he could and used the time to explore. Basil encountered endless trees from which he couldn't find his way back. Thankfully, certain landmarks aided him, like the leaf beds and the fire circle.

As he ventured through Golden Grove, Basil admired the forest inhabitants, observing physical characteristics he hadn't yet noticed. Their heights differed slightly, but most of them were a bit shorter than Basil.

The few nymphs and satyrs he passed threw him dirty looks. They'd sneer and stiffen when he approached. If they weren't alone, the creatures would mumble to each other. He had no other choice than to assume they were talking about him. The rejection wasn't any better in the forest than it had been in the castle. Royals and grove inhabitants were the same in that sense. And Scarlett was the one good thing about this mess, but she was gone. The nymph had vanished into thin air.

Who cares? The key is the only thing I need.

But that hardly felt like the case. Would it really have been so bad to simply stay in Golden Grove with Scarlett . . . forget about everything that concerned the castle?

Yes, Basil. It would *be bad. And it doesn't matter what I think, anyway; she's gone.*

There was no way to calculate the time. In the castle, it hadn't mattered; extravagant clocks stood at every turn, but there was no such thing in Golden Grove. His best bet was to observe the brightness of the day. But it was difficult because the same light filled the sky for over twelve hours, especially thanks to the springtime.

It was Basil's first time selecting food to eat on his own. He waited and waited for Scarlett, but when his stomach wouldn't stop growling, he had to continue without her. He traversed the underbrush until a small bush of berries stood beside him, and he couldn't resist. Each one possessed a smooth texture and perfect spherical shape.

The bush was pointy, and small berries decorated the green. Basil reached for one but wound up with many in his hands. Their touch was satisfying, and he simply couldn't stop picking them. Each one was tinted a vibrant pink and blotted his palms.

As they piled up in Basil's hand, a few of the berries squished, but he didn't mind. On a whim, he soon bared the entire bush.

About to put them in his mouth, Basil wondered what they would taste like. Tangy? Tart? Sweet? But before he could find out, he felt a harsh slap on his wrist. He looked up to find none other than Scarlett, her eyes wide. The pink berries went flying before smashing on the dirty ground. Covered in filth, they looked far from edible.

"In the name of Philip, what'd you do that for?" He looked to Scarlett, but his hungry eyes softened. He was grateful for her presence.

Scarlett sat on a nearby rock and slapped her forehead. "Those are ivlies!" Off of Basil's blank gaze, she clarified, "More commonly known as *death* berries?"

"Okay? What's wrong with death ber—ohh . . ."

"How could you miss it? I mean, their pigment, their—if I wasn't here, you'd be dead right now."

"So you've been watching me?" Immediately, Basil replayed the day thus far in his head: pounding the rocks, angrily talking to himself—

Was I talking to myself?

"She's . . . she's watching. I have to go," she said.

"Wait, Scarlett!"

But she stood and ran, trembling little sprints, her pointy heels imprinting the dirt. And Basil was left there, hungry and alone.

What could I have done wrong?

Basil was unsure of the time; the sun was almost down, but he could make out the colors and greenery as he trudged to the lonely bed of leaves. As dusk settled, he thought about home. He wondered how Bridget and Regis V and Lydia Rose were going on without him. Probably just fine—better, even. They didn't miss him; he was sure of it.

Basil gave up on Golden Grove. Forming relationships had been a mistake, and he knew that now. So he allowed his eyes to close.

But why did she simply run away? And who was watching? Ambrosia? Surely, she can't be that dangerous.

Tomorrow, Basil decided, would be the time to move along on his journey—out of Golden Grove and onto his next stop, wherever that may be.

But as his eyelids fluttered shut, he heard a *psst* coming from close by. It must've been a rustling of leaves, though they didn't usually sound like that. Still, Basil didn't allow himself to imagine otherwise. But the pesky noise became louder, and he was unable to find slumber. It became "Psst!" and eventually "Basil!"

When his name was called, he knew the source immediately. "Scarlett?" he whispered into thin air.

"Yes." Her voice broke. "Look up."

Basil forced himself out of the comfortable position in which he lay and turned his gaze to the tip of an adjacent sycamore. Scarlett's feet hung from the top branch. It couldn't be her. It couldn't be the same girl that had just run from him.

"What are you doing?"

Scarlett's voice was different, faltered, as she uttered the words regretfully. "We can't spend time together . . . hang around each other . . . talk . . ."

It was the last thing Basil expected to hear. He thought maybe she would say he had to leave Golden Grove, or she hated him, but not that they couldn't hang around each other. "What do you mean?"

"I mean, it's what's best. For you and me. And Golden Grove." But as she put on a strong mask, he could tell it pained her to speak.

He would never have suspected that a forest nymph would be his greatest weakness. "I don't understand."

"Come up here," she whispered, gesturing to the tree.

Basil was no longer tired, and he waited for Scarlett to conjure the enchantment. When a golden hue surrounded his body, he leapt to the trunk. It took no effort for him to reach the branch.

He was glad to be on the same level as Scarlett. The closer he was to her, the more he could appreciate her company. Each time Basil watched her speak, she became more and more beautiful, inside and out. But this time, her words disagreed.

"Ambrosia approached me late last night." Scarlett swallowed. "I can't talk to you."

Basil's chest tightened. He didn't know who this Ambrosia was, but he didn't like her. "Why?" It was all he could manage.

"I told you, she hates royals. If I knew why, I would say it." Something about her voice was off—insincere.

"Right." He gripped the base of his neck. She was just like Lydia Rose, too weak to make decisions for herself. If she felt anywhere close to how *he* did, Scarlett wouldn't have left. "Well, let me know when you—"

"Ambrosia doesn't take no for an answer," Scarlett interjected. There was more assertion in her voice this time. "Trust me, I know."

"Who even *is* she?"

The words caught Scarlett by surprise. "Have I not told you?" As Basil shook his head, she continued, "The queen—well, tyrant—of Golden Grove. The only evil part of this place."

As she explained, Basil remembered their first conversation. She'd talked about Ambrosia and become uncomfortable. "I think you did tell me," Basil said. He couldn't think straight.

"There's something you should know about her. I owe it to you," she whispered, hesitant.

"Okay?"

"She's the reason . . ." Scarlett shut her eyes for an excessive duration as her voice trailed off. "Ambrosia is cruel."

"Yeah, I've figured that much."

"Not cruel—brutal." She took a long, deep breath. "My father used to rule Golden Grove. Everything was different back then. It was a peaceful, blossoming place."

"It seems fairly peaceful to me."

"You've been here three days, Basil. And you've stayed in one, safe section. This is my home. I know it well," Scarlett said. "And so did my father—before Ambrosia." Basil didn't speak; there was nothing valuable for him to say.

"Ambrosia showed up in Golden Grove one day. She was the only human most of us had ever seen. Naturally, we treated her with respect because we'd always been taught that humans were better than us. I believed it until I met her." A silent tear slid down Scarlett's freckled cheek, and her voice began to break.

"It happened in a blur. One day, Father was there on the throne of leaves. The next day, he wasn't. The next day, the throne was dark green and black. The orange and red tones were nowhere to be found. Besides the scouns, all the leaves became wilted. Even now, they remain that way.

"Mother was pregnant with Phobos at the time, and I was only four. Phobos was born without a father. I wish I'd never known him, rather than losing him so young. But even now, I barely remember him.

"But I do remember finding his body . . . a massive *hole* in his stomach . . . his eyes wide open . . . I still see his face . . . mucus and saliva and blood and sweat and . . ." She wiped the tears from her eyes. "We thought she was kind at first—she brought us hope. When she began to sleep in Golden Grove, she made the forest brighter than it already was. But when the opportunity arose, she seized it. Power is dangerous. And my father is gone, all because she wanted his." The memory was difficult for Scarlett to speak of. But it all made sense to Basil— why she'd avoided speaking of her father and Ambrosia.

Unsure of what to do or say, Basil held out his hand for her to hold. They sat there in the quiet of night, and Basil thought about her words.

Power is dangerous. And my father is gone, all because she wanted his.

It seemed like Scarlett was speaking about him. Was his desire for power dangerous? Was he in the wrong?

Holding hands wasn't enough, and Basil embraced her tightly on the branch of the tree. Scarlett's head rested on his shoulder, and her body shook. He pulled her tighter with each tremble. "We can't talk again after this."

"Shh," Basil hushed. "It's going to be okay." But he was only lying to himself. Though they barely articulated the connection they shared, it was very much there. And no matter how much he promised himself the key was the only thing that mattered, it simply wasn't true.

Basil could never convince Scarlett to oppose Ambrosia; it would put them both in danger. She was ruthless—not afraid to kill if it meant staying in power. But Basil's body began to quiver with Scarlett's. It was Lydia Rose all over again; someone dear to his heart was taken away. The world didn't want him to be happy.

"I can't disobey Ambrosia. This is our last goodbye." And Scarlett choked on the words she despised.

IX

 olden Grove lost its magic without Scarlett. The beds of leaves were rigid and uncomfortable. The trees were bland and intimidating. The sky was the same color that it was everywhere else.

Dawn was rather cold for springtime. The outfit of leaves Scarlett had made still covered Basil. It began to shrink and wither on his body, but he had no idea where his clothes could be—or the location of his sword, water, and Prancer for that matter. Basil hoped his next spot would at least provide him with a sensible outfit.

The sun pulled Basil from his slumber and propelled his journey forward. He'd wasted too much time in Golden Grove, and there were only so many days before Regis V's coronation. Silverkeep was too vast to waste any time. The very thought never failed to remind Basil what he was there to do: find the key—not kiss a nymph or live in an enchanted forest.

Basil had no food, water, weaponry, or means of transportation. He could only hope that resources would be available

at his next location. And he could only hope there would *be* a next location. Basil had to carry on with nothing but his own body. And he did.

Golden Grove seemed endless, and Basil wasn't quite sure where it actually stopped. He walked and walked, wandering aimlessly, each step like a battle to survive. He needed Prancer. Or Scarlett. Frankly, anyone would have been better than nobody, even Regis. Basil wanted to collapse.

But then, "Wait!" A shadow loomed behind him, and from her voice, Basil knew it was Scarlett.

He turned to face her, and there she stood—the stunning redhead nymph, standing stiffly. "Don't leave," she whispered. "Not before you know the truth."

"Last night, you said it was our last goodbye."

Scarlett cleared her throat. "There's more I didn't tell you. I want to now, so you don't waste your life on this." She walked toward Basil, revealing red-rimmed eyes. "Ambrosia's ruined my life for long enough. My destiny isn't in her hands. If you do the right thing with this information, maybe you don't have to leave. You're my first real . . . friend."

Friend?

Basil could barely fathom that they'd only met three days earlier. At the very sight of Scarlett, he felt strong and weak all at once.

Too much feeling.

He shook his head, ignorant to think the move would push away all his emotions. "Whatever you have to say doesn't matter. I need to find the key." It wasn't the response Scarlett expected, and she flinched in response.

"You're not going to find it."

"I thought you were different, but you're just like the rest. You, if anyone, should believe me. King Philip's key is somewhere out there, and I'm going to find it."

"There is a key." Scarlett looked down with pursed lips.

"But you're *not* going to find it. Especially not if you leave Golden Grove."

With the latter sentence, Basil neared Scarlett's face. He was barely inches away as he placed his hands on her shoulders. "You know where the key is," Basil inferred, his heartbeat quickening.

He could tell it was a secret Scarlett wasn't supposed to share. She nodded, her eyes squinted. "That's what I was going to tell you. How do you think we have our magic?"

"But it can't be, it—" Basil was at a loss for words. His left eyebrow cocked, and he blinked rapidly. It never occurred to Basil that *magic* was contained in the key. But looking back at it, he wasn't sure *what* he had thought.

"It can be, and it is. The key is the reason for Ambrosia's violence and danger. None of us can fight it."

"And that's why Haldi laughed so violently when I asked her about it." The puzzle pieces were beginning to fit together. "Why would you wait until now to tell me? You've known it's what I've been trying so hard to find."

"Because, Basil . . . you wouldn't have believed me then. You wouldn't have listened to me. You would've tried to steal the key from Ambrosia. I didn't want you to end up dead." The words spilled out of her. But she slowed down to say, "Now, I'm hoping you'll make the right choice. If you trust me, you'll *forget* about it." Scarlett's voice broke with the last few words.

"If she has the key, why wouldn't she tell Silverkeep? Why wouldn't she become queen? Most would've killed for the opportunity."

Scarlett shrugged. "She absolutely despises Silverkeep, doesn't want anything to do with it."

Sweat condensed on the surface of Basil's forehead. "Where is she? Where's Ambrosia?"

Scarlett shook her head. "You can't get the key. Basil, you don't understand her power. She controls all of us in the forest. If there was a way to defeat her, we would've done it already."

"Which part of Golden Grove is she in?" Basil asked, blatantly ignoring her advice. "How far from the area we slept in?"

"Even I, a nymph with enchantment, obey her. Basil, you won't get the key. Maybe there's another way to . . . to get what you want. Maybe you can work things out with your brother and—"

"If I recall correctly, us talking to each other is a direct violation of her command. And you're the one that approached me today," Basil snapped. "What do you mean you 'obey her'?"

"Your temptation is more dangerous than I thought. You have to go home. Go back to the castle, Basil. I . . . wish you the best."

"I can't give up now, Scarlett! Do you not understand? I need to find the—"

"You need to find it just to prove something to your brother? It's pathetic, Basil. Truly just immature and—"

"It's not about Regis! It's about the kingdom. He will *ruin* it." But Basil knew that was a lie. His entire mission was centered around defeating his brother. And his unwarranted feelings for Scarlett—the value he recognized in her words—certainly weren't helping. "Besides, you just said that maybe I can stay."

"Before you made it obvious that you're not going to give up. Leave." Her red-rimmed eyes didn't stray from the ground. She started back the way she'd come, not daring to look at Basil.

But Basil couldn't give up. Not now. He sprinted to her, his voice strong as he said, "No."

"Basil, you don't know Ambrosia. I don't expect you to appreciate my concern. All I can say is that leaving will protect you, I—"

Basil chuckled.

"What?"

"It's just funny," he said, finally making eye contact with Scarlett, "how you think you can get rid of me like that."

Her gaze reverted downward, and a heavy silence floated between them.

Please. Please let me stay.

"*Promise* you won't do something stupid?"

Thank goodness.

"I promise." But his version of stupid was far different from hers.

Scarlett sighed and hugged Basil's torso. She was shorter than he was, so her head reached his neck. She leaned onto his right shoulder, and her red locks tangled in his face, but Basil didn't mind.

They stayed in an embrace for a few moments, and Basil stroked her hair. "Let's go back," Scarlett said, lifting her head from his shoulder. "I didn't think it would be so easy to make you forget about the key. Thank you for understanding."

Forgetting about the key? I never said that.

As they sauntered through the foliage, Scarlett and Basil held hands, and like a nervous youth, he was acutely aware of the moisture building up between their palms. Basil casually loosened his grip and wrapped his arm around her neck instead. "Will you show me around Golden Grove? I've barely seen any of it."

"Yes, but Ambrosia thinks you left, so we have to be careful." The minutes it took them to arrive in the forest felt much shorter than the time Basil had spent leaving—all because Scarlett was by his side. "Some parts of Golden Grove are not . . . welcoming."

Basil wasn't sure what Scarlett meant, but questions seemed unnecessary. "All right," he said. "Where's our first stop?"

Scarlett's lips parted slightly. "Follow me."

They walked in the direction of the beds of leaves in which they slept. "Do you remember the stream we swam in?"

"How could I forget?"

"It continues throughout Golden Grove." Scarlett gestured to her top-right. "You've only seen the beautiful part."

Though Basil questioned how any part of Golden Grove could be less than magical, he listened to Scarlett and followed her. A few minutes of silence later, they stood before a less beautiful part of the stream.

Distraught. Evil. Body of water—sure, but Basil didn't know what specific name would do it justice. The water wasn't clear and blue. Instead, the liquid that flowed was black—the opaque color of a midnight sky. There were no *uclinas* or sun rays bouncing off the surface.

"The stream," Scarlett managed. Her shoulders dropped.

"It's so . . ." Basil's eyes wandered from the wilted flowers to the creatures clinging to the rocks. "Just so . . ." He couldn't articulate the tragic sight before him.

"Those are the ogsues," said Scarlett, pointing to the slimy creatures that lived beneath the rocks.

A reminiscent flicker crossed Basil's face. "Like you said the day you healed me."

"You remember."

"I remember everything you've said to me thus far, Scarlett." Basil threw her a sagging smile. "Why is the water black?" He bent down in front of the water, his hands cupped together.

"Don't touch it!" Scarlett shoved Basil's hands away from the gooey black.

"Why? I'm curious about its texture."

"She wants you to be. She wants us to fall under her spells."

"How can you be sure?"

"I'm not. Come, let's go." Scarlett grabbed Basil's hand and tugged him upward. "I don't want to see this anymore."

Scarlett walked Basil to the blooming side of the forest, which welcomed Basil with familiar flowers and the innocent side of the stream—clear and flowery. "Well, we can swim now."

Basil jumped in straight away, and Scarlett soon followed. For a brief flicker in time, the two forgot. Forgot about everything. Time with Scarlett did that to him—it was why Basil felt so drawn to her. Scarlett playfully splashed him.

"Hide-and-seek tag?" Basil proposed.

Scarlett raised an eyebrow. "I don't think that's possible here."

"Just count to whatever number you please and try to find me."

"The water's clear, though," Scarlett giggled, the same little hiccup he'd heard several times before—Basil's new favorite sound.

"Well, perhaps you'll have an advantage." Without another word, Basil submerged beneath the waters, and Scarlett covered her eyes with her hands. She began to count down from thirty, but Basil bobbed his head up when she started speaking the numbers aloud. "I can't breathe underwater for that long," he said.

"I can use my daily enchantment," Scarlett offered.

"Or you can count down from a smaller number, like five or ten."

"All right," she agreed. Again, Basil disappeared in the stream as she covered her eyes with her palms. "Seven point five . . . seven," she said quickly. Little bubbles appeared on the surface by way of Basil's uncontrollable giggles. Now he had to move. "Six . . . five . . ." But before she said another number, Scarlett eagerly released her hands.

Basil's body was completely visible through the clear water, and she dove to catch him. Basil had underestimated Scarlett's swimming abilities. She breezed right through the water, her pointy heels causing fluttering waves atop the surface. Soon, she had a strong hold on Basil's foot. Scarlett tugged the foot toward her and pulled his entire body. As she did so, Basil turned back to her, face-to-face with the athletic nymph.

"You got me," he said. "You win."

They floated just above the surface. Scarlett's chin hid under the water, while Basil's stood barely above it. "Why'd you count from seven point five?" Basil asked with a chuckle.

"You said five or ten, and I couldn't decide, so I went right in between."

Basil snorted in amusement. "Interesting."

All it took was their eyes meeting to evoke the same feeling in Basil he'd had the night of the spoiled beef. Scarlett's face and hair were wet, as were Basil's. He was the one to subtract the space between them this time. And Basil brought his hand to the back of her neck. Her hair was tangled messily about her head, clinging to her nape and back, so she bobbed her head below the water. When she came back up, it trailed neatly behind her, accentuating her pale, freckled face.

Basil longed for the affection they'd shared once before, just as Scarlett did. And when they kissed a second time, Basil's mind went blank. He no longer thought about his brother, the key, or Silverkeep. Basil's hands lingered on her curves . . . her waist . . . her back. He caressed her neck and shoulders.

They stayed in the clear waters for quite a while—long enough for Basil to lose track of time. Scarlett and Basil didn't notice that dawn was upon them until the sun began to dip. They enjoyed the escape from reality too much to leave by choice, but they both knew they couldn't stay there forever.

When Basil reluctantly got out, his skin prickled with goosebumps. Scarlett wasn't cold when she exited, so she ran her hands back and forth over Basil's arms in an effort to warm him up. Leaving the stream was like a slap in the face, reminding Basil that he couldn't escape reality.

The food they ate that night by their leaf beds was a selection of plants, some new and some familiar to Basil. He was nervous to eat any food because of his incident with the ivlies, but starving wouldn't be much better. They lit a fire again, this time for warmth rather than cooking, and drifted off to sleep in each other's arms.

A golden key hung peculiarly off the naked branch, an emerald gem in the center, radiating power and magic into the air. Nobody and nothing surrounded it but a bare tree, free of leaves or flowers or fruit. "This can't be," Basil said aloud. "It can't be this easy." But he was talking to nobody. He inched toward the key, slowly and carefully, as if it were about to jump at him . . . as if it were alive. His arm trembled as it lifted to reach the branch. The texture of the key was foreign in his hands, but his grasp didn't last long enough for him to do anything more than touch it.

"What do you think you're doing?" a deafening voice bellowed. Basil melted to the ground, and a gold hue appeared around his body. But it was stronger than Haldi's or Scarlett's—almost blinding. Basil stood paralyzed. He tried to scream, but no words escaped his mouth.

Basil jolted awake, relieved at the sound of his own screech. He had no idea of the time, but the pitch-black sky said enough. Scarlett lay in his arms, her eyes shut, her mouth slightly open. She hushed Basil, but her eyes were closed, and her body lay still. Scarlett strung together random letters and spoke gibberish. He wasn't sure whether she was awake or not, but he stroked her hair until the words stopped.

Every time Basil closed his eyes, even for a moment, he envisioned that evil woman guarding the key. No matter how much he tried to think of other things, he couldn't stop picturing the same, fearful scene. Something about it made his body squirm. He'd let slumber take him for a bit and then jerk awake seconds later with beads of sweat lining his forehead. Basil preferred no sleep.

Lying awake, thoughts swarmed his mind. The dream had to be telling him something—a sign—for what he was meant to do. It reminded him of his mission: finding the key. The vision told him he had to order his priorities. He'd spent a day with Scarlett, forgetting about King Philip's key, and it couldn't happen again. *Wouldn't* happen again. The demand pounded at his head for hours on end until dawn arrived. He hadn't realized all the time that had passed.

"You're awake," Scarlett yawned. The sun was barely visible.

"I have been—for a while, actually."

Scarlett cocked her right eyebrow. "You? Awake? You've been sleeping into the sunny hours the past few days."

"I had a dream. It told me something." Basil's expression was stern, not in the mood for the humor that Scarlett offered.

She chuckled. "Told you something? What did it tell you? That nymphs are real?"

"I'm serious, Scarlett."

But she struggled to meet his tone. "Dreams are random. Everyone has them," she said, dismissing his claim. Basil was surprised she was so quick to disagree; magic was real—but dreams couldn't be?

"But it . . . it rerouted me. I need to find the key, and I don't have many days to spare before my brother . . ." He didn't want to finish the sentence.

"So, spending time with me was a waste?" Scarlett winced.

"No, that's not what I'm say—"

"I thought you agreed to forget about it yesterday."

"I never—"

Something changed in her as if it finally clicked that Basil wasn't going to give up. Not now, not ever. "It's all right. Just go. Try to find the key, and I hope you prove me wrong."

"You know what I meant." Basil reached for the back of her neck, but she shook her head to the side, and her flaming-red hair whipped his face. "Ouch!"

"I don't want you to die, Basil. I care about you . . . a lot. But if what you want is the key . . ." She sighed a dramatic, heaving breath, as if she was internally debating a response, and paused for a moment. "If I can't stop you, well, I'm not letting you go alone."

"No, Scarlett. It's something I need to do on my own."

"But you don't know where to go. What's your plan? To search the forest? You won't find her that way."

Scarlett was right. He didn't have the first clue where Ambrosia could be, and her guidance would be needed if he were ever to retrieve Philip's key.

"It's not like *I* want Ambrosia to have the key, either," Scarlett said. "But I've never thought of actually doing something about it. And if we do, we have to be careful."

"We have each other," replied Basil. "And I believe. I have to believe."

Scarlett slowly nodded. "She wakes up late."

"And we can find her when she does?"

To Basil's surprise, Scarlett agreed. "But you have to promise to take a careful approach. And you're going to need to talk with her. *Don't* expect her to be kind."

Basil asked Scarlett how long they had to wait just about every two minutes. Her response was the same each time: "A little while longer." But it was vague, and as they walked around the pretty parts of Golden Grove—flowery and full of chattering small animals—Scarlett refused to say anything else concerning Ambrosia. Basil scrunched up his face every time she avoided the subject, and it got to the point where the sun shone high up in the sky. Surely, the hour was approaching noon.

"Do you think she's awake now?" Basil asked, more emphasis in his tone this time. Scarlett didn't answer. "Come on, it's practically dusk." But that was quite the exaggeration; the day was young.

Remaining silent, Scarlett pivoted. Her pace slowed, and her eyes brewed terror. "Is this the way to Ambrosia?" But Scarlett refused to respond. Basil became rather tired of talking to a wall, but he followed. He knew that Scarlett was his only hope to find Ambrosia.

So many minutes passed before Scarlett offered an answer, that Basil nearly forgot what he'd asked. "Yes," was all she could manage between growing trembles. Her fear was contagious, and Basil's leg muscles tightened with every step. Scarlett made it seem like he was welcoming death.

As they walked, the scenery turned dark. They were entering the shady side of Golden Grove—the part that held the gooey black section of the stream. Blossoming trees and flowers were replaced with wilting petals and bare branches. They were similar to the branches from Basil's dream. But he assumed they'd appeared in the dream because he'd seen them before, maybe in his peripheral vision. He refused to imagine that his mind could have built the idea. But all bare trees had to look somewhat similar.

Scarlett stopped in her tracks, but Basil continued. He gestured to her to keep going, but she wagged her finger, shaking. "What are you—"

"Shh!" Scarlett interrupted. Basil pivoted so they were face-to-face, and he could feel the nervous heat bouncing off of her. Scarlett pointed to the clump of bare trees to their left. "She's right there!" she whisper-yelled. "I was there just recently, when she forbade us from . . ."

"All right, then let's go." Basil turned to the left and began to approach the tree, but Scarlett grabbed hold of his shoulders.

"Wait," she said in a hushed voice.

"What?"

But Scarlett had nothing to say. Basil knew she wanted to see him one last time before everything went bad. Scarlett closed her eyes and leaned on his leaf-covered shoulder. Her whole body shook, and Basil rubbed behind her pointy ears. Scarlett lifted her head and looked into his eyes. Her unsteady hand met the arch of his back, and she leaned into him, brushing her lips against his, softly kissing him. It seemed she was sure it would be their last, but he didn't know whether to believe the same.

Only a few moments passed before Scarlett pulled away.

"She's just around the corner," Scarlett said reluctantly. "It's your own risk now."

"I thought you were coming with me."

"Yes, up to here. But I can't go any further—we're forbidden from each other, remember?" Scarlett told him. "You wanted to go alone, anyway."

"So I just go in there and . . . and . . . what should I say?"

Scarlett thought for a moment. "I don't know, but don't rile her up."

"And if I do *rile* her up?"

"*Don't.*"

Basil nodded with a nervous understanding and squeezed her into an embrace. "Wish me luck."

Scarlett held up crossed fingers and pursed her lips. He had no idea what was in store. Would Ambrosia be noticeably evil or look like any other subject? Basil walked toward the tree Scarlett had pointed to and turned his head back one last time. He spotted a tear lining Scarlett's cheek. It took everything Basil had to resist the urge to wipe it away.

Basil fought his way through the pointy branches that flanked Ambrosia's lair. They poked his face and limbs, imposing red scratches all over his body. Once he got through the sequence of swirly black trees, Basil was surrounded by more shriveled greens. Tendrils crept up wooden stumps. He was enclosed in a perfect circle, and when he turned to gather his bearings, there she was.

Her dress was long and dark, similar to her hair. She sat atop a throne of bark, tied with deep green and black vines. Beside her was a black waterfall—like the water from the stream's dark side—decorated in haunted sparkles.

Does she just sit here all day?

Ambrosia radiated icy cold without giving off an actual temperature. And though Basil was reluctant to admit it, she was among the most beautiful women he'd ever seen, with a sharp jaw and perfectly pointed nose. Her eyes were silently glued to

Basil, even before he saw her. At the sight, Basil jumped back.

"Basil Avington," the woman said, her eyes wide.

His limbs trembled. "How do you know my name?"

"You have your father's lips . . . your mother's cheeks. And you don't have the brown eyes of your brother. I hadn't a clue until just now, though, that we had a *royal* among us." She let out a concise, evil cackle. "Looking for this?" She drew out her words, and the last sounded like a hissing snake.

Ambrosia pulled her arm from the black pool of fabric on her lap. Bracelets encompassed her entire wrist and forearm. But one stood out to Basil. It was gold, and charms hung from the bangle. One, very special charm, was in the form of a key with an emerald gem in the center. He could feel its power radiate.

It can't be.

"King Philip's key," he whispered before letting his jaw drop.

ᴛHIRTEEN YEARS ᴘRIOR . . .

 mber, have you saddled 'em up?" Gregory asked as he laced his equestrian boots. He was the only person to call her by that nickname.

"Yep," Ambrosia said, "And I fed Austin a couple cubes of sugar. I hope that's all right."

Gregory nodded. Horseback riding was the cousins' favorite pastime for sunny Sunday mornings like this one. They'd do anything to escape their noisy household.

Gregory's belligerent mother and father had agreed to take Ambrosia in after her parents had passed away in a chariot accident, and she'd coped fairly well. Ambrosia's only memories of her parents were their bedtime stories, ancient fables like King Philip's key.

The death was long enough ago to escape her memory, but it seemed all the time in the world wouldn't help her develop a

bond with her aunt and uncle—not that she was desperate to be noticed; in fact, she hated attention.

"It's so boring all the time, concealed in this . . . violent little home." Ambrosia sighed.

Her uncle did nothing wrong, but nothing right, either; he did nothing at all. Ambrosia spent every day in their tiny house, tidying up each room while her uncle sat on the couch sleeping. In some peculiar cases, he would have a broadsheet or book. Her aunt, on the other hand, could not be found without a pen in hand, glasses perched down the nose, and a stressed look on her face. It had to be exhausting; she never gave herself a break. Work kept her going, twenty-four seven. She did something with metalsmithing, though she never bothered to specify details, and Ambrosia never asked.

Gregory finished tying a bow on his boots and said, "You could always—oh, I don't know—work? It's not as hard as you think. I believe you would even prefer it."

Ambrosia shook her head. "No, your father needs me at home. He's said it himself."

"Yes, because the lazy pig won't get off his ass. But you're approaching twenty-four years of age. Do you really expect to spend the rest of your days here? You truly want to live here forever? You want to die here and grow old and—"

"Come on, Gregory. The horses are waiting." Ambrosia didn't want to think about the daunting future. She appreciated her aunt and uncle's kindness for taking her in and agreed to fulfill their needs. For now, that meant at home—dusting, sweeping, cooking, and cleaning.

Ambrosia was already outside the wooden door, climbing onto Austin. "Gregory!"

"Coming!" Moments later, the door slammed behind him. "Let's go," he said, clapping his hands together.

Ambrosia was dressed to ride with her thick raven hair pulled back in a tight bun. "Where should we go?"

"My favorite?"

Ambrosia grumbled. "All right," she agreed, dragging out the word. She hated riding through the land near the castle of Silverkeep—it wasn't encouraged, and the ground was unsteady—but Gregory grinned ear-to-ear when he mentioned it, and she didn't want to upset him.

Gregory and Ambrosia didn't bother to say goodbye to his parents. They were too eager to get going.

"Let's go, Austin," Ambrosia ordered. Austin was her aunt's obedient little horse, always listening to Ambrosia's commands. She was still learning, so Gregory always let her ride Austin; he was the more dependable horse.

Gregory climbed onto Jig, his horse, and nuzzled her nose. "Who's a beautiful li'l horse? Jiggy Jig, who's my cute li'l filly?" he said in a high-pitched tone.

"Okay, we get it Gregory. Come on," Ambrosia said. "Let's get a move on."

Without another word, Jig charged as if he'd understood Ambrosia's words. She struggled to keep up and yelled at Austin to go faster, but his maximum speed couldn't compare to Jig's. In a few minutes, Gregory was out of sight behind some trees.

Jig galloped out of control. "Slow down! Jig, slow down!" Ambrosia could hear Gregory yell, but the rhythm of Jig's gallops stayed the same.

Ambrosia called, "Gregory!" But Jig sprinted so fast, Gregory could no longer hear. The gallops began to quiet down, and soon, Ambrosia's surroundings went silent. She was enveloped in trees and blossoming flowers from all angles, and she had no sense of direction. Ambrosia always depended on her cousin for directions and followed him, but he was too far past her to help.

Ambrosia estimated the best she could, following wherever Austin decided to go. The castle was just on her right, and she could make out the top of it behind a tall sycamore. "Hut!" It was Ambrosia's way of telling Austin to stop, and it always worked. She wanted to admire the castle for a moment before continuing, but it only increased the distance between her and Gregory.

Even Austin purred at the beautiful sight. The visible part consisted of silver towers and three purple turrets. But Ambrosia forced herself out of the fantasy she was caught up in. She would never live in a castle—only her little wooden house, constantly reeking of cigar smoke and her uncle's cheap cologne. The thought sent a chill down Ambrosia's spine, and she cued Austin to keep moving. The trees to her left and right were flourishing, tall, and she began to understand why Gregory loved traveling here so much.

By the time Ambrosia glanced at the sun again, about an hour had passed since Jig had escaped with Gregory in front of her. She'd made several turns and changed routes; Ambrosia was almost positive she'd lost her cousin. But she barely stressed; they would meet again at the end of the day, when she returned to the house . . . if she could find her way.

Austin was the only company she needed, and he was the perfect horse. He stood beautifully beneath a shaft of sunlight. His mane shone white, while the rest of his fur was colored chestnut.

As the day continued, Ambrosia felt her skin absorb the sun, turning a shade darker. She'd always wanted to be tan; naturally, Ambrosia's skin was extremely pale—almost ghostly. She enjoyed wandering aimlessly; the horseback outing was the one, very small adventure of her average week, regularly consisting of nonsensical chores like excessive sweeping and wiping the same corners daily.

Ambrosia heard a horse's footsteps in the distance, and her senses heightened. "Gregory?" she yelled, hoping her cousin would emerge from the corner. But as the prances approached, she could tell Jig wasn't responsible. There were multiple horses, galloping simultaneously. Each stomp was in perfect unison.

"Hello?" She was surprised there was another rider; she

and Gregory seldom found any other equestrians in the land near the castle—it was forbidden by law of the king. She and Gregory regularly broke the rule.

Ambrosia continued to ride Austin, curious about the peculiar string of horses and who rode them. "Hello?" she repeated at the quickening horses, but there was still no response. Their gallops boomed through her ears. They were close. She kept riding, her pace increasing with each leap.

Moments later, the group of horses emerged from a clump of trees around the corner. The faces of the riders were barely discernible as they quickly pranced toward her. "Hut!" she yelled at Austin, but he wouldn't stop. Not even a hard tug on the reins did the trick. The sight of other horses excited him, turning him out of control. Ambrosia's breath rasped audibly.

The string of horses was arranged in a pyramid formation, a man at the point of the triangle. He rode a white horse and was dressed in a velvet cape. A jeweled crown sat atop his boxy brunette head. Ambrosia wasn't sure of his age, but he must have had a couple years on her.

Four others surrounded him, their horses and clothes all uniform: light brown steeds and purple and gray attire. They didn't seem to notice Ambrosia, riding straight toward them for a collision. Ambrosia was frantic, pounding at Austin to stop moving, but he only sped up.

"Come on, Austin. Come on!" Her tone grew fiercer with each word. If Gregory were beside her, he'd know what to do.

The group of horses was only yards away, and soon those yards dissolved. The riders still didn't notice her presence. The white horse in the front clashed heads with Austin, causing Ambrosia to fly off the saddle. She floated through the air for a few long moments before her body crashed on the hard, rocky ground with a *thump*. She didn't know what it was, but something had cut her forehead—something sharp.

"Oh my," the man in the front whispered, his eyes glued to

Ambrosia. She was curled on the ground, her arm covering her bloody forehead. Ambrosia let out piercing shrieks in agony.

"Bailey! Bad horsy!" he yelled, jumping off the white horse. The man sprinted to Ambrosia, noticing the damage he'd done. "In the name of Philip, oh my—servants!" He turned to the four riders, still atop their horses. With his words, they quickly jumped off.

"Let's go, Your Majesty," one of the riders said.

The man from the front looked at Ambrosia's bloodied head and then back at the servants. "You mustn't be serious, Hadwin. Do you see this woman? She's in need of some medical attention. We shall bring her back and heal her."

Ambrosia listened to the exchange in awe. Was the injury causing hallucinations? Were the people actually servants? And why would they call the man 'Your Majesty'?

"My sincere apologies, my lady. We'll clean you up in no time," the man said, placing his hands beneath her body. "I shall take you to the castle."

"Castle?" Ambrosia mumbled. It was all she could manage. The pain in her forehead pulsed through her body.

"Oh, my poor subject. She can barely speak," the man said. "Allow me to ensure your health. I'm terribly sorry if it's an inconvenience, but I'm not one to leave a pained woman on the ground." Ambrosia was awestruck. The man thought it would be 'inconvenient' to bring her to the *castle?*

"Your Majesty, I have dressings in my pack. We could use it here and be on our way," one of the men offered.

The leader shook his head viciously. "Nonsense! Can't you see she's not all right?" But Ambrosia was just fine. Her forehead bled a bit—sure—but a dressing could have solved it in no time.

The man beside Ambrosia lifted her body and stood to carry her. One of his hands was on her back, and the other nestled in the joint of her knees.

"We'll tie up your horse to this tree," he said, pointing to a nearby sycamore, "and he'll be right here when you return."

Ambrosia slowly nodded, squinting her eyes. One of the servants pulled a hefty string from a pouch. Ambrosia was surprised that they happened to have every necessary material with them. Austin was back to his obedient self when the servant wrapped the string around his foot and then around the trunk of a tree. He triple-knotted the string before shaking out his limbs.

The man didn't struggle to carry her. Ambrosia fit perfectly in his hands as she didn't weigh much over one hundred pounds, with a tiny waist and not much height. The man positioned her on the white horse. She sat behind him, her bleeding head leaning on his shoulder. The blood blended in with his velvet cape.

"Servants, we're off!" the man signaled to his crowd, and their horses pranced in unison. It must have taken loads of practice to get them all on the same page. "What's your name?" the man asked Ambrosia, simultaneously riding.

"Ambrosia. Ambrosia Cromwell," she whispered.

"Ah, like the food," the man said. "It's beautiful."

"And what about yours?"

The man chuckled and turned to face Ambrosia. He was still able to ride at the same time—this man's skill wasn't too shabby. When she could feel his breath on her, she knew it wasn't a hallucination.

"You're serious?" he asked as if they'd known each other forever. Ambrosia nodded. "I'm the fourth Regis, King of Silverkeep?" the man said, like a question.

Ambrosia's face reddened, baffled by the pure coincidence of it all. How could she be so stupid? The man was literally wearing a crown and commanding servants. Did he simply not care that she had been riding in forbidden land? Hadn't he been the one to create that rule?

"Of course, Your Majesty," she said, trying to redeem herself. "You are the best king Silverkeep has ever had. Thank you for everything you do." Ambrosia had no experience talking to kings. In fact, she was quite awkward speaking to anyone at all who wasn't her cousin, aunt, or uncle.

"Oh, please, there's no need." Ambrosia admired the man's humility. "It would do Philip—bless his name—injustice."

Ambrosia smiled—she was having a conversation with *Regis Avington IV*. And she had failed to recognize his face.

"Do no talking," he said. "It will tire your body. You must rest your head."

As they continued toward the castle, Ambrosia glanced behind her shoulder to find Austin tied up in the distance. His eyes and nose faced the ground. But soon, he was no more than a blip in Ambrosia's peripheral vision.

Ambrosia closed her eyes and enjoyed the rhythmic gallops of the royal horse. Soon, she lifted her head just enough from Regis IV's shoulder to see the castle standing before them. It was only yards away—Ambrosia could barely believe her eyes. She looked back down to pretend she hadn't moved and rested her head in the pool of blood she'd made on his cape.

"Ambrosia," the king whispered, "we've arrived." Her name sounded sweet as it rolled off his tongue.

"Oh." She lifted her head and couldn't help but squeal with excitement. Ambrosia tried her best to conceal the rest of her emotion. "It's . . . It's so . . ."

"Yes," the king said, "I know." He unwrapped Ambrosia's hands from his torso and jumped off the horse, landing on the cobblestone. "Fall to your left, Ambrosia. I'll catch you right here." Ambrosia did as the king advised and landed perfectly in his arms. She would have never expected the king to be so kind to an average subject. She'd done nothing to make herself worthy of the tender treatment.

"Oh dear, you must be in horrific pain." The king cringed at the sight of blood but visibly tried to keep his composure.

"We can take her to the chamber of medics," one of the horsemen said. It was the same man who'd offered dressings and thought it would have been best to leave her in the land when their horses crashed. Ambrosia remembered the king calling the man Hadwin.

The king patted him on the shoulder. "It's all right. I've got her," he told Hadwin.

"Whatever you say, Your Majesty."

The king held Ambrosia sideways, cradling her like a baby. "It doesn't hurt too bad," Ambrosia said despite the blood that continued to stream down her face.

"It must, after what my dear Bailey did. He's usually more mature, but it didn't stop him from knocking right into . . ." He looked at Ambrosia with curious eyes.

"Austin," Ambrosia answered.

"Austin." For a moment, the king simply stood outside the castle, staring into Ambrosia's eyes. He seemed to see right through the blood.

"Regis?" A woman broke him out of his trance. Ambrosia turned her head to find the speaker and locked eyes with the queen. She stood in the entryway of the castle, dressed in a blue gown. "Who is she?" The woman glared at Ambrosia, her eyes burning with something violent.

Ambrosia opened her mouth, but no words came out. Something about the queen sent a shiver to her limbs, and the hairs on her arms stood up. Luckily, the king spoke on her behalf. "Well, Bailey charged into her horse, and she *flew* off the saddle. Would you believe that?"

The queen faltered. "And why is she here?"

"Her forehead is completely bloodied. What kind of king would leave her on the forest ground?"

"Fair enough. Have her out by lunch," she said from the entryway. The queen's suspicious eyes lingered on Ambrosia for an excessive duration before she disappeared behind the door. The king let out a long breath almost as if he feared his own wife.

The king cupped a hand oddly around Ambrosia's black bun as he carried her into the castle. All at once, she took in the delicious scent. It was exactly what one would imagine royalty to smell like.

Ambrosia barely blinked; she didn't want to miss a single painting or gilded wall. Heated glares shot from everyone who walked past. Most of them were dressed in gray and purple with the exception of two young boys. She barely saw them for a second, but they stood out; they were the only children, and they looked identical. The king saw her notice them and pointed out, "My sons, Regis and Basil." Most subjects would know the two young princes, but Ambrosia was not "most subjects." And she could tell he didn't mind; it must have been refreshing—a change of pace.

"How do you tell them apart?" Ambrosia asked, her question mostly rhetorical.

But the king answered, "It's all in the eyes. Regis's are like mine—a deep hazel." He failed to mention the other son, but Ambrosia remained silent and simply nodded.

He carried her through the endless halls, and his hands began to shake. Ambrosia supposed she was getting heavy. "The chamber of medics is just around the corner," the king assured her.

"Great." At this point, Ambrosia was barely bleeding. Pain still enveloped her head, but she was getting used to it.

Momentarily, the king laid Ambrosia on a medical bed. Medics were seated on benches, but they stood and bowed their heads upon Regis's entry. "Your Majesty," they uttered in unison.

"This is Ambrosia," he said. "Fix her head. Now." He didn't express gratitude, but Ambrosia wasn't sure why she'd expected it; his kindness toward her didn't mean he had to treat his servants with great respect. Still, the way he spoke to them bothered her; it reminded her of her uncle, yelling and throwing chores at her.

The medics scuffled about the vast room in search of tools. The sight surprised Ambrosia as she expected the castle doctors to be prepared. Even the perfect wasn't so perfect. "Hurry up!" the king yelled, clapping his hands. When he turned his gaze to Ambrosia, though, his eyes softened. "Oh, Ambrosia. I'm so sorry." The king leaned over her, his face hovering only inches above hers.

"It's okay, really," she said. His face was extremely close.

"I shall never forgive myself." As the king spoke, a bit of his spittle landed in Ambrosia's eye. She flinched. Something about the situation was off; the *king* felt too sorry for his horse merely being immature. She was just a subject—a rather poor one, at that.

"Excuse me, Your Majesty," a doctor said, his hand trembling as it tapped the king's shoulder. The king snarled at him but backed away soon after. Finally, Ambrosia had space to breathe.

The doctor held a roll of cloth and unraveled a small bit from the end. Though Ambrosia was no longer giving up blood, there was quite the amount already covering her forehead and dripping down her nose and cheeks. Before the medic wrapped the cloth around her, another one came out of nowhere with a bucket of water. She poured it over Ambrosia's head, and Ambrosia shivered at the icy cold. The same doctor then took a towel to wipe away the blood and water.

In a few moments, Ambrosia's forehead was wrapped tightly, her face was free of blood, and the king gawked at her. "Dismiss yourselves," he ordered.

"With all due respect, Your Majesty, we're supposed to remain in the chamber of medics until—"

"I *said*, dismiss yourselves!" His voice boomed through the room, and Ambrosia flinched. The doctors filed out, almost running. He noticed Ambrosia's fright and whispered, "You needn't worry. I must be stern with my servants but not with you."

Ambrosia's thoughts froze. What did he mean? And why was she any different from the servants? Surely, she had to be of lesser wealth than the medics that resided in the castle. Maybe wealth wasn't what tickled the king's fancy. She smiled softly, but it didn't meet her eyes.

"Are you feeling better?" he asked.

"Y-yes," Ambrosia stammered, "th-thank you."

The king chuckled. "Am I really so intimidating?" He grinned widely, showing his pearly white teeth.

Ambrosia nodded, her face reddening.

"Please, don't fear me. It's the worst thing about royalty." His statement baffled Ambrosia. She would've killed to be feared by the population. She wished to be the woman to whom every subject bowed down. Regis understood this based on her cocked eyebrows. "It's true," he said.

Ambrosia still didn't understand why she'd been given special attention by the king of Silverkeep or why she lay in a room alone with him. But the king's motive became clearer with his touch and leering eyes. His hand trailed down her neck and arm. "You have such beautiful hair."

"And you have a queen," Ambrosia whispered. "I'm not sure what you're trying to do."

The king put a finger over her mouth and bent down, his lips brushing her ear. "Shh," he hushed, flashing her a roguish grin.

Ambrosia didn't hate the idea; he *was* the king—regal, intelligent, and not unattractive. But something in her said it wasn't right. Either way, how was a poor, orphaned young woman supposed to stand up to the king of Silverkeep?

"You *what?*" Gregory stared at Ambrosia in disbelief. It was later that day, and they sat together outside, still dressed in their equestrian clothes. Gregory had just explained how Jig turned around once he was able to settle. He'd been home for hours, worried sick about his cousin.

"I can barely believe it, either," Ambrosia answered. "And before he left for lunch, he asked me to come back soon."

Gregory's eyes widened. "And? You're not thinking of going back, are you?"

"He's the *king*. How could I not?"

His jaw dropped. "He's probably got a decade on you, and Bridget Avington is . . . I wouldn't cross the royal family." But the king was surely the most powerful of them all. "I still can't believe you didn't recognize him! Oh, Amber—all this time in the house hasn't done you very good."

"Oh, stop it," she said. "He liked that I didn't know him."

"Are you planning on telling—" Their conversation was interrupted by Ambrosia's uncle trotting down the stairs. He wore only a pair of stained drawers. The sight was repulsive.

"Have either of you seen my—oh there it is! My pen," he mumbled. Ambrosia fiercely shook her head at her cousin, hoping he wouldn't mention anything. She tried to be discreet, but the gesture was anything but.

Her uncle narrowed his eyes. "Do you have something to say?"

Ambrosia shifted her petrified glance to him. "N-nope," she stammered.

Any sensible person would recognize there was definitely something—and he might have—but the old bum was too remiss to care.

Once he disappeared up the stairs, Gregory let out the laugh he'd evidently been holding in. "Why do you care so much about my dad, Amber? If you can barely lie to him, how do you suppose you'll be able to lie to the kingdom?" he asked. "That queen seems *lethal*."

The forbidden affair happened again, continuously for weeks and then months. The visits were so frequent that Ambrosia had nearly forgotten how wrong they were. During their time together, Regis would read her Silverkeep fairytales. There was a day Ambrosia had asked about the Legend of the Key— whether he ever felt threatened by it—but Regis laughed at her stupidity and promised it was a myth, calling her a "silly, uneducated maiden." And from then on, Ambrosia never bothered to question the king.

Every time Bridget was out of the castle—on a tour or out speaking at some school—and sometimes even when she was there, Regis IV would send his white horse, Bailey, and a servant to pick Ambrosia up. He'd somehow located her dwelling, but she didn't question it; he was the king, so he could find out anything about anyone. She'd slip out of the house when her uncle wasn't watching her (which was the majority of every day) and battle the disapproving glares thrown by Gregory.

Today was no different than the rest, and a servant appeared outside, sitting atop Bailey. It was the same man that had taken her to the castle each time before, and he believed she was being picked up to do some specialized work in the castle. Ambrosia creaked open the half-broken door and waved goodbye to Gregory. Instead of returning the gesture, he slowly shook his head. Ambrosia knew her cousin was right—and she hated it.

She hopped on Bailey, behind the servant. By now, the injury that had started it all was nothing more than a small scar, sitting a few inches above her eyebrow in the shape of a distorted circle.

Not long after, she stood before the castle, and the servant reached out his hand for her to grab and hop off the horse. A knot formed in the pit of Ambrosia's stomach every time she locked eyes with Bridget, and this time was no different. The queen had been led to believe she was a servant, as everyone else thought, but she had a brewing suspicion—Ambrosia could read it in her eyes. She hated when Regis would call for a visit on a day Bridget was home; it felt incredibly risky. If a servant were to catch them, the king could easily swear them to secrecy, but if Bridget did . . .

Regis always told Ambrosia that the queen was only his partner in ruling, and his relationship with Ambrosia was no sin. She might have lacked knowledge on certain topics, but Ambrosia wasn't dumb enough to believe him; he lied to the whole castle about the purpose of her visits. She was reminded of the queen's place every time she saw the two four-year-old twins scurrying about the corridors.

"Come along," the king said, grabbing onto Ambrosia's shaky hand. "Let's go to my chamber, so you can . . . do work in the castle. Cleaning, perhaps?" he joked.

"Shh," Ambrosia hushed. The more Regis spoke, the less believable his claim would sound to the castle's servants and the royal family.

The king's chamber acted as Ambrosia's second home now. During the tedious chore-filled days that seemed as if they'd never end, she'd think about the castle, and hope would stir up inside.

"Is something the matter?" He could tell that Ambrosia was off.

She shrugged. "I just . . . every time I think about what we're doing, it's just . . . I mean, the queen is in this building. This is *her* bed."

Regis's face turned bleak, and his manners vanished. "Do you enjoy the time you spend with me?" he asked, a stern look on his face. He took her hesitation as an insult, as the great king of Silverkeep wasn't used to rejection.

"Of course I do, it's just that—"

"Good, then shut up about whatever *stupid* thing it is you have to say."

Ambrosia flushed. It was the first disrespectful thing the king had ever said to her. She couldn't say "Excuse me?" or "You can't speak to me like that!" to him . . . to the king of Silverkeep.

And just when Ambrosia had begun to think the connection they shared was genuine—maybe even love—she was reminded of the unfair hierarchy of Silverkeep and that their relationship was barely more than a careless fling—at least on his side. Ambrosia would never be on the same level as the king; she had no parents, no money of her own, and her best and only friend was her cousin, who strongly disapproved of what she was doing.

If it were anyone else, Ambrosia would have run and never turned back. But Regis Avington IV wasn't just anyone. He was the king of Silverkeep, damn it! And he was getting a bit too comfortable with their secret rendezvous.

Regis didn't even bother to lock his chamber doors. The liking she had just begun to develop for him was slowly turning into hatred; he was no longer the kind gentleman that saved her, and quite frankly, she wasn't sure he *ever* had been. His courtesy had been a facade. Surely, he didn't speak to the queen this way.

So, instead of opposing him, Ambrosia swallowed the minimal pride she had and nodded. The king and Ambrosia lay on the soft and lavish bed. But just as he adjusted his body to hover over hers, there was a loud swinging sound behind them. As if the king didn't notice, he remained lying over her, nestling his face in the arch of Ambrosia's neck, grabbing her black tresses tightly.

"Regis." But he neglected the whisper. "Regis!" At the yell, he lifted his head and glared at Ambrosia.

"What!"

Ambrosia slowly lifted her gaze to find the very sight she'd had nightmares about. It was the queen—Bridget Avington. She wore a tight purple gown, and her dark hair curled just below her shoulders, framing her perfect face. The more Ambrosia stared at her, the more she realized they looked alike, sharing a similar shade of hair and eyes, only the queen must have been a couple years older than Ambrosia was. But that wasn't what she was thinking about. In fact, she could barely manage to think at all.

She should have listened to Gregory before it was too late. He was right—the queen's stare *was* lethal. She had dark eyes, and fury swirled through her irises.

Mortified. Humiliated. She would forever be known as the king's mistress. A threat to Silverkeep. An evil, troubled young woman. Ambrosia mulled over the limitless possibilities of infamy.

Thank goodness they were clothed, unlike previous nights spent together. But nevertheless, the queen saw enough to analyze the situation. Once the king rolled off of Ambrosia, he locked eyes with his wife. All three of them were speechless, but the queen was the first to talk.

"What is she doing here!" It came out as a screech, barely comprehensible. She pointed her perfectly shaped fingernail at Ambrosia. The innocent girl felt like a bug being stomped on by a giant, despicable human. "Our chamber is not a place for . . . for . . . I *never* want to see her *hideous* face again!"

The whole castle probably heard her voice as it thundered and boomed.

"Yes, yes, of course, my love. I don't know what she's doing here, anyway. She just kind of wandered in here, and . . . and I was telling her to leave—"

"Good."

They both knew he spat lies, but the truth held little significance in the grand scheme of things. And somehow the queen "believed" her husband though he was on *top* of Ambrosia.

"Get out of this castle and never come back. *Ever*," were the queen's last words before she shot one last evil glare at Ambrosia and slammed the door shut.

It was Ambrosia's worst nightmare, but it occurred to her— maybe the secret would stay between the king and queen; all of Silverkeep knowing about the king's young mistress would do no good for his public image or the queen's ego.

Ambrosia looked at the king, unsure of what to do. But his expression was no different from the queen's. "You heard her!" he said. "You are banished from the kingdom of Silverkeep, you sinner! You shall never set foot in this kingdom again!"

Tears accumulated in her eyes, but Ambrosia remained silent. She struggled to hold in her shrieks of terror.

The king didn't walk her out that day. The man to whom Ambrosia had given herself wouldn't even say goodbye. He left his chamber and forced her out but didn't specify how. Ambrosia didn't want to pass anyone, but it was her only way of exit. As she walked through the lavish corridors, she dealt with murmurs and glares from servants passing by. They must have known from the queen's volume, but nobody would have the nerve to release the information to the subjects; if any of them were caught, their lives would be ruined.

Ambrosia was lucky not to pass the queen on her way out. She took in the aroma one last time before leaving through the front door. She passed rows of guards who, because of her tearstained cheeks, didn't question Ambrosia.

The servant wasn't there to take her home. Neither was the majestic white horse. And the innocent young woman had lost her innocence. She owed nothing to the cruel kingdom of Silverkeep, and a growing darkness brewed inside her. She wiped the tears from below her eyes, straightened out her maroon tunic, and raised her middle fingers high up in the air, for the entire palace to see.

Ambrosia struggled to find her way back home, but eventually, she stood before her crappy little wooden house. Gregory happened to be seated on the steps outside their dwelling, breathing in the crisp summer air.

Once Ambrosia told him everything, he seemed surprised to find her voice unbroken and her eyes dry. But it was because she wouldn't allow herself to suffer. She wouldn't allow the king to define her character, nor would she sit and mope around or grovel without dignity. Ambrosia made the conscious decision to put all her spiteful energy into *rage*—not self-pity.

Ambrosia had lost the only two real relationships she'd ever had. At first, Gregory had been her shoulder to cry on, but her mistake did more than harm her *own* life. The queen would send "surprises" to her home in the form of dead horses and threatening letters. Of course, Ambrosia couldn't get off so easily—not when the queen held an eternal grudge. Luckily the population of Silverkeep didn't find out, but the queen wouldn't forget.

Her aunt and uncle threw her out, but it wasn't the worst thing. Ambrosia left with only a bucket of water and a sharp sword—a weapon she'd stolen from her aunt and uncle—in hand. She was finally free to roam Silverkeep and seek revenge. But with no foundation to depend on, it wasn't so seamless.

As a vagrant, she was determined to seek revenge on the kingdom. Her feelings had been bottled up for quite long enough in the time she'd spent sweeping and cleaning, missing her parents. Gregory had been her one friend, but he'd never again see her as more than a foolish and poor young woman.

The first place she came across welcomed her—a bustling forest. They were oddballs, and therefore relatable. The men had hairy horse legs, and the women had pointy ears and leaves for fingernails. They called themselves *satyrs* and *nymphs*—words Ambrosia had never heard.

She became a part of their community—a family, led by a kind satyr named Zoz—in which one didn't need to provide money or intelligence. They already treated her as superior solely because she was human. For once, she *belonged*.

Ambrosia wasn't used to being treated as anything more than a poor maiden, and the one time she *had* been was taken away in an instant. But Ambrosia took advantage of their kindness and soon put all her rancor into the forest. Her heart shriveled up . . . Her spirit died.

The world had been cruel enough to her; she truly believed she deserved the chance to be cruel back, even if the nymphs and satyrs she terrorized were innocent. Morality became nothing more than a rare afterthought.

Gradually, after gaining their trust, Ambrosia turned their faith to fear. She threatened the creatures with the sword she'd stolen from her aunt and uncle before she left, claiming she'd injure anyone who neglected her demands. Ambrosia surprised herself with the power she possessed over the naive forest inhabitants. Swords were the nymphs' and satyrs' weakness, and caused them to fear her. She loved the feeling of superiority so much that she would protect her leadership at all costs.

And with time, her hunger for power got worse and worse. She couldn't get revenge on Silverkeep, but she could take out her anger somehow.

Ambrosia called meetings, demanding the presence of every nymph and satyr. She split them into small groups to scour all the land of Silverkeep in search of the key that her parents had told her about. She'd never forgotten her mother's bedtime stories, and the legend of King Philip's key was just about the only thing she knew about the history of the kingdom. She'd do anything to prove the king wrong.

Ambrosia had nothing to lose, but more power—the key—to gain.

The obedient nymphs and satyrs wouldn't ask a question twice or challenge her authority; the sword and her morbid promises were enough. And, with a whole team on her side, she was able to find the key on the top branch of an enormous tree—a tree that no human could ever have seen the top of, let alone reach it. Ambrosia could precisely recall the day: an adolescent satyr approached her with the key in hand, its power shining . . . radiating. Ambrosia grabbed it from his hands without a word.

With the key, she had the power she'd always longed for. And, as she held it for the first time, her last bits of humanity disappeared.

But to ensure her dominance, Ambrosia had to become the leader . . . which meant ridding the forest of the current one. She left Zoz's wife and young nymph daughter, Scarlett, broken-hearted, but so be it. Death no longer fazed her.

Ambrosia chose to wield the key for evil—not the good for which it was intended. She wanted nothing to do with Silverkeep and told nobody except the forest about her achievement. Ambrosia called "her" forest Golden Grove; she wanted to oppose *Silver*keep (and the name had a nice ring to it).

And with the key came mysterious capabilities she began to call enchantment—a type of magic that naturally distributed among the inhabitants of Golden Grove . . . but the heart of the power was in her hands.

BACK TO THE PRESENT...

 t is the key, indeed." Ambrosia's lips curled into a sinister grin, and she twiddled the key as if it were no big deal. "I was devastated to hear about your father."

She sat on her throne of bark and leaves, her black dress blending with the darkness of her circular lair.

Basil didn't see her point in bringing Regis IV into it. "You don't know him."

Ambrosia let out one derisive snicker. "Of course I do—well, I did."

"Sure, you know who he was. You're no different than the rest of Silver—"

"Don't say the name." Ambrosia extended her arm, facing her palm to Basil. "Never say the name in my presence." She gritted her teeth.

"What? Silverkeep?"

A golden gust of wind reached Basil, causing him to fly back and struggle to keep his balance. "Don't!" Ambrosia yelled.

"Um . . . okay, I won't say Silv—the name of the kingdom." Basil stumbled to his feet, not understanding why she was so opposed to it. But finding out wasn't worth the trouble.

"Good." Ambrosia dropped her arm, and the wind settled. "And *never* dare to tell me who I know. I watched you and your brother, sauntering stupidly around your little palace. I don't expect you to remember me. You were only—what—four years old?"

"You couldn't have been to the palace if you call it *little*."

The golden gust of wind again. But this time it was stronger, and Basil fell to his knees.

Shoot. I wasn't supposed to "rile" her up.

"Do not talk back to the queen of Golden Grove. You may be a prince in your bubble, but here you are nothing but a scrawny, powerless human."

Her words angered Basil, but he forced himself to conceal his rage. "Whatever you say." But he was sure Ambrosia was lying; she couldn't have known his father. And it was disrespectful to lie about such a thing.

The two glared at each other in silence, and Basil's lip quivered.

"Well? Have you come here to stare at me?"

"Uh . . . no. I need King Philip's key." When he spoke aloud, Basil realized how foolish he was, thinking such a task would be seamless.

Ambrosia let out a corrupted laugh. But when she saw the genuine look in Basil's eyes, her cackle softened. "You're serious?"

Basil nodded.

"You know, that's what your father said to me when I asked him his name."

"What is?"

"You're serious."

Basil nodded. "Yes, I'm serious. I would like to know what lie you're going to—"

"No, 'you're serious,' dingbat."

"I don't underst—"

"Just shut up and forget about it. You can look at the key, but you don't expect me to . . . to just give it to you, do you?"

He shrugged.

Ambrosia's tone of voice changed, and she spoke in a high, mocking pitch. "Oh, all right. Well, here's the key. Take it! Take it, please! What is it you're waiting for?" She went on to rip the glowing key off her bracelet with one tug and raise it in the air. When Basil remained stationary, she raised her eyebrows. "Take it!" she yelled, her voice deeper this time, booming through the circular patch of withering forest.

Basil, blinded by desire, trembled as he stepped toward the key. He glanced and flinched at every bare branch, afraid something would jump out at him with each further step. But nothing did, and he was face-to-face with Ambrosia, watching the key suspend from her claw-like fingernails.

As Basil lifted his hand to grab it, Ambrosia swiped hers away, along with the key, and began to cackle. Of course it wouldn't be that easy.

"What do I have to do?" Basil asked. "I *need* it."

Once she settled down and magically reattached the key to her bracelet, Ambrosia spoke. "As do I. There is nothing that will grant you King Philip's key."

"All right, look. You hate the royals. I hate the royals . . . If I have the key, Silv—the kingdom—will change."

"And you think I give a care? Listen, boy, whatever you plan to do with the key doesn't change the fact that you would have it and I wouldn't. You're still the son of your father, no matter what you think of him."

At the moment, Basil's priorities weren't straight. Obtaining the key felt more important than staying alive. Just as Basil opened his mouth to speak, there was a sound of rustling leaves. Ambrosia's eyes dashed about the area.

"Who is it?" she sang creepily and turned her gaze to Basil. "Is somebody lurking here? Someone that you know of that perhaps is watching to . . . protect you? Or something of the sort?"

"No." Basil hated lying but was rather good at it. Still, Ambrosia could see through one without a doubt.

"Is someone there?" she repeated with more emphasis this time.

Basil shook his head, but Ambrosia shouted, "Do not lie to me!"

"I don't know, maybe," he whispered. Basil hated feeling inferior.

"You must be making friends quickly, little prince. I did, too—although they didn't stay friends for long. I'm sure you can tell," she said. "Well, I wonder who it could be. Not my dear Scarlett—you two haven't seen each other since my demand, right? You said farewell and parted ways, correct?"

Basil swallowed, afraid to lie again.

"You're lucky I have pity for that girl. Or else the nymph would be . . . and you would be . . ." She extended her palm, from which smoke evaporated as if it were nothing. "Well, in any case, you should be on your way."

Too terrified to say another word, Basil turned to leave the ghastly lair. But something seemed curious to him. He turned his head over his shoulder and decided to speak. "What did you mean? About knowing my father?"

Ambrosia gazed into thin air, and Basil wasn't sure whether she didn't hear his question or was simply ignoring it. But it turned out she was thinking up an answer. "I'm not sure you're of an appropriate age to learn."

"I'm seventeen years old," replied Basil, a bit insulted.

"If you insist. Let's just say your father was . . . not very loyal to his dear Bridget."

Basil shook his head. It certainly wasn't the answer he expected from her, and it had to be a lie. Ambrosia was much younger than his father, and the king was incredibly in love with his mother. Besides, why would the king of Silverkeep involve himself with a fiendish, evil woman? But he wouldn't vocalize his opinions; he knew the harm Ambrosia was capable of, and she didn't like to be called wrong.

"I expected you wouldn't believe me. Now go," she said. Basil continued to walk, but it wasn't fast enough for Ambrosia. "Do you need some enchanted assistance?" she asked.

"No. Please, no." And Basil sprinted out of her circular haven, praying to leave unscathed.

Basil's limbs shook his entire way back to find Scarlett. Ambrosia's words swirled through his mind, and he couldn't forget them, no matter how hard he tried. But it couldn't be true, and though his parents hadn't always treated him with great respect or fairness, Regis IV had been his role model. Adultery would ruin the only happy memories of his childhood, deeming it all a lie. No. It couldn't be. Ambrosia must have worked out some twisted deceit to confuse him—and boy, was it working. But Basil was too smart to believe the lies she spewed.

He found Scarlett seated on a branch of a weeping willow, her feet dangling beneath her. Basil was too far away to read the expression on her face.

"Scarlett!" He sighed with relief. Though he'd assumed she would be there, growing doubt and fear had built up inside of him.

"Basil." Her voice was no more than a relieved whisper, even though nobody was around.

He wanted so badly to hug her, but he wouldn't be able to

reach the top branch of such a tall tree. As if she could read Basil's mind, Scarlett hopped off the top branch and floated to the ground. She ran into his arms, pleasantly surprising him.

"Well?" she asked, assuming he would have loads to tell her.

"She's . . ." Basil's voice quaked. Out of everything Ambrosia had told him, the thing that shook him was her mention of the king. "She said she knew my father. I know it was a lie, but I can't seem to . . . It won't leave my mind."

Scarlett looked down at her feet and hesitated. "The king's mistress," she said.

"Yeah, that's what she implied. But how did you—"

Her voice thin, Scarlett interrupted, "That's what she told us the first day she arrived in Golden Grove. Ambrosia explained her whole story, start to finish."

"But she was lying. For pity," Basil said.

Scarlett touched Basil's chin and lifted it to face her. For some reason, Basil had been avoiding eye contact. Scarlett shook her head once, slowly, but in an effort to protect him from the truth, she didn't speak. Instead, Scarlett reached for Basil's fingers, but he pulled away.

"I'll believe it if you can show me proof," he said. Scarlett remained silent, and Basil said, "Exactly."

"All that doesn't matter," Scarlett said. "But what did she say to you? About the key? I had to sprint back once Ambrosia heard me adjust my position in the bush."

"But she was lying, right? About my father?"

"For goodness' sake, Basil, I told you the truth. It's up to you now. Believe what you want."

"Good. Then I'm believing that my father never saw that awful woman's face. Because it's true." But Basil was convincing himself rather than Scarlett.

"Besides that," Scarlett said, changing the subject, "what did Ambrosia say about the key?"

"Well, it wasn't what I hoped. She showed it to me, dangling from her wrist, and tricked me into reaching for it. But she swiped it away just as fast." Words erupted from his mouth at a quickening pace. "And . . . and she pushed wind on me, knocking me down. Her enchantment was stronger than anything I've seen thus far."

"Woah. Slow down," Scarlett requested. "I heard *half* of what you just said."

"Which part didn't you understand?" he snapped.

"If I didn't understand it, how could I tell——"

"It sucks! The key is out of reach. It's impossible. Regis is going to be king, and I'll be watching as part of the audience. And when I get home, Mother will hate me even more than she already does. For goodness' sake, they sent a search team to find me! What will she think when I turn up?"

"Still heard about half," Scarlett said, placing her hand on his chin again.

"Why did I think this would be a good idea? I depended on the off chance—the *very* off, off chance—that I would get the key, come home, and become king. Nobody's done it. Why should I? Hell, it's a miracle in itself that I just so happened to stumble across this forest, the place that happens to house the key." This time, Basil spoke slower, and Scarlett took in every word.

"You're not doing this alone, Basil," she whispered. "I'm here. I'll always be here." Scarlett closed the distance between them and made for his lips.

But Basil backed away.

"No, Scarlett. I won't allow myself to get distracted. Not again." He plopped down in a pile of leaves.

Scarlett gnawed on her top lip. Basil's rejection stung, but she must have understood his worry. The last time they'd gotten caught up with each other, they'd wasted a day. And each day was one closer to Regis's coronation.

Basil didn't know how long he had left before his brother became king forever, but it had to be less than a fortnight; it'd been about that long when he'd left. It worried Basil—his un-awareness of the time of day and date itself.

"Should I go back?" Basil asked. "Should I go back home?"

"*Is* the castle your home? Or the mere place in which you live?"

Basil's mind was in a thousand different places, and he was in no mood for Scarlett's witty remarks. "I don't know, Scarlett. Can't you see I don't know? I don't know anything," he snapped.

"You know plenty." Scarlett ignored his sharp tone and comforted him as she often did. "Basil, you've been here for what, five days? The key isn't going to crawl into your hands, begging you to take it. No—you have to fight for it. And if you truly feel so strongly about that key, no matter the motive, you *will* have it."

"Since when are you on my side?" Basil asked.

"Since I realized how much passion you have for that key," she said. "Basil, I've always been on your side. I just . . . had a different idea of what was right . . . what was best for you."

Basil shrugged. "What does it matter?"

"It *matters*, Basil!"

Scarlett's newfound passion for his finding the key baffled him, and a laugh escaped his mouth. Their seriousness turned to giggles. "It matters, Basil!" he mimicked, throwing his hands the same way Scarlett had.

"Stop it." She pushed him playfully back. "Don't tease me."

Basil and Scarlett strategized for the rest of the day, trying to come up with ways to acquire the key. But it ended the same way each time, and the two had conflicting viewpoints that wouldn't allow them to agree. Basil didn't have enough time to go with Scarlett's *slow and steady* philosophy.

Basil and Scarlett began to yawn early that night, not long after dusk approached.

"Can we go to sleep now?" she asked, tired of their ongoing argument.

Basil nodded. "I'm taking that key tomorrow, though."

"No, Basil. We need to come up with a plan first. Trust me. Do *not* try anything." A mischievous smile spread across Basil's face, but he didn't say anything. "Promise me?"

"I don't know about that," Basil said. And Scarlett must have been too fatigued to express her opinions again. Besides, he suspected she knew he was too headstrong to listen to anyone but himself.

She slowly drifted off to sleep in her bed of leaves, but Basil lay awake, wondering why Scarlett's advice was so contradictory.

Basil didn't want to have the odd dream again. And he was plotting something of his own. She'd said it herself: 'The key isn't going to crawl into your hands, begging you to take it,' which was precisely why Basil couldn't wait around, even if Scarlett thought differently.

Golden Grove was home to a few nocturnal animals, and they were the only ones awake when Basil decided to take action. He'd lost track of time, lying and thinking of nothingness, but it must have been past midnight. As he emerged from the messy bed of leaves, Basil was careful to make no rustling noise.

Basil remembered what Scarlett had said about Ambrosia's slumber schedule; she always slept in. It would be a perfect time to capture the key.

Basil navigated the best he could toward Ambrosia's lair based on what he remembered of the short walk. It took some trial and error, but he had quite a bit of time on his hands.

All of Golden Grove was quiet when Basil arrived at the wilting leaves surrounding Ambrosia's circular area. The dying nature was how he knew he'd arrived. For some reason, he was even more scared than he'd been the first time.

Basil wasn't prepared for what he had to face. And when he arrived, he clamped his hand over his mouth so he wouldn't gasp. The entire lair was enclosed in a massive golden bubble. It floated around the circle like an expanded version of the bubbles he'd blown with Regis as a child. The memory—the reminiscing—sent a chill to his spine.

The bubble was translucent, and he could make out Ambrosia's body, sleeping on the same throne she hadn't once stood from when Basil came to speak with her. Basil reached out his trembling finger to poke the bubble, and tremors ran through his body. He wasn't sure whether it came with dangers, but there would be no other way to reach Ambrosia.

The bubble was incredibly resistant, and after poking it, Basil was sent to the ground. He barely felt its texture before his body crashed into the rocky and dark forest floor. There had to be a way in, but he didn't know it. And if just one poke sent him flying, trying to push his entire body through would only bestow more danger.

Scarlett. She would know how to get in the bubble—with her enchantment. But would Scarlett agree to such a treacherous task? Besides, it was nighttime, and she had to be fast asleep.

Discouraged, Basil stumbled to his feet and kicked the ground. He watched the dirt paint a picture before his eyes, spreading through the air.

Scarlett, Basil concluded, would never agree to wreck the bubble; she didn't even agree with him trying to visit Ambrosia's lair. Was she even cognizant of the bubble? And did Ambrosia always have it up? Or only because of the rare occasion?

Basil stormed away from her guarded lair, struggling to stay quiet in his footsteps. But no matter how hard he tried, he couldn't help but express his rage somehow, and that was in rather loud strides.

Most of the inhabitants of Golden Grove were deep sleepers, but there were exceptions. And a tiny, foreign creature was the first to catch Basil's attention. It seemed to flutter awake with just Basil's stare.

Chirp, chirp. Because of the darkness, Basil couldn't make out what the creature looked like, but he assumed it was a bird because of the noises it sang.

"Shh," Basil hushed.

"Mi friends deen't wake up 'till morneen, anyway," the creature squeaked.

Basil flinched, taken aback. "You *talk?*"

"What kind of questeen ees that? Of course I do—ya mustn't be from around here." *Chirp, chirp.*

An idea popped into Basil's mind. It was questionable, but he was desperate.

"Do you think you could . . . help me?"

"And why would a seetyr requeest help freem a foolish bird? Your keend has never been courteous to us. Shouldn't we reteern the favor?"

"I'm not a satyr," Basil tried. "I'm human." He said the words before thinking.

"Even weerse!" the bird chimed. "Yee're keend *eats* us— poaches and *eats* us. And you want mi *guidance?*"

It wasn't something Basil wanted to admit, but roasted quail was a regular meal in the castle—his brother's favorite, actually.

"Look, birdy, I'm sorry about whatever grudge you hold against humankind. But . . . okay, do you like Ambrosia?"

The bird squeaked her own version of ironic laughter. "It's Zena. And weew, you *really* areen't from around here, now are ya?"

In the kindest voice he could manage, Basil pleaded, "Please, help me. I might have a way to take Ambrosia's powers away." He even clasped his hands together and bowed them to the bird. He was unsure whether the creature would be able to see in the dark, but nonetheless, attempted everything he could to win the bird over. It might be his only way at a chance to obtain the key.

"Ya theenk it's that easy?" the bird scoffed.

"What if I give you something in return? Something only a human could give?"

"Ye humans, ye think ye're all si meech better than us." Realizing she would get nothing from squabble, Zena said, "What's yeer proposition?"

Basil sighed, about to offer something he most definitely did not want to. "A trip to the castle?"

"Eend how do you suppose that'll happeen?" Zena asked.

"I'm Basil Avington, the prince of Silverkeep." For once, he used his name to his advantage. "And once I have the key, Ambrosia will be gone, and you'll be able to see the castle. Is that such a bad thing?"

"Yee're really the preence? I feend that hard to believe." Zena's tone shifted. "But if you promeese, it will have to do. What'd'ya want me to do, anyway?"

"I need you to erase the bubble that protects Ambrosia's lair." Basil finally had a chance to say the words he'd been waiting for. "Can you do that? With your enchantment or whatever? Do birds even have enchantment?"

Zena was insulted. "Of course we do. But ya deen't really theenk you can defeat Ambrosia, do ya?" The bird gasped, and she said, "Oh—are ya the one who heeld a sword to Haldi?"

"Why does everyone know about that? But yes. And yes." Zena was beginning to get on Basil's nerves with her inane questions and whatnot. But he needed the help.

"Well, ya're lucky I deedn't use up my deely enchantment. It would be seelly of me to refuse an offer to veesit the castle of Silverkeep—I'll see what I can do. But whateever you get into with Ambrosia . . . do *not* mention mi name. She'll sleece me open and eat me for lunch."

"Well that's . . . graphic. But yes, I won't mention you."

The same golden hue Basil had now seen several times

highlighted the bird's body. Before Basil could say another word or ask whether she had a certain plan, Zena was off. Her wings fluttered through the dark night.

"Right *now*?" Basil asked. But the bird was no longer listening. Zena's bright gold border lit up the space around her as she flew, gleaming, through the sky. In the light of her enchantment, Basil could see her bright blue wings and little green body.

It looked so easy—too easy—when the bird escaped into Ambrosia's lair. It was difficult, from Basil's perspective, to see everything going on; the sky was nearly pitch black, and inside the bubble, a hazy layer covered everything.

Zena's yellow beak was so long, it popped the bubble moments before her body entered. And when it did, there was a fragile noise. The burst echoed throughout Golden Grove. The only person it woke, though, was Ambrosia Cromwell.

mbrosia's skinny, tightly clothed body roused from slumber. Basil tasted the smoke-like taint that wafted through the air. In the blackness, Ambrosia's eyes glowed green—it wasn't her irises, but the part meant to remain white. It had to be sourced from her enchantment.

The same swirly black trees and creeping vines surrounded her lair, but the darkness of night and the illumination of the bubble induced all the more terror.

Ambrosia gritted her teeth and jutted out her palm, just as she had the day before when she'd sent the gust of wind to Basil. All at once, Zena's tiny glowing body was compressed.

Zena let out horrific shrieks of pain, and guilt stabbed at Basil. But still, he cared mostly for his own safety. After recognizing he was in Ambrosia's direct line of sight, Basil sprinted quietly behind a bush—the same bush Scarlett had hidden in during his conversation with the devil spawn.

"What do you think you're doing?" Ambrosia shot a red

beam to Zena, zapping her body and causing her to plummet to the ground.

She squawked. "I . . . I eem . . . I deedn't mean to—"

"I am so generous to keep you talking creatures alive, and this is how you repay me? *This?*" The rage in her eyes increased, and Ambrosia smashed Zena to the ground, using her enchantment from a distance.

Zena squealed. "Ya'r Majesty, please spare me!"

Basil cringed from the bush when he heard the bird call Ambrosia *Your Majesty*; nobody should be called the honorable name besides the authorities of Silverkeep.

"Why should I?" Ambrosia asked. "You're nothing but a pesky bird who can't speak right."

"Because," Zena squeaked, "I deen't want to die." It was all she could come up with.

Ambrosia giggled. Everyone in Golden Grove seemed to have a thing for ironic laughter. "None of us do."

"Mi wasn't going to do anytheeng. Mi promeese!"

But Ambrosia was obviously smart enough to recognize the lies. It must not have been the first time Golden Grove inhabitants had tried to defeat her. "Who put you up to this?" she sneered.

No. Please don't give me away. Please don't—

"Basil Avingteen, Ya'r Majesty."

Basil's heart pounded in his chest.

"That castle boy? The prince of Silverkeep?"

"Yees, ma'am. He . . . he forced me to do it."

Basil subconsciously curled his hands into fists, a spark of ire rushing through him. How dare she give the prince away! He had by no means *forced* her. He should've known asking for a bird's guidance would be a bad idea.

"Where is the rascal?" Ambrosia asked.

The glow around Zena faded as Ambrosia became more focused on catching the prince responsible. "I . . . I deen't know."

"Where *is* he?" Ambrosia ramped up the golden hue. "Tell me!" The green in her eyes brightened. "Tell me at once!"

Surely, Zena would tell Ambrosia momentarily. He needed to get away before it was too late, but it would be difficult to do so silently. Basil crept out of the bush, avoiding the dark leaves and branches. He began to tiptoe. He'd have to leap across a patch of grass in Ambrosia's direct line of sight to make it. The best he could do was hope she wasn't looking. And in a state of panic, Basil jumped.

"Son of Regis!" Ambrosia howled.

And Basil knew he was done for.

Mid-leap, Basil was frozen in the air. He opened his mouth, but no words would escape. Ambrosia's palm reversed and beckoned Basil. With a swift motion, she reeled Basil in like a fish. A new, stronger bubble formed around her entire lair, but this time, Basil was inside.

"You thought you could *steal the key?*" she roared, and Basil didn't understand how the forest inhabitants remained fast asleep. As if she could read his mind, Ambrosia yelled, "The bubble is soundproof. That's right, no cries for help will save you." She snickered. "Zena!"

The helpless bird flew quickly to her shoulder, her beak trembling. "Yees?"

"Should I kill him?" Ambrosia asked as if it were no big deal. "Should I chop him down the middle or perhaps make him explode from the inside?" She cackled.

Zena hesitated. "I deen't know, Ya'r Majesty."

"I think that would be fun, don't you?"

Zena cooed in fear.

Ambrosia pursed her lips for a moment. "But then, the castle would worry. They wouldn't stop until they found me. And then, they would find the key. But with the key, Silverkeep would be . . . perfect," she said. "I'm not sure you're worth all that trouble, *Prince.*"

Basil swallowed in relief. With death out of the picture, he could stay rather calm—or, at least calm*er*.

"My hard work would be meaningless. You know, the key wasn't always as powerful as it is."

Basil stood silently.

Ambrosia's eyes darted to him. "Did you *know?*"

"Uh . . . now I do."

Ambrosia smiled a sinister grin. "Good," she whispered. "When I found it—or, when it was *found*—all it could do was a few handy tricks here and there. But through practice, I made the key what it is: able to do anything and everything—well, most things—with just my mind. King Philip left it for a great, ambitious man to find. I suspect he didn't imagine a meek woman."

"Meek?"

"Ah, yes. Before my history with your father, I was different—a kind and orphaned, weak young maiden. He's responsible for this . . . for all this. For my *cruelty*." Ambrosia cackled again, each shrill sound echoing through the bubble. Basil struggled to refrain from plugging his ears. He couldn't tell what bothered him more: her redundant lies about his father or her deafening laughter.

Basil hated being helpless. He despised inextricable situations like this, and he wasn't used to them, either. Every time he tried to move his arm or leg one way or another, Ambrosia's invisible grip would tighten, and movement would become even more impossible.

"Let me go!" Basil begged.

"Do *not* tell me what to do! Your family likes to do that, you *Avingtons*. It seems the tables have turned."

"What can I do?"

"Leave. And never come back. It's quite a reasonable offer."

The golden bubble brightened Ambrosia's lair as she strengthened it, and the scene turned completely visible. Her black hair levitated, swiveling through the air in unnatural ways.

"I'll banish you like your father banished me. This is the gift the world has finally given me—a chance of revenge, for you are the son of the king—the king who turned me into who I am."

Zena let out a squall of terror.

"Shut up, you good-for-nothing bird!" Ambrosia hissed. And with one hand motion, she smashed Zena to the ground. Blood splattered onto Ambrosia's face, but she didn't seem to mind. And just like that, Zena was dead.

"You see this blood? This filthy gore all over my face, splattered on my forehead?"

Basil nodded quickly, his lip quivering. Subconsciously, his hands were in front of his body as if they were protecting him from Ambrosia. But they would do no help.

"This is the state in which your father found me. The blood on my forehead—it's quite nostalgic, actually," Ambrosia recalled. "He was too kind."

At this point, Basil couldn't utter a single word. If he tried, it would be a stammer of fear.

"So, shall I banish you now? Should I release this bubble and trust you will go?"

Basil needed the key, but his top priority was to get out of there. He would come back later under less life-threatening circumstances. He nodded furiously, desperate to exit her lair.

"On second thought," Ambrosia thought aloud, "I don't believe you will listen. Basil Avington, I suspect you'll crawl back to Scarlett, asking for her advice."

Basil shook his head rapidly.

But ignoring the gesture, Ambrosia grabbed a hold of him with her enchantment. "What would you have done if I hadn't woken up? Stolen the key off my wrist? You think that would've worked?"

Again, he shook his head. Sometimes a lie was better than the truth.

Ambrosia drew Basil closer. Once she let his trembling body down, he could see every detail of her appearance. Beneath her piercing black-and-green eyes was a soul. Behind her devilish black dress was a person. But that person was far out of reach. And Basil could tell she wouldn't come back.

And maybe what she'd said was true—about his father. Maybe Regis IV wasn't as noble as he led Silverkeep to believe. But the truth didn't matter. And there were no plausible justifications for the way Ambrosia treated the forest inhabitants.

"I thought the key would cure me. But there's never enough power, Basil. You wouldn't be satisfied with it. I know because I'm not," she hissed. Basil could smell Zena's blood on her face, wafting through the contaminated air. "You and me, we're greedy." The golden hue brightened, and Ambrosia's eyes narrowed. "We'll always need more and more."

In the past week, Basil had cried more than ever before. And in the face of Ambrosia's enchantment, he struggled to hold back tears.

"No, I don't trust you. You must stay here, with me." She removed the glow from Basil. "Don't *think* about trying something."

A wave of relief washed over Basil, but it didn't last long. And soon, plant tendrils climbed up his heels, anchoring him to the ground. He looked up to watch Ambrosia and found her black hair sticking straight up, forming the shapes of leaves.

Ambrosia cackled again, this time louder than any of the other times. Basil tried to cover his ears only to find his hands brought together in front of him by hissing vines that slithered up and down his body. They were covered with thorns, but the scratches were the least of Basil's worries.

He should've learned his lesson the first time. Scarlett wouldn't save him—couldn't save him. He was alone this time. It didn't matter if he was a prince or a poor subject—in this moment, he was Ambrosia's victim. Basil knew what she was capable of. Ambrosia wasn't merciful; she'd hardly hesitated to kill Scarlett's father solely for power.

No. She won't kill me. She said it herself.

"You will stay here!" Ambrosia bellowed.

Basil opened his mouth to speak, but a sharp vine sprinted to cover his lips, scraping his tongue along the way. He tasted his own blood and bile in his mouth and couldn't even spit it out. When he tried, it ricocheted off the vine, which sent it straight down his constricted throat.

The tears increased, and Basil couldn't help but let them flow down his cheeks.

"You're *sad*? You're *crying*?" Ambrosia purred. "I used to cry!" Her voice was thunderous.

Basil's lips twitched in times of fear, but this wasn't fear—it was terror. Basil's lips quivered so much that he thought they might shake the vine right off.

"Ya!" Ambrosia yelled as she extended her arm.

Basil's stiff body fell to the ground. *Boom.* A cloud of dirt filled the air.

"Sleep tight," Ambrosia hushed. This lady was a mental case. But Basil had to be loony himself if he thought mere ambition would acquire him the key.

"Eat it! Eat it, or you'll *starve*!" Ambrosia screeched.

She held a wilting black flower inches from Basil's mouth. It had been half a day since he'd last eaten. And Ambrosia was "so kind" to lean his body against a rock as opposed to leaving him in the dirt.

The ironic part was that Basil couldn't eat it—not with a

vine strapped across his mouth. "O-okay!" Basil's scream was muffled.

"Good boy." Ambrosia retracted the vine with her enchantment and revealed his scratched up, bloody mouth. Basil spit out all the blood and saliva he'd been holding in. She fed him a crumpled pile of black "flowers." They were revolting, but Basil had no other choice.

The sun had been up for a few hours, and Basil's rage grew with each passing moment. The bubble was gone, but trees and bushes still sheltered Ambrosia's lair. She must have wanted it the night before to protect her as she slept. But now she was awake. Now her pale cheeks and deep green eyes were in front of Basil's fearful face.

Even if anybody *could* see him, nobody would stand up for the human stranger that'd appeared in Golden Grove five days ago. Zena had taken a lot of convincing. No, Scarlett was his only hope. And would she sacrifice herself for a liar? For a cause she'd discouraged? Scarlett had been right all along, and Basil hadn't acknowledged her entire life of experience.

The tendrils hissed all throughout the day, scraping and scratching Basil everywhere. *Everywhere.* At this point, his leaf clothing was crumpled and dysfunctional. And besides his visits to the stream, which already seemed so long ago, Basil hadn't had a bath in far too long.

He needed to escape Ambrosia's lair; each day concealed in her circular haven would be another day closer to Regis's coronation. All he cared about was getting *out* of there. But he couldn't—not alone, anyway. Basil should never have left the castle.

The one thing that sitting there gave him was time to think. And in his minutes pondering, it occurred to Basil he hadn't thought of Lydia Rose for quite a while. And even now, as he closed his eyes and envisioned her, she was beautiful—sure— but the sight of her didn't break him. And in each memory of Lydia Rose, he focused on the happiness the moment had once brought him, not the sourness it evoked now that it was over. Lydia Rose wasn't even the person he wanted to think about. No, that person was Scarlett. Basil found himself imagining a future with her—one that was most definitely impossible.

As the tendrils climbed up his legs, Basil snapped back into reality. He was in Ambrosia's lair. And he would die there—maybe not tomorrow, but someday—if he didn't do anything. And if he did stay, would living there with *her* be any better than death?

Yes; he couldn't die. Basil couldn't let his father see him fail. And he didn't want to meet his father up there yet. But would he see him up there? Basil had to be going to hell, while the king was surely in heaven. Then again, if what Ambrosia said was true, Regis IV could be in a scorching hot, red and sorrowful afterlife.

Basil's thoughts were all over the place. It took him a while to realize that Ambrosia was gone from her lair. But he knew Ambrosia was smart, and it must have been a trap; she wouldn't have left him there unattended.

Still, it quite possibly could've been his only chance of escaping. Basil jerked his body from the tendrils, but with each attempted rip, they only tightened.

"Where do you think you're going?" the vines hissed in unison.

"In the name of King Philip—why does everything talk here? Birds . . . plants?"

Of course Ambrosia hadn't left him. She was too evil.

Zena's bloody feathers lay sprawled on the ground before him. The bird wouldn't have died if it weren't for Basil.

What's going on*? Why do I care about a* bird*?*

Rock bottom. Nothing could be worse. Any hope Basil had about finding the key had perished.

Damn you, Ambrosia!

He kicked the dirty forest floor. Basil had nothing to do with his time, so he started etching images into the dirt. He'd hated anything to do with art in the castle, but now it was the only thing that kept him sane. With his bare feet, he illustrated King Philip's key on the ground. But it was difficult to draw something with such complex nooks and loops and nuances. Angered, Basil erased his drawing with the sole of his foot.

Instead, he started illustrating Scarlett. But even the most adept artist wouldn't do her justice sketching in dirt; she needed color—her scarlet hair, her piercing eyes.

Basil was convinced his drawing manifested Scarlett as he saw her red hair peeking through the bare trees bordering Ambrosia's lair.

"Psst! Basil!" she whispered.

His eyes widened, but he couldn't utter anything more than some muffled screams because of the vines strapped across his lips.

"Come on!" She clearly couldn't tell he was immobilized by the tendrils that crept up and down his body. But Scarlett figured it out at once and used her enchantment to create a golden hue around Basil.

"Now. Move!" she ordered, her voice quiet.

Basil wasn't sure Scarlett's enchantment would work, so he was awestruck when his limbs moved freely. Scarlett had outsmarted Ambrosia's enchantment.

As the magic peeled the vine off Basil's mouth, he let out heavy gasps for air; he'd only been able to breathe through his nose.

"How can I thank you?" he managed between short breaths.

"Don't be a bonehead again."

Together, they sprinted out of Ambrosia's lair, the pokes of the bare and sharp trees feeling like nothing after what Basil had just withstood.

Once they were just out of Ambrosia's haven, the evil woman appeared in his peripheral vision. Ambrosia's black dress trailed behind her back, and a noxious expression sent redness to her eyes. In her hands was a basket of "food" she'd planned to feed Basil.

The audible crash of the basket with the ground would stay with Basil forever. With all her rage, Ambrosia formed the bubble around her lair again. But Basil and Scarlett were just beyond it—barely—but safe.

Ambrosia couldn't reach them—not in time. Scarlett grabbed Basil's hand and zoomed over the cut branches . . . through the tangled grapevines. Ambrosia must have known where their beds of leaves were at this point; they had to go somewhere else.

"This way!" Scarlett yelled, running ahead of Basil.

But Basil looked behind his shoulder to find empty sky; Ambrosia wasn't close behind them—in fact, she wasn't behind them at all.

"It's okay . . . we can . . . slow . . . down," Basil managed between heavy pants. "She's not chasing us."

Ambrosia was, in fact, seated on her throne of bark and leaves, wearing a demonic grin, her arms crossed. Ambrosia's black tresses stuck straight up toward the sky, and as he turned around, Basil could've sworn he saw small flames appear on the tips of the thin strands.

XIII

unning by foot wasn't a prime skill of Basil's, but Scarlett's aid helped him. "We just made it," Basil said, his entire face red and perspiring.

"Barely by a second," Scarlett said.

"Still made it."

"A moment later and we would've both been dead," she countered. "I can't believe I . . . I can't believe I risked my life for you."

Despite everything that sucked, Scarlett's words sent a rosiness to Basil's cheeks. It was barely noticeable; his whole face was already burning red. "*I* can't believe it, either. I wasn't expecting you to come."

"I guess, I don't know, you make me want to do crazy things." Scarlett took a seat on a tree stump. The way they spoke so freely was unlike anything he'd had with Lydia Rose. And Basil could barely fathom that, less than a week ago, Scarlett had been a stranger. His cheeks flushed.

"What were you thinking? That you could get through her bubble with no consequences?"

"How was I supposed to know about the bubble?"

Scarlett simply shook her head.

"What do we do now?" Basil asked the dreaded question.

And even Scarlett, who seemed to know everything about Golden Grove, had nothing to say. Scarlett told Basil they were sitting on the outskirts of Golden Grove, where Ambrosia wouldn't find them.

"I'm not going to Ambrosia's lair again. I can't," Basil said.

Scarlett pursed her lips. "You're getting that key."

"I thought you said—"

"Ambrosia killed my father. I won't let her kill either of us," she whispered.

Basil didn't understand. "Exactly—it was you who told me she was too dangerous. *You're* the one that made me promise not to go to her lair impulsively."

"Impulsively," Scarlett emphasized. "A well-thought-out plan is different from a rash decision."

"Isn't she after us this very moment? She's probably coming up with a plan of her own to destroy us."

Scarlett sighed. "Basil, I've been alone my entire life. Yes, I've hung around with nymphs and satyrs, but nobody like you—nobody human, to be honest."

"Me, too—well not the human part. But how will getting the key—"

"I see how much you want it," she interrupted. "The hope that key brings is what keeps you going. I've never had something like that—a dream, a goal."

Basil let out one concise giggle. "Dreams aren't that great, actually."

Scarlett's head cocked to one side, and her brows furrowed.

"It's blinding. I can't see anything else," Basil explained.

"Nonsense. You can see *me* just fine."

Basil looked to his feet and gulped down his saliva. "Are

we going to stay here?" Basil surveyed their surroundings with contempt. The area was muddy, and the small pond that sat between them was murky and brown.

"Let me clean it up a bit." Scarlett focused on the water and extended her palm. All her muscles tightened up as she mustered all her energy into the water. But no golden hue appeared—not one flicker.

"Wait a second," Scarlett said, looking down at her hands, mesmerized.

In disbelief, she tried to cast the enchantment on Basil, but nothing happened.

"Your enchantment—it doesn't work," Basil inferred.

"We're not in Golden Grove anymore." Scarlett took in their surroundings. She looked at every work of nature as if each leaf was some type of miracle. "In all my life, I've never left."

"I thought this *is* Golden Grove—the outskirts, you said."

"I thought so, too." Scarlett's eyes darted about the greenery. "It barely looks different." She walked up to one of the trees and touched it hesitantly.

"So your powers only work inside Golden Grove?"

"Yes," she said, "but this means Ambrosia won't find us— she would never suspect I would leave. After all she's told us about the outside world, we've all sworn we'd stay forever." Scarlett shook her head slowly as if it were the first time she'd ever been outside, because, in a sense, it was. "And there are no monsters? No poisonous air or venomous invisible snakes?"

"Well, if they're invisible, I wouldn't know, but—"

"Do you know what this means, Basil? She's been lying to us all along."

"No kidding."

Scarlett sat on a rock with a gape of the jaws.

"And if she *does* find us?"

"She won't," Scarlett retorted, curt and fierce.

Basil crossed his fingers and hoped she was right. If Ambrosia hadn't planned to kill him before, she'd definitely try to now. It surprised Basil that Scarlett didn't agree, especially as she was initially the main advocate for being better safe than sorry.

And just then, Basil felt at ease. Even amidst the danger and chaos, Scarlett was there, by his side, on the same page. Each time Basil had made an impulsive decision, he'd challenged Scarlett to her limit. But now, that limit was stretched so wide that it was expanded, redefined. He could tell that Scarlett, like him, cared about retrieving the key. Though their motives may have differed slightly, they shared a common goal.

"She won't find us because we're not going to be here for long. I have a plan."

"And you thought it up just now?"

"No," replied Scarlett. "I've been considering it for quite a few days now—it seemed too . . . too risky at first. But I *want* to be risky. I want to put myself at stake—I haven't had an adventure my entire life, Basil."

"Neither have I," he said. After a deep breath, Basil added, "But if we're doing this, we have to execute it properly—I don't want to put my life in any more danger."

"I will—put my life in danger, I mean." She barely hesitated. "If there's one thing I want to do before I die, it's this. And if I live knowing I could've done it—could've gotten the key—but decided to be a coward, it wouldn't be living so much as, I don't know, regretting."

Basil shook his head; he wouldn't let her risk her life.

"I'd rather die knowing I lived . . . truly *lived*," she whispered, "but I won't die. I promise." Scarlett walked toward Basil, holding a regular flower from this regular, unenchanted forest. She slipped it in his hair, and he allowed it. The stem prodded the back of his ear, but Basil didn't mind.

"Hey," Scarlett whispered, placing her hands on each of Basil's cheeks, "you're okay."

He closed his eyes to take in the moment. He didn't want to admit it, but Basil was slightly reluctant to think of leaving soon. Once he found the key, it would mean abandoning Scarlett . . . and his newfound home.

"It won't be goodbye," she said as if she could read Basil's mind. "Just a . . . a see you later." But they both knew Scarlett was lying to herself; once he found the key, he'd be on his way. Basil wouldn't come back to Golden Grove—not once he became King Basil Avington.

Still, proving himself to Regis V—or what Basil referred to as "maintaining order within Silverkeep"—was his top priority.

For different reasons, neither of them could wait more than a day, and that one day was filled with feasting on leafy fingernails and constant talk of ideas. Scarlett and Basil were incredibly anxious to execute their plan—a plan that manipulated Ambrosia's Achilles' heel. And with each minute that passed, the threat of Ambrosia brutally murdering one of them became increasingly daunting.

"Wait." Basil stopped in his tracks as they prepared to re-enter Golden Grove. "Won't she have some protective layer around her lair?"

"Not to *burst your bubble*, but there won't be one." Scarlett laughed at her own joke, but Basil's expression didn't waver.

How is she kidding around right now?

His limbs trembled though Scarlett would be the one risking the most. "Not in the daytime. Besides, even if there is one, she'll let me in if I'm alone."

"If you say so." Basil had his doubts; the odds hadn't been working in his favor. But Scarlett might be luckier than him.

Basil and Scarlett could immediately tell when they entered

Golden Grove; it was as if Scarlett's body sprang to life, and energy and enchantment filled her body. A glowing smile appeared on her face.

She must be hiding her terror for my sake.

Phobos was sitting atop an oak tree as the two of them passed, and he playfully threw an acorn down at Scarlett's head. After flinching, she tilted her head toward her brother.

"Whatcha up to?" Phobos asked.

"Oh, nothing. Just a leisurely walk," Scarlett lied. Her acting skills impressed Basil.

Phobos raised his bushy brows. "Why are you coming from . . . wherever that is. Isn't that the outskirts?" He pointed a finger in the direction from which they had come.

"Yes," Scarlett said, "we were trying to find . . . Basil's sword, the one he lost after—"

"Holding it to Haldi," Phobos finished. Everyone seemed to know about that. "Well, have fun, younguns!" he called out after they were yards away even though Phobos was fourteen, three years younger than Scarlett.

Once they were out of his earshot, Scarlett said, "Good thing it wasn't Batellia—I swear that four-year-old never stops asking questions."

Scarlett tried to get a laugh out of Basil, but it didn't work. He found nothing about their adventure funny. In fact, Basil struggled to even move.

"Ambrosia's lair is just a few yards away," Scarlett whispered. "You'll have to find a better hiding spot than I did last time—one that won't make any noise."

Basil's hands tightened to fists. "Why didn't we think about this before?"

"It doesn't matter. We're thinking about it now. You should stay here—you'll be able to see and hear if you just lean your head from"—Scarlett glanced around—"that tree."

The sycamore she pointed to had a thick trunk; Basil's whole body would be invisible behind it. "Are you sure I shouldn't go any further?"

"Yes, Basil. Would you rather risk both of our lives or one?"

"Stop saying that. You're going to come out fine. You'd better, or I'll never forgive myself," Basil whispered.

"I know." Scarlett gulped—her first sign of fear—and planted a kiss on Basil's forehead.

Scarlett continued in front of him, and Basil's teeth gritted at the sight of Ambrosia, seated neatly on her throne. Scarlett wore a crying facade as she ambled toward the cold lair, letting out bursts of fake hiccups and tears. Her idea impressed Basil; he was eager to see how it would play out. Scarlett looked over her shoulder and winked at Basil one last time before approaching the forest tyrant.

Scarlett appeared powerless to Ambrosia though she was the most powerful (and only) nymph Basil had ever known. But at this point, she was more than a mere nymph to Basil. He would agree she was more resilient than anyone he'd known.

"Scarlett!" Ambrosia called, her lips curling into an evil grin. "To what do I owe the pleasure?"

"Basil's back," she cried. "He's wandering about the forest, trying to hunt me down. He's so dangerous . . . won't leave me be."

Though Basil and Scarlett had originally disagreed on how to manipulate Ambrosia, Scarlett promised that touching her soft spot would do the trick. Ambrosia knew what it felt like to be the girl Scarlett pretended to be; to feel controlled by the desires of others—others who were considered of a greater status.

But it wouldn't work *flawlessly*.

"Liar!" Ambrosia yelled. "You saved him from my lair. When I took him, you—"

"No, you don't understand. When you kidnapped him, I was happy . . . *elated*. My goodness, I was finally . . . at peace. But now he's stalking me, he's—"

"Do *not* interrupt me, you nymph!" Ambrosia screamed, ironically hypocritical. When she yelled at Scarlett, the surrounding nymphs and satyrs heard her voice thunder and listened intently to the conversation. But Scarlett and Ambrosia ignored the nosy forest inhabitants.

Scarlett bowed her head to Ambrosia. "Yes, my great queen."

Scarlett had previously promised Basil that her plan would work—that Ambrosia wasn't always evil, and bringing out empathy in her would make the forest ruler vulnerable. But Basil began to question Scarlett's idea.

"Are you telling me the truth?" Ambrosia still spoke doubtfully, but it seemed she began to ponder the possibility of Scarlett being sincere.

"Why wouldn't I?" Scarlett wiped away her fake tears. "Please . . . I need help."

Ambrosia was beginning to unravel, but she was still herself. "Why should I believe you? I'll need you to prove it in some way. Prove that Basil is your enemy and not your friend."

Scarlett had come prepared. She revealed Basil's sword from behind her back. After he'd threatened Haldi with it, the nymphs had taken the jeweled weapon and stored it inside a tree. The forest inhabitants had been nervous the Ambrosia situation would repeat itself; a human, a sword—it all seemed too familiar to them.

Yesterday, Scarlett and Basil had spoken to Haldi and retrieved the sword from the tree as they devised their plan.

Ambrosia gasped. "This . . . this isn't just any sword." Her mouth dropped open in awe. "Do you know what this is, Scarlett?"

Scarlett shook her head. "I know it's Basil's sword, and I stole it from him so he wouldn't hurt me."

"The kings' sword." Ambrosia's eyes widened almost as if she was . . . happy. "May I?" She eagerly reached her hand toward Scarlett.

Don't give it to her.

The innocent nymph's arms shuddered as she handed the sword to Ambrosia. It was heavy, and Scarlett struggled to fully extend her arm. What bothered Basil wasn't that he was giving away the sword—once he had the key, that wouldn't matter—but the fact that Ambrosia could hurt Scarlett with it.

Ambrosia grabbed the hilt of the sword and lifted it, point facing the sky. "Wow," was all she could manage as she rotated the blade, observing each detail, each nuance.

But after her initial astonishment faded, Ambrosia shifted her focus back to Scarlett. It seemed she truly wanted to believe her, but she wouldn't without reason. "Why do you give me this? What does this prove?"

"Basil Avington threatened us with it. He tried to kill us, he—"

"I *saw* you run out of my lair with him. I swear you rescued the boy when I kidnap—" She cleared her throat. "When I kidnapped him to *protect* Golden Grove," Ambrosia argued.

They had thought of this, too. Scarlett and Basil had known she'd ask provocative questions as they'd rehearsed the conversation for hours on end.

"This I cannot justify. I just hope you'll believe me when I say he forced me to help him." But Ambrosia wasn't satisfied. "He said that if I didn't, when he did escape, I'd regret ever refusing him . . . ever . . . denying him of freedom . . . Yes, those were the exact words he used."

"I don't believe it. Close, but not quite. You could be telling the truth, but I must be sure of it before I gift you with my help and expertise," she snapped back.

Basil hid behind the sycamore, his arms and legs stretched in a thin line for dear life.

Plan B.

When physical proof failed, speech was the way to go. The power words possessed was forever greater than anything else.

Come on, Scarlett.

"I understand," Scarlett said. "I guess you don't know what it feels like to be treated like nothing by a royal . . . All the royals—they're despicable."

Because, if there was one thing Ambrosia despised, it was being spoken to with no recognition, with negligence. Ambrosia wanted Scarlett to recognize she'd been through the same thing, the same pain.

Scarlett turned to walk away, but Ambrosia lifted her palm. "Wait!" she called, so loud that the already nosy nymphs and satyrs practically gathered around Scarlett and Ambrosia. The two barely seemed to notice, though.

Scarlett struggled to hold back her smile as Ambrosia used her enchantment to summon her back. Scarlett knew the internal scars Regis IV had given Ambrosia had never faded. She knew that Ambrosia was only evil because it was easier. And that more and more power only meant more and more loneliness. And because Ambrosia was so lonely, being able to relate to another—even if it was just a free-spirited forest nymph—was comforting. Scarlett knew this because, though she wasn't an evil beast from hell, she was lonely, too.

"Yes?" Scarlett turned her head back around and spoke innocently.

"I understand . . . better than anyone," Ambrosia whispered. Tears spilled from her eyes for the first time that anyone in Golden Grove had ever seen. All of the inhabitants watched in awe as their queen struggled to keep her composure.

Basil and Scarlett didn't quite expect her to cry, but it wasn't the worst that could happen. "Come." Ambrosia beckoned to Scarlett.

Scarlett nodded. Ambrosia held the kings' sword in one hand, and her bracelets were stacked on the other. This was it. This was Scarlett's chance. And it would be the only chance she'd ever have.

Ambrosia opened her arms to embrace Scarlett, and Scarlett accepted the hug. She was just a bit taller than Ambrosia, so the queen's head rested on her shoulder, which was dampened with Ambrosia's flowing teardrops.

Basil's body, already so tense, stiffened further as he craned his neck ever-so-slightly to watch from behind the tree. It wasn't him in Ambrosia's lair, but it felt like it.

What looked like the entire population of Golden Grove was circled around Ambrosia's lair, amused at the sight of her emotion. They all hated the queen—maybe not a loathing as strong as Scarlett's or Basil's—but a hatred all the same. So, if they saw Scarlett make a run for it with the key, they would only help her.

Ambrosia's muffled cries and mucus met Scarlett's scalp, but she paid no attention. Basil's eyes were glued to the key, which dangled from the forest queen's wrist, the emerald gleaming an unnatural glow.

Ambrosia's sobs progressively became heavier and heavier. Scarlett's hands lingered on Ambrosia's back, and they trembled as they trailed to the queen's shoulders, then her arms. Ambrosia was distracted in her regret, failing to notice Scarlett's hands moving toward her most valuable possession.

Basil watched Ambrosia's lair, just like the rest of Golden Grove. But unlike Basil, the other inhabitants didn't know what Scarlett was after.

Ambrosia would only be crying for so long. And Scarlett needed to act. Now.

Her hand reached for Ambrosia's wrist, and the evil queen barely noticed. Scarlett fiddled with Ambrosia's bracelets until she felt the key. Her hand naturally gravitated toward it as if the key was begging to be saved.

And all at once, Scarlett ripped it off Ambrosia's golden bangle. The key easily detached from her wrist like a berry plucked from a bramble; Ambrosia hadn't worried about protecting the key, for nobody had tried to oppose her. But Ambrosia noticed the moment it was gone, her eyes bulging from their sockets, her hands dropping the sword in astonishment and turning to claws.

Scarlett shrunk in terror.

"Give it here!" Ambrosia ripped her body from Scarlett's and inflicted her hands on the nymph's throat. "Give it!" Her screech was petrifying.

"N-n-no!" Scarlett stammered, almost strangled by Ambrosia's grip. Ambrosia's sharp nails scratched the skin on Scarlett's neck.

Let her go.

Basil tried to jump into the melee—he really did—but his body wouldn't move.

Ambrosia lunged for the key, but Scarlett pulled her hand back. The forest tyrant tried to conjure the key's enchantment on Scarlett. It didn't work, though; she no longer held the key. And all the power was in Scarlett's hands.

Scarlett wrenched away from Ambrosia—revealing to Basil the lines of blood on her neck.

"Basil!" she called out.

He emerged from the tree and revealed his quivering body. "Toss them!" he suggested.

The key flew through the air, as if in slow-motion, and landed rattling in Basil's shaky hands. The hopeful and curious eyes of the nymphs and satyrs remained fixed on the emerald and gold wonder.

But now, Scarlett and Ambrosia were equal in strength and power. And the only thing she could do was run.

"Come on!" Basil yelled. "Let's go!"

Ambrosia attempted to impose all sorts of tricks and injuries on Scarlett, but nothing worked; she was just as powerless as all the other forest inhabitants with only a daily allowance of enchantment she'd most definitely already used.

Her best weapon was screaming. And her voice thundered throughout the crowd of nymphs and satyrs. "Seize him! Seize her! Do something!" she demanded.

But nobody listened.

Scarlett sprinted for her life, faster than Basil had ever seen somebody run. He wasn't sure if it was due to her enchantment or her mere athleticism, but Basil was impressed either way. The red hair behind Scarlett whirled as she reached Basil.

And as Scarlett approached him, all Basil could see was the blinding light that shined from the key—the burst of magic it emitted.

This. This was what he'd wanted for so long. And he had it, literally, in the palm of his hand.

"The texture," Scarlett whispered, catching her breath. "Feel it."

Basil was speechless as he grasped the key with everything he had. It was beautiful, detailed, and centuries old—the same masterpiece the great King Philip had once held. And it contained all the power he would ever want . . . ever need.

The nymphs and satyrs scurried to Basil and Scarlett with a desire to see the coveted object. *Wows* and *I can't believe its* spread throughout the crowd.

But Ambrosia curled her lips and stared at the happy girl and boy with cold and harsh eyes. "You'll regret this!" she howled. "This. Is not. The end!"

But Basil and Scarlett, hopeful and naive, stupidly disregarded every word the forest tyrant hollered.

Ambrosia bolted toward them, and Basil halted her sprint with a thrust of his palm. He hadn't known it would be so easy.

"She's right," Basil hushed. "It's the beginning."

"The beginning of something beautiful," Scarlett whispered. "You'll do great things with this key." And she embraced Basil, bittersweet tears dripping down each of their faces. But neither of them could compare the heartache of departing to the hope and endless possibilities that came with the key.

Basil turned toward Ambrosia, standing nervously on the edge of her lair, one last time and said, "Perhaps you weren't lying about my father after all." Though he had initially been in denial, his father's flaws and failure at nobility had turned out to be the strongest weapon. And only Scarlett had been wise enough to use Ambrosia's past against her.

Ambrosia let out a growl. Now that he had the key and she didn't, Basil could've killed her. But no matter how triggering and abrasive the woman could be, the boy wasn't a murderer. The decision to spare Ambrosia's life wasn't the first mistake Basil made. And it certainly would not be the last.

XIV

hese look painful," Basil said, inspecting the marks Ambrosia's fingers had imprinted on Scarlett's neck.

"I know," replied Scarlett. "The woman's got quite a grip."

"You were so brave today." Basil brushed his hand through Scarlett's fiery tresses, but she only looked down at the ground with nowhere near the amount of pride she should've had. "Really, Scarlett."

"Thanks, but . . ."

They were on the outskirts of Golden Grove—*actually* this time—away from the rest of the intrusive inhabitants. Scarlett and Basil sat on their butts, chest-deep in blooming greens. They alternated with the key, taking turns observing its beautiful features. They'd done the impossible, and Basil's heartbeat was quick in amazement.

"What?"

"But . . . I'll never see you again," Scarlett said.

Basil didn't want to think about leaving her, but, at the same time, returning to the castle with the key stirred up plenty of excitement. He had everything he'd always wanted . . . except Scarlett; Basil would have to leave soon, without her.

Unless . . .

An idea—crazy and probably unrealistic—crossed Basil's mind. "Come with me," he proposed, stroking Scarlett's scalp.

Scarlett raised her eyebrows. "I don't understand."

"Come," Basil drew out his words. "With. Me." His voice was a delicate hush.

"Are you serious?"

"To the castle. Come with me, Scarlett." Basil's hand brushed down her shoulder to reach her open palm. Their fingers gently interlocked. "I know we've only known each other for a short time, but I've never felt this way. Ever."

Scarlett shook her head. "I'm a nymph, Basil. It seems you've forgotten."

"Of course I haven't forgotten—it's what makes you *you*. And it's beautiful." He reached his other hand to the tip of her pointy ear. "You have nothing to be insecure about."

"But my family, my—"

"You've spoken to Phoba and Batellios once since I've been here. You've barely mentioned your mother. They'll be all right. And they can come visit, and—"

"Phob*os* and Batelli*a*," Scarlett corrected. "And . . . you're getting ahead of yourself."

"How?" he asked. "We need to get out of here before Ambrosia finds some way to outsmart us. And I only have a bit of time before Regis's coronation."

"I'll need to think about it," Scarlett compromised.

"Think about it all you want," he said. "But think quickly—we'll need to get out of here."

It was a beautiful image, Basil's daydream of Scarlett in the castle. She wouldn't hide her nymph features—no—she would accentuate them so all of Silverkeep would see her leafy finger-nails. The servants would embroider green forest-like gowns, resembling the leaves she wore on a daily basis. Her hair would curl around a tiara, and her ruddy locks would trail behind. Scarlett would be the most beautiful queen. And Lydia Rose would be nothing more than a princess.

The crazy thing was that it didn't feel impulsive; though Basil had only known Scarlett for six days, everything felt perfect between them. Basil realized *time* wasn't always necessary to strengthen connections. The spark they shared—the experiences they'd endured together—did the trick.

That night, they barely slept. Scarlett and Basil filled the night hours experimenting with the key, exploring the possibilities of what it could do.

Neither of them understood how Ambrosia had been able to figure it out so quickly; the key didn't exactly come with an instruction manual. But after some time, Basil and Scarlett realized the key was quite simple. And it worked in a manner similar to all the nymphs' and satyrs' enchantment though the power was significantly magnified.

"Can it bring people back to life?" Basil asked, curious for no particular reason.

"It can heal—I've heard she can use it for healing—but not once somebody's dead, at least I don't think so," replied Scarlett. "Anyway, are you going to try it out? The key, I mean—not the resurrection."

"Okay, I'm thinking of something."

"Focus all your energy on it. Every bit of concentration you have," Scarlett said.

Basil nodded, and slowly, the flowers on the ground levitated. They floated off the grassy field and hovered in the air, surrounded with a bright golden hue. Then, they arranged themselves in a pattern—yellow, red, purple, yellow, red, purple—around Scarlett. They swirled and swirled around her like a tornado.

Basil looked to the side, and the flowers fell right back to their stems. But they didn't scatter on the floor; they reattached neatly.

"*That's* what you wanted to do?"

Basil shrugged. "Your turn." He handed Scarlett the key.

The nymph stood from the ground and brushed the dirt off her behind. "Let's go."

"Where?" Basil asked, reluctant to stand from his comfortable position.

"I'll show you."

Basil let out an overdramatic groan as he stood. He followed Scarlett, who ran at a pace with which Basil could barely keep up. "For the love of King Philip, where are we going?" Basil managed between short breaths.

But soon they arrived—at the depressing, dying part of the stream. Basil had seen it once before, but not for long. And he wasn't catching on.

"*Why* are we here?" he asked, poking his tongue in his cheek.

"The key was meant to be used for good, right?" And Scarlett, the key in her hand, focused her energy on the black water filled with wilting white lilies stained gray. Dusk had nearly fallen, and the stream was barely visible.

The water began to gleam, and the black liquid turned clear just before their eyes.

"I—" Scarlett was speechless. The wilting gray flowers sprang to life. The black pigment was extracted and swirled through the air, diminishing like an essence.

"You just did that. That's . . . incredible," Basil whispered. "If that's possible—"

"Anything is," Scarlett finished. "Anything is possible."

"Come to the castle with me," Basil tried again, hoping that this time, Scarlett would be more open to the improbable.

And she nodded, first slowly, but soon rapidly. She jumped like a koala into Basil's open arms, tears shedding down her cheeks. Scarlett had experienced more this past week than she had her entire life. The hope, affection, accomplishment—it was all so new and foreign to her.

Tucked in Basil's embrace, Scarlett yawned. And the contagious action spread to Basil, too.

"Dream of me," she whispered.

And soon, they fell asleep, her head nestled in Basil's chest, just like the night they'd shared the spoiled meat. Slumber took them quickly, and they drifted off with hope of endless possibilities.

What they failed to consider were Ambrosia's promises. She'd sworn she would get revenge—that this wasn't the end. And the next day, Ambrosia wouldn't have the power she possessed before, but her enchantment wouldn't go away immediately. She'd have the daily enchantment that every other nymph and satyr had, and *she* knew how to harness it into something destructive.

Basil hadn't realized they'd fallen asleep in the middle of Golden Grove the previous night. And if he had, he hadn't thought it mattered. But when he woke up, countless nymphs and satyrs loomed over him. Some of them he hadn't seen before, while others looked familiar.

All of the forest inhabitants seemed terrified of Scarlett and Basil though they didn't have any reason to be; the two weren't going to abuse the key's power as Ambrosia had. But the nymphs and satyrs were used to the key being a weapon, not a tool.

Basil flinched at the many pairs of eyes glued to him. "Wha—what are you all doing?" He yawned. Basil's hair was floppy, and his shoulder was achy; he hadn't paid attention to the awkward position he'd slept in because, though his body wasn't, his heart was comfortable as Scarlett lay with him. She was still asleep.

"You're our hero," one of the satyrs said. "You've saved us."

"Thank you, but really, I didn't do much. It was all Scarlett." And with the mention of her name, Scarlett bolted awake. When she glanced upward, she, too, flinched at the stares.

"What's going on? And why were they . . . watching us sleep?" she asked Basil as if he had a clue. Basil thought it was funny—it was the same way he'd first met Scarlett a week ago.

"Our true savior." The same satyr bowed his head to Scarlett. She wasn't used to compliments, and her freckled cheeks blushed.

"To the new rulers of Golden Grove, we'd like to celebrate the commencement of your rule, Basil Avington and Scarlett."

Basil looked to Scarlett with questioning eyes and then back at the crowd that stood above him. "I'm not sure what you—"

"You two will be the best rulers. The youngest we've ever had!" the satyr yelled. Nods spread throughout the clump. The speaker was confused at Basil's expression. "Not to say you're unqualified—you very much are!" He tried to catch himself, thinking his words were misunderstood, that that was the reason Basil's brows remained furrowed.

"No, um . . . I'll be out of here in a few days—one, probably," Basil guiltily informed them, still lying on the grassy ground.

The crowd exchanged mumbles, concerned. "What do you mean? I thought you wanted to take down Ambrosia?" a satyr asked.

"I did, but for different reasons than you."

"But—"

"Ambrosia is powerless. Is that not what you all wanted?" Basil tried to redeem himself.

"But it was for selfish reasons, huh?" A nymph chimed in,

pushing her way to the front of the crowd. Her long face and chestnut skin were familiar, and Basil could've sworn he'd seen her before—talked to her before. She had long, brunette hair.

Yes. It was the first nymph Basil had seen—Haldi. She hadn't liked him from the start.

"Look, I wasn't trying to mess with your forest dynamic, but I needed that key. Won't you all still have your enchantment when I leave?"

But none of them knew; it hadn't been tested before.

"*Mess with our dynamic* you did, Basil Avington. Ambrosia was right about you royals," Haldi sneered.

Basil didn't want to be hated by the forest inhabitants. "What? I saved you all, I—"

But he wasn't heard above the angry clamor of the nymphs and satyrs. Just two seconds ago, they'd been applauding him. But now it appeared they wanted to destroy him.

"It's all right. You don't need their support," Scarlett whispered in his ear. "Don't forget all the power is in your hands. Not theirs."

And she was right. Basil had no valid reason to stress over the opinions of funky-looking nymphs and satyrs.

With one summoning of the key's enchantment, Basil could've scared them all away. But he didn't; he wanted to be as different from Ambrosia as humanly possible.

"Say something," Basil whispered back, thinking the forest inhabitants would listen to one of their own over the stubborn and selfish prince.

Scarlett nodded and looked up at them. "This boy is good, I promise. I would trust him with my life. In fact, I did. And I'm still here, now aren't I?"

The nymphs and satyrs looked to Haldi and the satyr that had spoken initially, unsure of who and what to believe. But within moments, they scattered about the forest as if they'd forgotten the matter at hand.

"They're like that, my fellow nymphs and satyrs," Scarlett said once they were gone. "Nosy, but they want the best. They're quite loving, really."

"Okay. Well, we're leaving now," responded Basil, agitated.

"Excuse me?"

"You heard just fine." But Scarlett crossed her arms. "Look, Scarlett, we've got to go before Ambrosia does anything else. And I've been away for too long—the searchers are wasting their time with each passing moment."

"Oh, please. You don't give a damn about the *searchers*," Scarlett accused. "You're just eager to be king."

"And if I am?" Basil questioned. "Hmm? What's wrong with that?"

Scarlett shrugged. "Nothing, but just *say* it next time. You don't have to lie to me," she said. "And we can't leave yet. I haven't said goodbye."

Basil rolled his eyes. He'd been in Golden Grove for long enough; now that they had the chance, he was ready to get out of there, still petrified Ambrosia would pop out of nowhere. "Come on, Phobos and Batellia were probably in that clump—they must have seen you. Besides, I didn't say goodbye when *I* left the *castle*."

"Well, that's the difference between us. Like a normal person, I actually love my family." Scarlett pouted. "But all right. Go back without me, I guess." Basil knew she didn't mean it.

With a dramatic sigh, Basil agreed, "Fine. Say goodbye, but then we're off."

Scarlett sprang to her feet and dashed across the field. She glanced over her shoulder to find Basil, still buried in plants. "You're not coming?"

Basil whined before following Scarlett.

As they made their way into another part of the forest, neither Basil nor Scarlett expected the alarming sight that appeared before them: the blooming flowers no longer bloomed, and the trees were bare. It was like the dark side of the stream Basil had seen before, bu*t much* worse.

Birds and creatures hung off the branches, poached and bloodied. But nymphs and satyrs were nowhere to be seen; they must have left to find somewhere safe.

Scarlett was speechless, but Basil said, "Ambrosia promised it wasn't the end." His eyes brewed fear. "Come on, let's get out of here."

"Are you kidding?" Scarlett asked.

"What? You want her to hurt us?"

"I'm not going to leave Ambrosia to ruin the forest. If she can still do this, she can still kill my friends—my family."

"Woah—who said anything about *killing?*"

Scarlett waggled her head side-to-side. "We have to fix this."

"So use the key, like you just did for the stream."

"And just let her do it again when we leave?"

Basil was beyond the point of frustration. All he wanted was to get out of there, and he didn't care about anyone besides Scarlett and himself. Everything was so close to perfect—and the perfect life awaited them at the castle. The rest of the forest inhabitants were nothing to him.

"She doesn't have the key! Don't you see, Scarlett? She can't kill anyone."

"That's not true. People can kill without enchantment—poison, swords, literal hands!" Scarlett cried.

"But they're protected with enchantment."

"Once you leave with the key? I'm not so sure." Her pace quickened.

"Regardless, Ambrosia will be on the same level as them."

Scarlett no longer cared what Basil had to say. She jogged in front of him through the depressing forest. Phobos and Batellia were nowhere to be found—no satyrs or nymphs were.

Scarlett turned back to Basil. They were separated by cut

down branches and mud. Ruins. "We should've killed her when we had the chance," she whispered.

"Look, Scarlett," Basil said, trying to catch up to her. "Once I'm king and you're queen, we'll fix this—all of this. On the throne, we'll be able to do anything and everything. But we have to go."

Scarlett swallowed her salty teardrops. With the key in her hand, she made one last fix. Scarlett focused on her surroundings, and they began to glow. Within moments, every fallen tree reconstructed itself, the leaves blooming in sunlight. The mud below their feet disappeared, tall grass replacing it.

"See? We're more powerful than Ambrosia will ever be again," Basil said.

"Look, I'm excited to live in the castle with you. I am, okay? I promise. But there's something I have to do first. I'm sorry, I—"

Without further explanation, Scarlett ran. Her lengthy flaming hair almost reached Basil, but the rest of her was far beyond him. With the key clutched in her hand, she didn't stop—not once for a breath.

Not again.

"Where are you going? Scarlett!" But she just ran faster. *"Scarlett!"*

Golden Grove was her home—it always had been. And she wouldn't leave the rest of her kind to suffer; she was too compassionate. Scarlett didn't bother fixing the dark and soggy land she sprinted through; she likely knew that once she left, the same would happen. Any of the nymphs and satyrs had the power to destroy the forest, but they didn't have the skill, ingenuity, and sick mind that Ambrosia had.

"She's trying to lure you! It's a trap, Scarlett!"

As Basil continued to follow, the distance between them grew; she was incredibly fast. And soon enough, Basil understood where she was headed.

"No! Nothing good will come of it!"

But she didn't listen.

And soon, when Basil finally caught up, Scarlett's back was to him, her front to Ambrosia Cromwell. The forest queen still sat on her throne of bark and wilted leaves, her eyes swirling with rage and a sly grin on her face.

"You've come to your senses, haven't you?" Ambrosia said, her arm outstretched, ready to receive the key. But Basil became calm again when Scarlett pulled it out of her reach.

"You have to stop. Whatever you're doing to the forest—it's not fair," Scarlett asserted. Basil was impressed by the strength in her tone.

Ambrosia huffed. "*Not fair*," she jeered. "The *world* isn't fair. Now give me that. Come on, now, give it here."

"Never."

Basil smiled; he liked the dominance Scarlett had over Ambrosia. The evil forest queen had no more power than the rest of the forest inhabitants.

Ambrosia mustered faux puppy dog eyes as she sat on her throne of bark and leaves. "Come on, Scar. What have I ever done to *you*?"

"You *killed* my father. And don't call me that."

"I—" Ambrosia had nothing defensive to say, and she didn't try. "You took advantage of my kindness. And if I didn't know it already, you taught me how useless benevolence is. I tried to help you and you—"

"Benevolence?" Scarlett's eyes widened. "You?" she scoffed.

"I *need* that key. You're too young to know what you need—you know simply what you *want*—both of you." Ambrosia gestured to Basil, who stood behind Scarlett. Scarlett turned around to find him, caught off guard by his presence.

"Get over yourself. You will never get this key back, but you *will* stop destroying Golden Grove, or whatever it's really called," Basil said, stomping in front of Ambrosia until his face hovered inches from hers. "We're leaving soon, and once we do, you'll only be hurting the innocent nymphs and satyrs, not us."

"No!" Ambrosia squawked. "You're not *leaving*."

"You will fix it," Basil demanded. But Ambrosia stuck her tongue out, an immature expression when she could obviously think of nothing else.

"Or we'll *kill* you," Scarlett added. Even Basil was surprised by her sudden harshness, and he turned around and raised his eyebrows at Scarlett.

But somehow, Ambrosia was unimpressed. "No, you won't. You're too—"

Before she could finish, though, Scarlett slashed the key across the air in front of her, and a bloody cut appeared across Ambrosia's neck. Then, hissing tendrils curled over her feet, trapping Ambrosia in her stance. They were the same sharp and spiky vines that had crept up Basil's body when he'd been kidnapped. Now, Ambrosia would know how it felt. Basil stepped away and scurried to Scarlett's side.

"If you haven't already figured, I *did* save Basil. And he was never anything besides a kind friend to keep me company. Or perhaps more than a friend, but that's not any of your business, is it?" Another slash, this one across Ambrosia's forehead. "Anyways, he wasn't a stalker, not an evil royal." Scarlett stretched out the word *evil*. "In fact, I really like royals." One more cut, straight across her stomach. "They're beautiful people."

Ambrosia clenched her stomach and gritted her teeth. Her raven hair stood up, and this time, Basil was *sure* the tips began to flame. "Killing your father," she managed, "was the best choice I've ever made."

Now the fury belonged to Scarlett. Basil watched the two women, awestruck.

"Go along, kill me, darling," Ambrosia said, all too calm. "Kill me already! You coward!" Her voice turned to a shriek.

And Basil saw that Scarlett was close to doing it. It would be easy with the key. But, like Basil, Scarlett couldn't will herself to murder someone.

"Just fix what you've done to the forest. I'm not going to kill you—not because I'm weak, but because I'm strong—stronger than you'll ever be."

And, to both Basil and Scarlett's surprise, Ambrosia agreed. "I will fix it." But there was something hidden behind her tone.

"And?" Scarlett asked.

"And I will never do it again." Though there was nothing sincere about her resolution.

Figuring that's the best they would get, Scarlett smiled. "By tomorrow, I expect to see the forest restored to its original state."

They stood in silence—the three of them—tension rising between eye contact.

"Well? What are you two lovebirds still doing here?" Ambrosia shooed them away with her hand. And Basil knew something was awry; she shouldn't have been smiling so wide. She shouldn't have been smiling at all. Could it really be so simple? But Basil told himself the concern was only in his head.

Though there was nothing else to discuss, the conversation seemed unfinished. Basil was impressed with the part of Scarlett that had shone through in front of Ambrosia. It was a part he'd never seen, but every second he spent with Scarlett—every new aspect of her character—drew Basil in more and more and stirred up desire inside him.

They walked out of Ambrosia's lair with the advantage, and this time, Ambrosia didn't call after them. Still, it seemed remains of her power lingered as the tendrils and thorns dissolved around her. She didn't promise revenge or claim they would soon regret what they've done. Instead, she sat on her throne, contemplating.

When night fell, Basil and Scarlett were still in Golden Grove. After Scarlett had bidden farewell to her mother and siblings, they'd spent the past few hours discussing what life would soon be like. Scarlett knew nothing about the castle, being queen, or the kingdom of Silverkeep as a whole. But Basil was sure Bridget would teach the girl everything she needed to know.

"The servants will be enamored of you," Basil said at one point in their conversation.

"And why is that?"

Basil shrugged. "I just know it. We're all so . . . headstrong. My brother especially. Oh, you'll get a kick out of my brother. But, in any case, the servants will appreciate a queen as kind as you are."

"Is it really so easy? Can I become queen just like that?" Scarlett asked.

Basil didn't think about it too hard. "Well, if I'm king, wouldn't that make the decision up to me?"

Later that night, Scarlett taught Basil how to braid hair by demonstrating on her own. She took one side and quickly twirled three strands to form a twist. When she let Basil try with the other half of her fiery locks, he didn't hesitate to agree as it allowed him to ramble on. With each sentence, he found a way to mention his brother. "Regis V will be a mere prince," or "the seven minutes don't matter, after all," or "Lydia Rose and my brother will be sorry for ever crossing me."

Once Basil tied Scarlett's second tangled and messy braid, dusk had fallen. The two twists were far from symmetrical, as Scarlett's was neatly tied up, starting at her forehead, while Basil's had pieces sticking out and started halfway down her face. It ended with an excessive amount of tangled hair below the tie—which was a piece of grass.

Neither of them had realized the amount of time they'd spent talking about their future together. Scarlett advised Basil to stuff the key in his ear or nostril; nobody would find it that way. And if Ambrosia was plotting something, she'd never suspect it. Reluctantly, Basil poked it up his nose, and due to the key's enchantment, he felt no pain.

"What's going to happen to Golden Grove without the key?" Basil asked.

"The Forests of Ethereal Paradise," Scarlett whispered.

"What?"

"Before Ambrosia changed the name, my father ruled The Forests of Ethereal Paradise. Not Golden Grove."

"That's beautiful."

Scarlett paused before saying, "It's never happened before, but I assume the enchantment will fade, perhaps gradually. And as it does, Ambrosia won't have any more power than the rest. But it's okay—we were all fine before magic, and they'll be fine after it. Better, even." She shut her eyes with a smile on her face. "Goodnight, Basil. I can't wait for tomorrow."

"Sleep tight, my love."

My love. I just said love. *Out loud.*

Scarlett fell straight off to sleep in his arms. Tonight, they were on the outskirts of Golden Grove. And tomorrow, they'd be in the castle of Silverkeep. It would be a thrilling day; Basil would reappear at the palace with Scarlett by his side and the key in his hand. What would he say to his mother? To his brother? Would Bridget be mad? Or impressed?

Basil thought of different scenarios as he drifted off to sleep. And each one was perfect. He mumbled ideas to himself. Was he to simply show the key? To prove its magic?

And the final, beautiful sight that put Basil at ease was the picture his mind created of Regis V, fuming with jealous anger. He'd finally know how it felt. Basil would pull the key from his pocket and allow the emerald's power to radiate through the castle entryway. The servants would be stunned; Bridget's jaw would drop, and Regis would . . . what would Regis do? Perhaps he would curl his hands into fists and lunge at Basil. But he would be powerless and scrawny.

No matter his family's reaction, Basil would be King. And he and Scarlett would grow old together as the best king and queen since the reign of King Philip. Their connection would last forever, until death did them part.

asil woke up and instantly remembered what the day would entail. The prince—soon to be king—let out a squeal of excitement. King Basil.

The first thing he felt for was the key, which was still rammed up his nostril. He stuck his fingers up and pulled out his mucus-stained, magical prized possession. So Scarlett wouldn't notice his nasty mucus covering the key, he rubbed it on the grass; he didn't want to disgust her, though she was probably still asleep.

Yes, she was. Basil looked to his right where she lay. Scarlett, her back to him, looked peaceful in her slumber. Basil was surprised; the sun was up high in the sky—Scarlett would usually be awake at this time.

"Scarlett," he sang with glee. "Today's the day!"

But she remained in place. "Scarlett, wake up! You can sleep all you want when we get to the castle. Oh—our room will be glorious. We can even decorate it with, I don't know, trees!"

No sound.

Basil rolled to his side and playfully tugged on Scarlett's two asymmetrical red braids. When the action failed to wake her, Basil put his hands on either side of her waist from behind and lightly shook her. As his shakes became heavier, Scarlett's body rotated to face him.

And with her body fell a pool of deep red blood. Gory liquid poured out from a gash in her stomach.

No.

Her mouth was open, lips slightly parted. Blood spilled from there, too. Basil's heart plummeted through his body. It had to be a dream.

Basil's trembling fingers dropped the key and made for the right side of her neck. His index and middle fingers felt her vein, but the pulse was absent. Desperate, he tried her wrist . . . her chest . . . her temple . . . the joint behind her knees. Nothing.

Her body lay lifeless.

Cold.

Stark.

Numb.

Pale and moribund.

Stiff and inanimate.

Scarlett is dead.

Every bit of color was drained from her lips. And her dead eyes stared at Basil, wide open and apathetic. The only pigment existed in her hair, which remained flaming red. Her two braids, one of Basil's tying, were still intact.

"Wake up. Wake up. Wake up. *Wake up.*" Basil pinched his own skin until he screamed in agony. "Wake up!"

But he was awake.

And she wasn't. She would never be. Ever again.

It was then when Basil realized the tree behind her was no longer a tree but a pile of ashes—it must have died with her; she'd said she was 'one with nature.'

Basil, flailing, snatched the key from the ground and did

all he could think of. He focused on Scarlett's body with all his attention. But her body didn't glow—no golden hue existed. Not this time.

"No." His voice began to break. "No."

After his initial state of denial vanished, Basil allowed tears to well up in the bottoms of his eyes. He'd never cried as hard as he did for Scarlett. He'd never thought a human could produce so many tears.

Basil would've given anything to see her body jolt awake, to see her spring to life, to watch her wipe the blood from her stomach and say she'd smeared some berries by accident. She could've coughed them up, too—the smashed berries. She could've said her ghostly white skin was due to some arrowroot powder she'd covered her body with, intentionally washing out her complexion.

Basil inched closer to her heavy body. He wrapped his arms around Scarlett and let the blood saturate his outfit of leaves. The short amount of time he'd spent with her had been the best—and most risky—days of his life. He'd felt at home with her. And now that she was gone, he'd never feel at home again.

"Please," he whispered in her ear, his voice cracking. "Please, be alive. Please, be my queen. Please, come to live in the castle with me."

But nothing he could say would bring her back to life. The key could heal, but it couldn't revive. She was no longer dying; she was *dead*. And no amount of enchantment could reverse her tragic fate.

He was too late.

The key was useless if it wouldn't save her. It didn't matter if he was king or a poor subject—without Scarlett, Basil was nothing . . . because he'd been nothing before her, and she was the one who had brought out his good and charming side. Scarlett gone meant Basil becoming nothing again—becoming a jealous, selfish boy.

And if not for his selfishness, Scarlett wouldn't have been dead.

He leaned his head on her back, his hands wrapped around her waist. Scarlett's vibrant braids tangled in his face.

This section of the forest was completely empty besides Basil and Scarlett. And though he didn't want to get up, he had no idea how to deal with this on his own.

"Help!" he cried, incomprehensible. "Somebody! Anybody!"

Hiccups broke up Basil's words, his body drenched with Scarlett's blood and his own tears.

How had it happened? Had Scarlett felt pain? Had it been Ambrosia? It must have been Ambrosia.

He'd never dealt with a situation like this one, and therefore had no clue what to do. He didn't want to leave her frail body lying on the ground, but he couldn't go through this alone.

"I'll be back," he whispered to Scarlett. And Basil tried his best to run, but it was difficult.

His limbs trembled.

His vision was blurry.

His stomach lurched on his way to seek help.

It wasn't but a few minutes before Basil found a group of forest inhabitants. All the nymphs and satyrs sat in a circle on imperfect benches made from bark. None of them noticed Basil at first; they were focused on a satyr—the same satyr that had approached Basil yesterday morning—announcing various topics in the middle of the circle.

Save for the leading satyr, Batellia was the first to catch Basil's eye. She couldn't sit still; the young nymph sauntered around the circle, singing to herself. Phobos watched her, silently urging her with facial expressions to be mature, but Batellia didn't listen. She was easily the youngest nymph of the bunch. But her cheery smile wouldn't last much longer.

All it took was Basil clearing his throat. And the head satyr stopped talking. His gaze shifted to Basil, dropped jaw, widened eyes. Following his lead, the eyes of every nymph and satyr turned to face Basil. The heads of the forest inhabitants all turned in unison, and gasps echoed through the crowd. Haldi's expression was especially violent; she'd never trusted the prince.

Basil realized immediately that his appearance could've been misinterpreted; his body was covered in blood, and the key was in one hand. The nymphs and satyrs were quite possibly nervous he'd come to kill them.

The head satyr pushed through the crowd of inhabitants, sprinting toward Basil. His horse-like legs propelled him at a quicker pace than most. In awe, the rest of the nymphs and satyrs remained on the benches, children crying, mothers and fathers comforting, though they were terrified themselves.

"What have you done?" the satyr whispered, his eyes wide. "What did—"

"Scarlett . . . she's . . ." But Basil couldn't bring himself to say it. He wouldn't utter the word *dead*. He *couldn't*.

It didn't matter, though, because the satyr understood from the blood that covered Basil. "How did it happen?"

Basil shut his eyes. He hadn't yet accepted it. The boy shook his head, teardrops diving down his cheeks.

"Where is she?" The satyr kept his composure. He seemed experienced as if he had decades on his hands. Basil assumed he was the voice of the forest inhabitants or something of the sort.

Basil sighed as he cocked his chin in the direction of Scarlett's body.

Without another word, the satyr followed Basil to Scarlett. And when they arrived, they saw her, in the same position he'd left her: slumped by what used to be a tree, her mouth open, and her gaze deadened.

"Oh my goodness, I—" And the satyr, too, began to let out uncontrollable gasps. Basil didn't know if they'd been close, but it seemed everyone in Golden Grove had some relationship; it was a small, tight-knit community of fascinating creatures.

Both of their eyes were on Scarlett. The wind started to pick up, causing her braids to swirl around in the air.

"This is the same way we found . . ." the satyr whispered, unable to finish.

Basil leaned his head down and raised his eyebrows, wanting answers.

"The way we found Zoz."

"Zoz?"

"Scarlett's father," the satyr said, wiping tears from below his eyes. And Basil wished he'd known more about Scarlett when he'd had the chance; how was it possible he'd never heard the name of Scarlett's father? He'd never seen or heard of her mother, either, and *she* lived in Golden Grove.

"Ripping of the stomach, bleeding through the mouth and the laceration." The satyr shook his head. "Ambrosia's trademark." He was tearing, too, but not as violently as Basil.

Basil was frantic. "What can we do? How can we save—"

But the satyr interrupted him and placed his hands on Basil's shoulders. "She's gone, Basil Avington."

The boy shook his head. Scarlett had been a day away from becoming queen of Silverkeep. If she'd made it just one more night, the rest of her life could've been perfect. It *would've* been perfect.

"I'll gather Scarlett's family. Stay here with her," the satyr said before disappearing behind some trees.

And Basil was left alone with the beautiful, deceased nymph. He thought about her slaughtering. If Basil had hugged her tighter in her slumber, would she have been alive? If Basil wasn't such a deep sleeper, would he have been able to protect her? If he'd urged her harder to leave the day before, would they have arrived safely at the castle?

Now Basil knew what love was. Lydia Rose had taught him pain, but their relationship was nothing more than affection, lust, and friendship. Scarlett was different than anyone Basil had ever spoken with; they just clicked as if they were meant to be. The week he'd spent in her company felt like so much longer.

Snatching Basil from his thoughts, the head satyr appeared with Phobos, Batellia, and another woman behind him, who Basil assumed to be Scarlett's mother. She had ruddy hair, just like Scarlett's, only a bit shorter—though Scarlett's mother seemed to be at the age in which one would expect some graying. And Basil couldn't make out her eye color; her eyes were tinged red, filled to the brim with accumulating tears.

Batellia was too young to fully understand the situation—and she couldn't have been alive at the time of Zoz's death—but still, she whined, her eyes drained, her cheeks red and puffy. Phobos stood beside her and kneeled to match her short stature, but he, too, was broken.

"Your fault!" Batellia whined, pointing her leafy fingernail at Basil. "You came here and took her from us! You—"

"Shh," Phobos hushed, hugging his little sister.

Scarlett's mother looked Basil dead in the eyes as tears fell from her own.

"And she was about to be queen, too," Scarlett's mother said. "She was so excited yesterday."

A pit of guilt formed in Basil's stomach. If not for him, Scarlett would've been alive. If he hadn't pushed Scarlett past her limits, she'd have been safe. She'd always tried to protect others—to shield Basil from danger—but ended up falling into the danger herself.

"What do we do now?" Basil asked, breaking through the heavy silence.

"We must say goodbye," responded the leader nymph.

Scarlett's mother's nostrils flared, and she broke down, falling to the ground. Her daughter was too young. It was far too many years early to say goodbye. Phobos hugged his mother with one hand and Batellia with the other.

The satyr walked over to Basil and whispered quietly, trying not to interrupt the family's mourning, "When a forest nymph dies, her tree dies with her."

"And this is her tree?" Basil sniffled.

"Scarlett never had one of her own—she was birthed from a mother and father, rather than a tree. So the tree that dies with her is the one closest to her location of death."

There was still so much Basil didn't know or understand about the forest, but learning these matters now wasn't his top priority.

"And she's just . . . dead? Do we bury her?" Basil's voice was broken.

"Her body may be deceased, but her essence will live on. In the form of—well, I'm not sure she'd decided on a life form yet—she wasn't expecting her . . . end to come this soon."

"Uclina," Scarlett's mother muttered, looking up from her daughter's stark body. Basil hadn't realized she'd been listening. "Scarlett loved uclinas."

Basil remembered the time they'd spent together in the stream; Scarlett had picked him a uclina and told him they were her favorite.

"Are you ready for the funeral? Tonight or tomorrow?" the satyr asked delicately.

Basil's heart ached for Scarlett's mother. She'd lost her husband already; her daughter shouldn't have perished this soon.

"Tonight," she decided. "I must get it over with."

Basil wondered what life form Scarlett's father was.

"We will conduct it by the fire circle," the head satyr informed, approaching Scarlett's mother and then kissing her forehead.

Basil's second funeral in the span of a few weeks . . . or days—he'd lost sight of time at this point—hurt worse than his first. His father's death should've broken him, and it did. But Basil had honestly been less concerned with the death of his father than the fact of his brother's coronation approaching.

Both deaths were unexpected: Regis IV's sudden pulmonary embolism and Scarlett's brutal murder. And he loved them both in different ways. His father was, well, his father. But he and Scarlett shared a short-lived yet indescribable bond. And Scarlett's death didn't just break him, or tear him, or shatter him; it *destroyed* him.

Nymphs and satyrs sat in the fire circle atop wooden benches, their fingers intertwined. It seemed the whole community was closely connected. In the center was Scarlett's body, sending tears to his eyes every time Basil looked at it. And whenever Basil locked eyes with any of them, their expressions weren't pleasant.

It's my fault.

Basil hated himself. The boy was selfish and full of envy and spite. He couldn't think of anything that made him much better than Ambrosia herself. Sure, he wasn't a murderer as Ambrosia was, but truthfully, Scarlett's death was all thanks to him. *He* was the murderer—of Zena, of Scarlett . . .

"My dear Scarlett." The heartbroken mother could barely get the words out. "I can't even describe how much . . . I . . . I can't."

Scarlett's body lay on the ground, wiped of the blood that spilled from her mouth and stomach, and her hair fell free, framing her face. When Basil had untied the braids, Scarlett's hair was crimped beautifully.

An array of flowers and greens surrounded her body, and in her hands was a bouquet of blossoms, pink and green. A purple and orange uclina was tucked behind her pointy ear, sticking gracefully out of her hair. Scarlett was dressed in a beautiful dress of leaves—her mother had crafted it.

Scarlett's mother had to take a moment before speaking again. She pursed her lips and squinted her eyes. "Scarlett is a flower."

The forest inhabitants sat on the benches around her, solemn and sorrowful.

"She's always bloomed," she said. "Scarlett is the strongest of all of us. She gets it from her father. He sacrificed himself for the forest . . . for all of you."

Scarlett's mother's use of the present tense broke Basil's heart.

"And every day, I think she's done blooming. I think she's finished bringing light to our world. But she is one of the few that continues, and will continue, to bring light to Golden Grove, even after she's gone. The light she's given us will remain eternally."

Everything she said resonated with Basil. He'd felt the same way about Scarlett; she'd always surprised him, enticed him, introduced him to something new. He'd just never been able to put it into words as her mother could.

"Scarlett made a new friend these past couple days." She gestured to Basil. "You all may know him—the prince of Silverkeep, rising king. And Scarlett came to me yesterday, claiming she was about to depart from the forest." Scarlett's mother stopped for a moment. "She died for all of you, just as Zoz did. The key is in safe hands now.

"Ambrosia has no power over us anymore. She will have the same enchantment that each of us has—no key, no nothing. She . . . she killed Scarlett with her bare hands." After her excessively graphic imagery, Scarlett's mother needed another moment.

The speech went on for a little while longer, and after she finished, Scarlett's mother nodded her head to Basil. It was his turn, and he had to transform Scarlett into a uclina. The forest didn't grant him a chance to speak, but he didn't have a way with words, anyway, especially at a time like this.

Scarlett's mother had granted Basil the honor to transform her, but it had nothing to do with the key. Nymphs and satyrs had been transformed into other life forms after their death long before the key had arrived in Golden Grove; it was their natural way.

But Scarlett's mother led the chant. It was a beautiful song—one everybody seemed to know. Basil was the only one to remain silent, but he knelt beside Scarlett, picking the uclina out of her hair and placing it in her mouth. It felt awkward, shoving the flower down Scarlett's throat, but Basil did it.

The song repeated and repeated until Scarlett's body began to shrink. Her mother refused to glance at Scarlett's weakening, withering figure, but Basil couldn't take his eyes off of her. Her arms turned paper thin, her bones diminished, and her limbs bound together. Soon, her bottom half fell green. And as a part of her shrunk, her hair grew. Parts of it turned purple, while some remained red. And her stomach . . . knees . . . chest . . . flattened.

And slowly, Scarlett disintegrated into the most beautiful uclina Basil had ever seen. The sight was almost as miraculous as it was terrifying. Basil choked on his messy tears and hiccups, stealing the stares of the nymphs and satyrs.

A red center existed on the unique flower instead of the usual orange one. It must have been because of her flaming-red hair, Scarlett's most beautiful external quality. Her fiery tresses mirrored her internal character, as well; Scarlett hadn't been afraid to take risks and sacrifice herself for her loved ones.

The uclina lay aside many other plants and flowers. Basil easily inferred they were other dead nymphs and satyrs. The sight was sad and mesmerizing all at once. He wanted to be alone, but Scarlett's mother, brother, and sister surrounded the uclina: the insignia of Scarlett's life.

"You promised," Basil whispered to the uclina. He was almost numb. "You promised everything would turn out all right. You promised you wouldn't die." Scarlett's family didn't hear him over their cries.

Basil needed space to breathe, so he left the grassy field and returned to the place they'd slept that night; he wanted to reminisce.

When he arrived, though, the area wasn't empty. Ambrosia sat in front of the tree, her eyes fixed on the drying pools of dark blood. Basil wiped his tears and flared his nostrils.

"I expected you'd come here," she said.

"What are you doing here?"

Ambrosia snickered. "What am *I* doing here? This is *my* forest."

"Leave!" It took all his self-control to refrain from attacking Ambrosia. He wished to see her bloody and dead, and he would have killed her, but Basil was drained of all energy.

"Leave!"

But Ambrosia didn't listen. She remained seated, her back leaning on the trunk of a tree. It was the closest one to Scarlett's place of death that hadn't diminished to ashes.

"I *hate* you. Why would you do such a thing? Why wouldn't you kill me instead? Why would you . . . lay her next to me for me to find?" In his mind, it was a shout, but Basil could manage nothing more than a cold hushed tone.

"I tried to—kill you, I mean. But it didn't work. I assumed you had the key, but I couldn't find it. You must have hid it somewhere good." Ambrosia offered a sinister smirk, amusing herself and only herself. "And I thought you'd want to see her one last time—dead."

Silent tears dropped from Basil's eyes.

"What? I did it out of generosity!"

The woman was insane. Deranged. Psychotic.

"You're cruel." Basil could finally muster a yell again, but nothing else. "Get out!"

"*Why* is it such a surprise to you? I promised two things: that your stealing of my key was not the end and that I'd restore the natural condition of the forest. Have I broken either of my promises?"

Basil didn't say a word.

"Exactly." Ambrosia crossed her arms, appeased.

"I'll leave you alone," Ambrosia agreed, "to whine like a little boy."

As she walked away, her black dress trailing behind, Ambrosia turned her face over her shoulder and made firm eye contact with Basil. Her green eyes staring straight into his, Ambrosia scoffed, "And you say you'll be king. Ironic how you still whimper like a baby."

Basil ignored her. Fit for king or not—it didn't matter. Only Scarlett mattered. And she was gone.

Compared to today's events, losing Lydia Rose seemed like the best day of his life. Why had Basil fretted over such a small, trivial matter, when in the end, it didn't matter?

It wasn't long after Ambrosia left that Scarlett's two younger siblings came to sit with Basil. Batellia was hesitant, and it took Phobos's strong tug to get her to do so.

"Scarlett is dead because of you," Batellia accused, not for the first time, as they approached Basil, who lay slumped on a tree trunk. Batellia was a wreck, her miserable expression no different from the rest of theirs.

"Shh." For the second time, Phobos couldn't control his younger sister.

But Basil knew Batellia was right. Everything was his fault; even a four-year-old could tell. "It's all right."

"For what it's worth, you were good for her," Phobos said. His words only made Basil's tears stream faster . . . harder.

"No, *she* was good for me." Basil never would've thought he'd fall for a nymph—in fact, he never thought such creatures existed—but since he'd left the castle, Basil's life had been a blur of chaos and surprises.

Phobos embraced him by the tree, like the brother Basil had always wanted. Their shoulders shook in unison. A prince—possibly king—and a satyr, a human and a creature, but ultimately, two friends. None of it mattered—wealth, species, habitat.

Batellia was too young to understand love, but death she could grasp. Basil recalled his studies in the castle; one time, he'd learned that most children began to comprehend the idea of death at around age four. And Basil understood that all Batellia saw him as was an outsider who came into Scarlett's life, and soon after, bestowed upon her a tragic demise—but expressed with a lesser vocabulary.

Basil cried himself to sleep that night. Once Phobos and Batellia left, he lay alone. He didn't know where to go or what to do; he didn't have Scarlett by his side, always knowing right from wrong. And it would be like betrayal for Basil to leave straight away. Although there were matters more important, the forest would never forgive him if he left right after Scarlett's death, which had all been his fault in the first place. Batellia had already hated him, even since the night they were supposed to share dinner, not to mention Haldi.

And days passed—days that felt they would never end. They continued for an eternity, yet lasted an instant all at once. Each day was one closer to the coronation. Each moment was a second closer to the crown being placed on Regis V's head. But time stood still in Golden Grove. And he took dear care of the key though he barely knew how it functioned.

It would've been easy to leave; Basil could've taken the key and gone on his merry way. But the forest trusted him now, and he would have to wait just a bit longer before it would seem moral to depart.

XVI

hobos was the only person that knew when Basil was set to leave. During the few days since Scarlett's death, Phobos and Basil had developed a bond. The two connected because of their common sorrow for Scarlett. Tragedy was more endurable when Basil could share it with another.

Scarlett visited Basil every night—sometimes in sweet dreams of what could've been, sometimes in nightmares of her death.

The sudden friendship between Basil and the satyr was difficult to explain as Phobos viewed him differently; Basil was a royal with more power and age than the young satyr had. Still, Basil enjoyed having someone with whom he could relate.

Basil's journey hadn't been at all what he planned, though he hadn't exactly had a plan to begin with. Sure, the books in the royal library had mentioned casualties, but those were centuries ago. Nobody was looking for the key anymore, and

Silverkeep was—to Basil's knowledge—no longer violent. Because of the union of kingdoms, there hadn't been war for a very long time.

The past few days, Ambrosia had been nowhere to be found. Haldi and the head satyr led daily fire circle meetings for all the forest inhabitants, and though Basil possessed none of their physical attributes, he felt as if Golden Grove was a part of him. In the short time they'd spent together, Scarlett had become a part of Basil as well. And now that she was gone, a part of Basil was gone, too.

It hurt. It hurt so much. As if his heart were literally broken into two pieces—both of which were missing.

Basil woke up early on the day of his departure. He tapped Phobos on the shoulder to say one last goodbye, even though just the night before Basil had given his "last" farewell. Basil was surprised when Phobos rolled to his side right away; he remembered the forest inhabitants as rather deep sleepers. But Phobos was unfazed when he turned to find Basil standing over him. It was barely the crack of dawn, and everyone else rested in slumber.

Nymphs, satyrs, and other creatures were sleeping in all sorts of odd ways. He'd never noticed when he'd spent time with Scarlett—they were usually isolated, and if not, weren't the first ones awake—but some creatures hung upside down from tree branches, and others had only their heads pop out of the grass; the rest of their bodies were connected to the roots of a tree.

Basil had forgotten about Phobos, who faced him, patiently waiting. He was too polite to speak to Basil with hostility, but said, "You tapped me?"

"Uh . . . yes. I'm leaving today."

Phobos pouted. "So you've said. It's a shame."

"No. You'll all be better off without me." Basil wrenched the key from his nostril. At this point, he'd gotten used to it, but Phobos hadn't.

"Um?"

Basil wiped the mucus on the grassy patch beside him. "Sorry, it's . . ." He debated explaining the purpose of hiding the key in his nostril but decided against it. "Well, anyway, I'm leaving. In moments."

"I'll be sure to avoid the grass," Phobos joked.

Basil could've easily cleaned up the mucus-stained grass with one golden hue, but he didn't want to risk disturbing other forest inhabitants from their rest.

"I'm going," repeated Basil. "I wanted to say goodbye to you." And he stood and began walking.

"Wait," Phobos whispered. He shot up and jogged to catch up to Basil. "I'll walk with you to the end of Golden Grove."

Basil smiled. He wasn't sure whether he wanted Phobos to come along, but nevertheless, the offer was kind.

They walked in silence as if neither of them could think of something appropriate to say. Everything seemed too unimportant, trivial.

Basil maundered—beside Phobos—through Golden Grove. He tasted its natural scent and observed its artful creatures for one last time, glanced at the willow trees—weeping as he'd been. Scarlett was supposed to be by his side, accompanying Basil to the castle. She should have been preparing for her reign as queen, not lying in a field as a uclina. Every time Basil thought about it, his blood boiled.

The same things—plants, flowers, trees—that were once beautiful, seemed ugly.

"Sorry for ruining everything." Basil cut through the silence as if he were ripping off a dressing while the wound was still bleeding. His words wouldn't cure his mistakes, but they would acknowledge them. In this moment, Basil was admitting to himself and to Phobos that he wasn't free of regret.

Phobos, with his horse-like legs, walked at an awkward pace beside Basil, careful to avoid the sleeping nymphs and satyrs whose bodies lay sprawled on the field. He was observably careful about his selection of words. "You shouldn't be." Phobos spoke plainly, unsure.

"It was all my fault, wasn't it?"

Phobos exhaled. "Most definitely."

Basil looked to his feet. It wasn't the answer he'd expected. He dug his fingernails into each of his palms. "I'm a terrible, selfish——"

"Let me finish," Phobos interrupted. "It was your fault that she woke up with a smile on her face for days on end . . . that she was truly happy for the first time in a while . . . that she had the thrill of excitement. And, it's also thanks to you that she's in that field now, lying as a uclina."

"You're wise for fourteen, and too forgiving."

"I'm stating the mere truth."

It was quiet again, and Basil and Phobos neared Ambrosia's lair on their way out. She was still asleep on her throne, a demonic grin plastered on her face. Basil could've killed her, but there was no need for another dead body, and no matter how evil Ambrosia was, Basil still didn't want to be a murderer.

"Let's not wake her," Basil whispered. And Phobos silently agreed with a simple nod.

Together, they tiptoed through the rest of Golden Grove, and it wasn't long until they reached the end.

"This is where I leave you," Phobos said. There weren't any nymphs or satyrs around; it was rare for the inhabitants to sleep on the outskirts.

Unsolicited teardrops fell from Basil's eyes—so much crying these past few days. To his left was the first tree of Golden Grove he recalled seeing. Basil remembered Haldi emerging from behind it and letting out uncontrollable laughter. So much had changed since then—since nearly two weeks ago. Basil had arrived in Golden Grove with a sword, Prancer, and a drawstring bag of food and water. But he left with none of that. Decamping from the forest that had become his home,

Basil realized he'd learned love and grief; more than all his life in the castle had taught him.

Basil was on his own again. But he wasn't the same Basil Avington he'd left the grand castle of Silverkeep as, and it wasn't solely because of the key that dangled from his left hand.

"Goodbye, Phobos."

Scarlett's brother turned around, disappearing into the forest with high, springy steps.

"Wait!" Basil called out. Phobos turned around with a slight twinkle in his eye.

Basil opened his arms and didn't bother to wipe away his streaming tears. Phobos ran into his arms for a warm hug. In the few days since Scarlett's death, they'd developed a genuine brotherhood.

Though Basil enjoyed the hug, Phobos lingered there a bit too long for Basil's comfort. Basil patted the satyr on the shoulder a few times, trying to inform him of this with courtesy. Phobos took the hint and lifted his face from Basil's shoulder, revealing crusty eyes and puffy cheeks. Neither of them wanted his time in Golden Grove to end this way.

And when Phobos pulled away, it meant it was time for him to leave Golden Grove. Finally—after so many days of thinking he would leave in moments—Basil was really going. And he didn't plan on coming back.

Basil spent the day traversing the foliage between Golden Grove and the castle. He'd discovered that, even though he'd felt as if he were in an entirely different universe, the forest wasn't very far from the palace of Silverkeep.

Occasionally, Basil would take a seat on a tree stump to catch his breath. Everything reminded him of Scarlett—the leaves, the flowers—they stole teardrops from him. And with only himself for company, Basil wasn't embarrassed to let himself go. The tears came and went when he least expected.

The hope was almost gone, and having the key didn't feel as good as it would have if Scarlett were there, walking beside him to the castle. In fact, it barely felt good at all. Ironic—because his whole journey had been rooted in hope, but now all of that had vanished . . . disappeared into thin air.

Because of the uniform scenery, Basil could barely tell how far he'd gone and how far he had left to go. He traipsed—no sword, no Prancer—through the endless meadows for what felt like an arduous eternity.

But at once, after who knows how many hours, Basil shimmied past his last tree. And there it stood, plainly, his "home" that seemed nothing like one. He looked to the top turret window that peeked inside his room. From what he could see, nothing had changed. The same flowers decorated each terrace—no uclinas or scouns. The same purple roofs pointed to the sky, and the same fancy windowpanes stood, gold tinted. An odd emotion overtook him—close to comfort but not quite.

When Basil saw the neat line of guards protecting the castle of Silverkeep in full armor, he crept behind a tree, careful to remain unnoticed. He hadn't decided on his entrance yet, but the very thought sent a chill down his spine. Should he slip into his room silently and appear at breakfast the next morning, pretending everything was fine? Or perhaps Basil could do some magic with the key and fly into the castle, giving some elaborate speech simultaneously. But as Basil emerged from the tree and brought himself into view of the guards, he wasn't thinking about the best way to enter; the only thing on his mind was the destruction he'd caused.

Still, when the guards saw him, Basil stopped dead in his tracks—froze. The guards broke their regal and ordered stance and turned to each other. Basil couldn't make out their mumbles, but he didn't need to hear them to understand their confusion.

All at once, the front two lines of guards made for Basil in unison, faces puzzled. This was it. His time in Golden Grove was over, and he was back to his harsh realities. Scarlett's death he could not undo—the past was in the past—but he could take what he had and use it for a better future. And his life would be different—the whole *kingdom* would be different—now that King Philip's key was in the hands it had always been meant for.

XVII

"ou sure we're s'posed to do this?" A quintessential guard asked another as if Basil weren't squished between them, listening.

"Yup. The queen commanded we must do whatever's possible to return him safely to the castle." His voice was unusually guttural.

Did she really?

Instead of the heroic, dazzling entrance he'd been hoping for, Basil would have to be embarrassed and ashamed in front of his family. But he had to remember that he carried the key with him; the humiliation would vanish the moment Basil was to reveal the prized possession.

Several guards yanked on Basil from a multitude of angles, and Basil groaned with each ache. They were the royal guards—not in a position to hurt him.

Every time Basil blinked and opened his eyes, he was a step closer to the castle, and eventually, he stood mere inches from the main doorway. This wasn't the way he'd hoped to return, but it would have to do.

"We've got him from here," the strongest, broadest guard demanded. Basil felt most of the guards let go of him and watched them return to their formation. Only two guards—one buff and one scrawny—held him now by either shoulder and side of the waist. It was as if Basil were outside of his body, watching everything happen with no reaction. He was still numb.

And, as if it were nothing, the two guards swung open the royal doors and continued inside. Basil was enveloped in the wintry, royal air, and the taste of bittersweet royalty lay on the tip of his tongue. The guards pushed Basil alongside the walls and artwork in the corridors he knew too well. But he regarded the paintings of previous kings with a new outlook, imagining his own face on the wall.

"Your Highness, our searchers have been looking for you for twelve days," the talkative, smaller guard said.

Basil remained silent, unsure of an appropriate response. Had it really been twelve days? It felt longer but shorter all at once.

"Where should we leave him?" the other one asked.

The first guard cocked his head toward the auditorium. "We'll bring him to the queen."

Why would they be in the auditorium? The vast space was only used on special days. His father's funeral had been Basil's third time in the auditorium in his entire life. The only special day he could think of was—

The buff guard cracked the gilded door open just a smidge, hoping to avoid making a scene. But he could've swung the door open and yelled; it would have borne the same effect, because one glance at Basil from Bridget, and then all eyes were on him. It wasn't just the royal family—it wasn't even just Silverkeep—it was the union of kingdoms, gathered for Regis V's coronation, their gasps and murmurs echoing through the room.

Basil had arrived at the perfect time; Hadwin held a velvet embroidered cushion with two sturdy hands, the king's crown sitting atop it. But at the sight of Basil, Hadwin's hands lost balance, and the invaluable diadem fell from the cushion. It plummeted to the ground, too fast for Hadwin to catch, and its impact echoed through the auditorium.

Still, the expensive crown wasn't the most alarming part of that moment. Basil, who'd been missing for almost two weeks, was back in the castle, dressed in withered green leaves and blossoms.

Regis V shot up from the throne and sprinted down the velvet walkway, darting from the auditorium. He didn't look back at the many pairs of eyes on his back. "Basil!"

Though it wasn't yet official, Regis was, at the moment, the new king of Silverkeep. So when he grabbed Basil's arm, the guards let go and returned to the outside of the castle. Basil's twin pulled him out of the crowded room and into the empty corridor.

The sight of Regis on that throne had made Basil's skin crawl, but it wouldn't matter in a bit. And though he despised the image, there was a certain comfort that seeing Regis gave him. His brother was in the castle, alive and healthy, and still the spitting image of Basil. When Regis stood in front of him, Basil felt as if he were looking in a mirror. It was a feeling Basil should've been used to after seventeen—now eighteen—years, but it had been a while.

It's my birthday today. Both of our birthdays. I'm eighteen.

"What did . . . I mean where . . . What happened? And what are you wearing?" Despite everything happening, Regis let out a small giggle at Basil's leafy ensemble. Basil would have, too, if it were a fortnight before.

And then Basil did something remarkable—something he would've never thought to do a week ago. Basil hugged his twin. *Hugged him.* Scarlett's death had made him think—if Regis were to suddenly die, Basil would be heartbroken, even though they didn't always see eye to eye. And Scarlett had often talked about her perfect relationship with Phobos and Batellia.

As they hugged silently, Basil could hear Bridget addressing the audience in the distant auditorium, saying, "My deepest apologies for the disruption. The ceremony will resume shortly."

"What . . . what are you doing?" Regis asked, standing awkwardly stiff as Basil clutched onto him like a leech.

"Sorry." Basil lifted his head from Regis's shoulder and wiped the tears from his cheeks. "It's been a crazy twelve days."

"It's all right, brother. It's okay," Regis said. "But seriously, where have you been? And why are you . . . crying?"

"I couldn't possibly explain everything now. But . . ." Basil's voice dwindled, and he decided to let the key do the talking. And as he pulled out the glowing piece, so masterly crafted, Basil felt a tinge of some odd, foreign feeling. Could it possibly be . . . guilt?

"Is that . . . It can't be the . . . Did you find—"

"King Philip's key."

Regis stumbled backward. "No. Basil, that's impossible. It's not even real. It's a legend—the books have said it. Nobody's found it for centuries. It can't be—it's an ordinary key, not King Philip's . . ." Regis rambled and rambled until Basil proved him wrong.

"Would an ordinary key do this?" Basil debated between cutting Regis or levitating, but he decided on the latter.

He focused on his own body, and momentarily, the golden hue was produced around Basil. His feet hovered a few inches above the ground, and he stayed there for a bit; Basil enjoyed having some height over his brother.

"You're lying. It can't be true. It can't be!" Regis paced back and forth, his eyes glued to Basil, his cheeks flushed in anger. After gaining nothing from his racing steps, Basil's brother dropped to lay sideways, his cheek touching the marble ground. His eyes were level with the space separating Basil's feet from the floor. Regis extended his hand through the air, disturbed by the existent space.

"How did you even . . . *Why* did you even—we're *brothers*, not enemies!" Regis's cheeks were fully reddened . . . his teeth gritted . . . his fists clenched. A moment ago, Basil had been hugging him, but now, he was back to the sour spite he was used to.

Before either of the boys could say another word, angry footsteps became audible, and the clinking heels could only belong to one person: Bridget.

Sure enough, as she turned the corner, Basil read the cross expression on his mother's face. Quickly, he jumped down from his levitation and put on a fake smile.

"Mother!" Basil exclaimed, "I have loads to tell you."

But her expression was far different from his. "What in the *world* happ—where were—I mean, I was worried sick!" Bridget could barely finish her own sentences, almost as if she . . . *cared?* Her hair was curled neatly below her shimmering tiara, and she wore an elegant purple dress, representing the colors of Silverkeep.

"I can explain, but it's a long story." Basil could barely remember for himself how his journey had commenced.

"Regis, how incredibly irresponsible of you to leave your audience hanging like that! Come back at once! We can deal with this later," Bridget said. And though he wouldn't admit it, Basil felt a tinge of neglect stab at him; he'd been gone for over a week, but Bridget only cared about what the union of kingdoms thought of her older, better twin.

"It doesn't matter, Mother! None of it does!" Regis yelled.

"What do you mean? Of course it matters! I can't believe this is happening." She reverted her attention to Basil. "I can't believe you just leave and then . . . and then show up here on the day of—"

"Did father have an affair?" Basil interrupted.

All at once, Bridget was taken aback. "Excuse me?" It

seemed she'd forgotten what she was about to say. Her cheeks blushed, and she avoided eye contact.

"Ambrosia Cromwell." Basil drew out each syllable of her name, for it would be the last first chance he had to say it.

"Do not speak her name," Bridget muttered quietly. "Regis, go back!"

"Mother, what's he talking about?"

"It's nothing. Go back, you're becoming king, honey! Go!" Bridget wore a fake smile as she placed both her hands on Regis's shoulders and shook him. "Go on! The auditorium's that way." And she cocked her head toward the room that held their grand audience.

"I'm not sure I'm becoming king," he whispered, spitting and ripping his mother's hand off his shoulder.

"That's ridiculous. Come on, darling. I've told them the ceremony will resume shortly."

"Is it true?" Basil asked again. "That father had a mistress, I mean?"

"Nonsense, Basil. Come on, Regis!" Bridget was beginning to lose it. Her whole face reddened, and her voice sounded oddly suspicious.

"Look at what's in Basil's hand, for goodness' sake! Just look, Mother!"

"We. Will. Worry. About that. Later! Go and entertain the union!" Bridget screeched, likely for the entire audience to hear.

"Life isn't about entertaining the union, Mother! Open your eyes. Look around. Your son has just been missing for over a week, and you barely care! You care about nothing but your public image."

Could it really be possible that Basil's brother was on his side? After Basil had brought home King Philip's key and was actively trying to defeat him?

"I am *protecting* you!" yelled Bridget, defensive.

"Protecting? Mother, Basil has King Philip's damn key!"

"Nonsense. I swear you're going to drive me mad, the both of you!"

Regis nodded rapidly, while Bridget shook her head left and right. But Basil levitated again to stop the confusion. The golden glow . . . and then he was up.

Bridget's jaw dropped at the sight, but she shook her head. "King Philip's key is fictional. It's not real, Basil. It's—"

"So he can naturally just . . . fly, then?"

"He's not flying. He's an inch above the ground. Go to the auditorium, now." Her voice was low but vehement.

"You can't tell me what to do!"

"Excuse me?"

Basil had never seen his brother fight with Bridget; Regis had always been the perfect child, but the sight didn't fail to entertain him. Perhaps while Basil had been gone, Bridget had needed a punching bag, and Regis had been there for her to take her anger out on.

Finally, the touch of hot water burned Basil's skin as he dove into the tub that a servant had filled. But with the long-awaited bath of lavender oil and mineral salts also came the washing away of any traces of Golden Grove. He watched as the leaves fell from his skin and into the water. The uclina Scarlett had given him his first time in the stream—gone. Basil worried not about the leaves leaving his body but about them withering, disintegrating. They'd be gone.

He'd never felt so soothed yet miserable at once. Scarlett should have been there, bathing in the castle for her first time. Instead, she lay as a uclina. The saddest part was that there was nobody in the castle to share his grief with. If Basil were to tell his mother or brother, they wouldn't care.

Basil picked out small twigs and bugs that were tangled deep in his floppy nest of brown waves. The strangest pieces of nature were nestled atop his head. But after that bath, every lingering piece of Golden Grove he had once worn was gone. No more vibrant leaves, tiny twigs, or chunks of dirt existed.

Basil rubbed his face so much with his purple towel that his cheeks and forehead turned red in irritation. And on that towel fell the grime that had been buried deep in his pores. As he looked in the mirror, Basil could only imagine how stupid he'd looked dressed in leaves and dirty all over.

Though he'd miss his links to Golden Grove, he gratefully slipped into his crisp white blouse and comfortable tunic. And he finally had access to a clock again—it was ten minutes to seven; dinner was soon. He combed back his hair and admired his reflection. What would the night entail?

Hadwin was already seated when Basil entered the dining room five minutes early. It felt as if his father's death in this very room had been a lifetime ago.

"Hello, Hadwin."

"Greetings."

"How are you?"

"Doing just fine, thank you."

Hadwin managed an awkward smile to conclude the stilted exchange. Basil knew that Hadwin was not content with him; the poor timid man had been left alone in front of the union, sharing the stage with only Lydia Rose. He'd had to cancel the coronation and send everyone out of the castle; there was no way the celebration could have continued normally after Basil's unexpected entrance.

But the empty air was filled when Regis entered the room,

his elbow interlocked with Lydia's. Surprisingly, the sight no longer made Basil want to die—only thinking of Scarlett's death did such a thing.

Bridget entered soon after, two minutes past seven. It was unusual for the queen to be anything besides perfectly punctual, and it was even more unusual for her to be dressed in her same day clothes. Bridget's hair was styled no different than it had been at the coronation, and messy pieces fell out the sides. Nobody commented on her atypical appearance.

The dinner was unpleasant. An awkward silence carried through the first two courses as nobody had the nerve to speak. Bridget consistently gnawed on her fingernails as she did in times of trouble.

The first sound was a servant, barging through the dining hall door with an announcement. "Your Majesty," he said with deference, "the crown is chipped."

"All right." Her reserved response was not of Basil's expectation; he practically expected fumes to escape her ears.

"What would you like us to do?" the servant asked.

"I would *like* you to be gone."

"Uh . . . very well." And he was off, shutting the silver door behind him.

Hadwin swallowed. "I'm so sorry, Your Majesty. It was terrible of me, I should have—"

"Enough," Bridget interrupted. "If the crown had been in my hands, it would surely have escaped my grip. It's not *your* fault." And she looked to Basil, her eyes burning with accusation. In her defense, Basil *was* to thank for the startle.

"I'm sure they'll be able to fix it—the craftsmen are very well qualified, Your Majesty," Hadwin said.

Bridget nodded twice and began to pick at the roasted eggplant. The uncomfortable silence was back.

Regis V placed his silverware down and sat up straight. "My goodness, I can practically hear the elephant in the room trotting behind me. I can see its two tusks . . . feel its trunk!"

"Is that so?" Bridget asked.

Basil hadn't said a word since his first greeting to Hadwin.

"Yes, *Mother*. Is anyone going to discuss what happened to-day . . . why my coronation was halted?" he shouted. "Basil has King Philip's key! Don't you all know what that means? I mean, *he* certainly does, otherwise, he wouldn't have just run away."

Lydia Rose stroked the top of his hand in an effort to quell Regis's stress, but he ripped it from her grip.

Bridget heaved an exaggerated breath. "All right, there's a lot we have to discuss, but I need time to process—"

"No! There *is* no time, Mother! I want answers . . . *need* answers! Don't you get it?"

"Do *not* disrespect my intelligence."

Regis stood from his chair and stomped on the ground. "Stop, Mother! Stop acting so perfect! Damn it, why are all of you acting so *perfect!*"

"Because," Bridget said, "we are the royalty of Silverkeep. If we're anything but flawless, how can we expect our kingdom to function smoothly?"

Regis released a short spurt of sarcastic laughter. Basil liked this new version of his brother: rebellious, angry—maybe he finally understood how Basil had felt his entire life.

"Am I king, or not?"

"You are king!" Hadwin shouted, slamming the bottom of his knife to the table. The heads of everyone in the room— Basil, Regis V, Bridget, Lydia Rose—turned to him; Hadwin seldom spoke when he wasn't spoken to, much less yelled at a member of the royal family. "I'm . . . I'm sorry—"

"No, you're right. It is settled. Unless an opposing fact exists, your coronation is to be rescheduled for another day this week," said Bridget, softly.

"And if an opposing fact does exist?" Basil chimed in. "Do you even care enough to ask where I've been for the past days . . . weeks?" Bridget remained silent. "I have King Philip's key! I can do things with it that haven't been done—that we know of—since Philip's reign centuries ago." He pulled the gold and emerald beauty from his tunic pocket.

"Centuries ago, *exactly*—the legend is long forgotten. It's a bedtime story, not a fact," Bridget said.

"My goodness, Mother! I'd sooner fly through the midnight sky than have you believe me . . . believe the *truth*."

"Your brother is becoming king this week. It is final, Bas—"

"You're *ly*ing! You're lying to yourself, and us, and the *king-dom*! It doesn't matter how many years ago King Philip ruled Silverkeep—his key has remained the most coveted item since he described it on his deathbed. Time has done nothing but make us doubt the legend. The centuries have not *erased* it!"

"That's not so, Basil. Your brother is to become king. You will be—"

"It's in your own darn law books! One of the oldest laws—look for it yourself. I've memorized King Philip's words: 'My power has been compiled, stored in a hidden key. Whoever has the virtue and intelligence to find—' "

"Interrupt me once more, and you will not be dining with us."

The legs of Hadwin's chair screeched as he scooched back and rose from the cushion. "You are both correct—only the books of law can settle this." And he disappeared behind the door.

It was enough to silence the mother and son. Basil returned to his eggplant, purposefully scarfing it down and chewing improperly. But Bridget kept her composure.

Still, though Bridget and Basil were temporarily done, Regis was not. "Mother, I don't understand. What's to happen? What will I—"

"Just wait for Hadwin to return. The matter can only be settled with words of law."

"And if Basil is correct? If the key makes him king?"

"Then it shall be so." It wasn't the reaction Basil expected, but it perturbed his brother to say the least, along with Lydia

Rose, who could be found fixing her blond waves every other second. Regis V was red and sweaty all over, while Basil failed to hide his excited grin. The roles had been reversed.

When Hadwin entered back through the door, four sets of eyes darted to the scroll he held. After pushing aside his silver, eggplant-smeared plate, Hadwin laid the scroll on the mahogany table. "Page seven, page seven," he muttered beneath his breath. Hadwin knew just about every law; he was the kings' prime advisor—practically the human law book of Silverkeep.

Hadwin used his clean second fork to trace the cursive text, preventing the natural oils of a finger from smearing the delicate ink on the parchment. "The Deathbed Law," Hadwin read aloud. "My power has been compiled, stored in a hidden key. Whoever has the virtue and intelligence to find it must take the throne, for he who can do so much will be the most fit to rule, with everything I have and more."

They were the same words Basil had memorized.

"What else does it say?" Regis asked, desperate.

"That is all. The law is vague—before anyone could ask Philip questions, his world turned black," Hadwin answered.

"But that's from hundreds of years ago. It can't possibly be relevant, right? Mother? Hadwin? It doesn't matter that—"

"No." A blank look sat on Bridget's face, and her eyes twitched. "I love you, Regis, but the law is definitive. King Philip's words must not be forgotten."

Basil's lips curled deviously, but a tinge of guilt stabbed at him.

"Basil, you are to be king," she whispered.

"No. No! He can't be! Basil is *not* the heir! What he did was treacherous! He ran away from the kingdom, and you reward his betrayal with what *I've* worked so hard for . . . with what is rightfully mine! You can't steal this from me—I'm the *heir!*"

Worked so hard for? You were born into the position.

But he wouldn't say anything.

"Enough."

"This family is just—" Regis V scoffed. "If Father were here—may he rest in peace—he would never have allowed this insanity to continue to this point. I mean, Basil can't take me out with a sword. He can't paint a damn cheese plate, and he doesn't know the first thing about ruling."

Basil ignored his brother. Regis didn't know how to rule, either. He'd thought a dress for Lydia Rose would be more worthy of expense than artillery for the noble protectors of Silverkeep.

"Is nobody going to speak?" Regis shouted, his fists tightening, sweat accumulating on his shiny skin. But Bridget's eyes were glued to her empty plate.

Regis excused himself, throwing his napkin down with all his strength and might. But the cloth only glided to his cushion, making little noise but a soft swoosh.

As he stormed off, his loud stomps and nonsense yells were audible to all the royals that remained at the table.

"Make sure he's all right."

"Yes, Your Majesty," Lydia Rose squeaked. She, too, perspired with tears of dread but listened to the queen. It was difficult for anyone to feel comfortable around Bridget—even Regis IV had been scared of his wife.

Lydia's exit left the table with Basil, Bridget, Hadwin, and two empty chairs. Nervous servants scurried to the table to clear the silverware the two had left behind.

"We have matters to talk about," Bridget said to Basil. "There are things you are yet to understand and things you will have to learn with time. I would've liked you to prepare, but alas—what's done is done."

Was that all her favoritism had been? Had Bridget treated Regis with more respect merely because he was the heir? Now that Basil was to be king, Bridget spoke to him like all her ill will had vanished.

"Yes, Mother, of course."

"Hadwin, I would like you to teach him everything he must

know. Work your magic, and I'll arrange a coronation. When do you think he'll be ready? It should be as soon as possible— next Saturday?"

"That should be good," Hadwin said.

Could it really be so easy? Of course, it wasn't *easy*; he'd had to risk his life and the lives of others, fall in love only to lose her, and find comfort in a new, mysterious forest—but all that was done now. And the part that remained—the approval of his mother—seemed quick and fair compared to what he'd just been through.

"And if you still have your heart set on Lydia Rose, I assume her father will be more than pleased to give her back to you."

"*Give* her?"

"Yes," Bridget responded as if she saw nothing wrong with her proposal.

"First of all, I don't want her. But even if I did, it kills me how you offer her to me like she's some . . . object."

"Basil, once you learn the ways of the world, there is a lot with which you will be displeased. The first, and perhaps most important, thing you should know is that the kingdom is unfair. You'll have to make decisions, and an answer that benefits everyone will likely not exist."

It baffled Basil that after his life-altering journey, all Bridget had to say concerned what to do when faced with adversity. Did she not care for her son? Was she not curious about where he'd been? Did she not have questions about his adventure? Basil had nobody to talk to, not even Bridget, who seemed to have gotten over her loss quickly. He knew *he* would never, in all his life, get over losing Scarlett.

"You truly don't want Lydia? Her dear father Derek will be disappointed."

"You hate Derek."

"I hate nobody," Bridget said.

"You hate *me*."

"Nonsense. But I suppose I'll allow Derek to be upset. He should be for all he's done."

Basil and Bridget hated Derek Searle for different reasons but shared their loathing all the same.

"You've done a great thing, Basil. With the key, you'll be able to bring order to Silverkeep."

"It will be like King Philip's reign. He said it himself."

"Now now, don't become too big-headed. But I believe in you, darling."

"You do?"

Her acceptance was all Basil had ever wanted. "Of course I do." And she kissed his forehead. It didn't cure his lifetime of negligence thus far, but it was a start—a good, maybe great start. Conditional love was better than nothing.

"Rest up, darling—Hadwin will begin your instruction at tomorrow's crack of dawn. Isn't that right, Hadwin?"

"Yes, Your Majesty."

"Good night, my boy." And Bridget exited the dining hall, Hadwin following close behind.

I should be thrilled. Why do I feel a strain in my lungs?

It didn't feel right without Scarlett.

Basil remained seated for a little while out of pure laziness. Moments after Hadwin and Bridget were gone, a servant emerged from the kitchen with a tray. Atop the silver platter were five small pastries.

"Oh, Your Majesty, I'm sorry—I didn't realize the rest of you had gone."

"It appears you're a moment too late. Not to worry, I will eat for the rest of them." Basil chuckled, his mouth watering at the pastries. Before tonight's dinner, Basil's last real meal had almost escaped his memory; he was so used to forest berries and flowers, he'd almost forgotten the sweet taste of *real* food and desserts.

It wasn't difficult for Basil to devour the pastries in record time after the servant left him alone in the dining hall. When she retreated to the kitchen, Basil was brought back to his last memory in the castle before his world had been turned upside down. He remembered gathering up the loaves of pumpernickel, fetching water from the royal well, stealing the kings' sword, and getting Prancer, which reminded him—his horse, along with the bejeweled weapon, was lost somewhere in Golden Grove. The sword hardly mattered now; with the key, it would be easy to redeem himself and make up for his trivial misdoing. But he would never forgive himself for losing Prancer. Hopefully, he was safe in Golden Grove—hopefully not in *Ambrosia's* hands.

As Basil finally gathered up the muscle to stand from his chair, he rubbed his palms together to rid his hands of sweet crumbs. That night, walking through the gilded corridor to his room, Basil thought about Regis—he'd been so excited to become king, but all that had been taken away in a single day—the crown had been inches from his head, seconds from his scalp. But Basil would not allow himself to pity his brother, not after all he'd done. Basil could not forget that Regis had left him on the field to bleed out after their sword fight. He could not forget that his brother had destroyed his painting, or that—though it no longer mattered to Basil—Regis had stolen his first love.

So Basil was at peace—or at least the *most* at peace he'd been since Scarlett's death—when he entered his lavish chamber. But as he changed into sleeping clothes and cuddled up beneath his soft sheets, he couldn't help but imagine Scarlett lying beside him. They could've had a perfect life together. Scarlett would've been the best queen, ruling by his side in the best reign since King Philip.

The thought of beginning studies tomorrow should've excited him more than it did; the only thing he could think about was Scarlett—her flaming-red hair . . . her perfectly imperfect freckles . . . her pointed ears. And the image of her lifeless bloody flashed before Basil's eyes with every blink.

Out of pure habit, Basil shoved the key painlessly up his nostril. For sure, Basil had missed his bed. After spending endless nights on "beds" of leaves and sticks, the castle sheets gave him comfort like nothing else. But that comfort didn't last very long.

Basil's eyes were in the process of shutting when he heard a storm rumble. The roaring thunder was especially peculiar because it didn't usually storm this season in Silverkeep—not since many years ago. But even if the season were different, the weather was unnaturally harsh.

Basil couldn't have simply fallen back asleep, not when he was soon to be king. And even if he tried, the cursed noises wouldn't allow his mind and body to find peace. So he sat up atop his silver comforter and rotated to face the window. Basil peered through his parted curtains and watched lightning accompany the crashing thunder. There was somebody in front of the castle . . . a vague silhouette that was difficult to distinguish in the darkness.

But her yells were so strident, it didn't take the light of day to identify the face behind the thunder. Basil recognized the woman before another flash of lightning could strike.

XVIII

 asil rushed out of his chamber, rage boiling in his veins. He leapt onto the balcony, his feet barely shy of the edge.

Basil assumed he'd awoken the rest of the castle with his jump. "*What are you doing here?*" he bellowed. The boy hardly cared if he pulled the royals and servants alike from their slumber.

Three rows of guards, mounted in their stance, protected the front entrance of the castle of Silverkeep, but they did nothing to stop Ambrosia; they couldn't. The perplexed men watched her with her black dress and growl. She sat atop a horse.

Prancer. At least he was back.

"I believe we have some unfinished business . . . affairs that are yet to be sorted out," she called from yards beneath. Bits of fire appeared on the ends of her hair as it swirled about the black wind.

"Our business was finished when you killed Scarlett. Believe me, what you did was more than enough punishment."

"Our business will be *finished* when I have King Philip's key . . . *my* key."

Before Basil could say another word, the air beside him illuminated; Regis V must have lit up his chamber. Basil turned his head to find his trembling brother, rushing out the door to his balcony. It mirrored the structure of Basil's.

"Brother? What's going on?" Regis asked.

"Go inside, Regis!"

"I'm not moving until you tell me what the hell is happening!"

"Well then, don't move."

Lydia Rose, in her velvet plush nightgown, scurried outside her and Regis's chamber and grabbed onto her lover's shaky hand.

"Is this a dream? This whole day is a dream . . . a nightmare, isn't it?" Lydia squeaked to Regis. "*Isn't it?*" But he didn't answer.

"Really, you should go inside. It's for your own good!" Basil shouted. "It's my order. As king, I demand it of you." He felt guilty expressing his dominance over his brother, but it was the only way Basil thought he could protect him—though it did quite the opposite.

"It's funny, really!" Ambrosia cackled from below. "The way you two squabble—so petty, yet you expect to be a good king."

"How did you do that with the thunder? And lightning?"

She snorted. "I can do a lot of things. You think that without the key, my power is gone? My dear, you are sorely mistaken. You see, my beloved forest inhabitants have been kind enough to give me all their daily enchantment today."

To bother Basil further, Ambrosia began to scratch Prancer. She prodded his eyes and pulled on his mane until he let out whinnies of pain, sounds that broke Basil's heart.

"They would never."

"They did." But Basil knew it must have been because of a posed threat.

"Your enchantment will run out soon, Ambrosia. And when it does, you'll be powerless."

"*I* decide how it works!" Ambrosia yelled illogically, contradicting all Basil knew. She couldn't have control over the enchantment; it was probably fading gradually as Scarlett had said.

Regis grasped the railing of the balcony tight in his palms and roared, "*Who is she?*"

"I'll explain later. There's no time to waste. Regis, go inside—you too, Lydia. This woman is a murderer. She's already killed a nymph very dear to my heart. You have the chance to protect yourself. Take advantage of it."

"I'm not going anywhere!" Lydia yelled, her voice breaking. It was the first time she'd shown outright courage.

"What the *hell* are you talking about, Basil? Nymph? Murderer?"

"Go. Inside. Regis, we may argue, but I don't want you killed! Not because of me! I can't bear the guilt of more blood on my hands."

"So that's what it is then, *guilt?* And what do you mean by *more* blood on your hands?"

Knowing there was no chance his brother would obey, Basil decided his best bet was to ignore him. The rest of Regis's shrieks went in one ear and out the other.

"Give me the key, and it will make this whole process much easier," Ambrosia offered from the cobblestone, becoming impatient. But Basil struggled to hear her from such a distance.

"Pardon?"

With that, the familiar golden hue formed around Ambrosia. She glided through the night sky and landed on Basil's balcony.

"Deal with Prancer!" Basil called to the guards below him. They obediently sprinted to the horse.

Lydia shrieked in terror and escaped back into the chamber, but Regis remained on his balcony, his eyes blooming with almost as much intrigue as they did fear.

"Can you hear me better now?" Ambrosia scowled, so close that her wisps of hair tickled Basil's forehead.

"What have I done to you?"

"Are you truly asking me that question? Have you forgotten the shame you've brought me? The damage you've done to Golden Grove?" She lunged into Basil, but backed away, probably remembering it was impossible to kill him—as long as he held the key.

"You still have powers and just as much authority over The Forests of Ethereal Paradise. Everyone fears you—is that not what you want?"

"*Don't* call Golden Grove by such a name. And the powers are fading. I need the *key!*" Ambrosia lunged toward Basil, grabbing for his neck, but he pivoted away.

"Give it up. You will die tonight if you don't leave."

"Little prince boy, you don't scare me." She smirked, wedging Basil into the outer-left corner of his gilded terrace.

But with focus, Basil used the key's enchantment to blast her backward. He'd learned the gust of wind tactic from Ambrosia herself. She fell onto her butt, coughing up bits of dust. The magic ripped the seam of Ambrosia's long black skirt.

With the loud impact of Basil's shove, Regis hurried into his room. "I'm g-getting Mother," he stuttered. And before Basil could advise otherwise, Regis was gone.

"Where are you hiding my key?" Ambrosia whispered through gritted teeth.

"It's not *your* key. And you will never find it." But Basil knew it wouldn't be below Ambrosia to pull the key straight from his nostril and lick it clean of mucus.

"I'd sooner die than leave here without it. My dear, one of us is going to die tonight. And it won't be me."

"Then spare yourself the time and energy." Out of everything she'd said, her use of kind words like *my dear* made Basil's blood boil. But he had the key now. There had to be a way to take away her enchantment—if only he knew how . . .

"Are you suggesting I shall die? Voluntarily? That I will give up my pursuit so easily?" Off of Basil's silence, she continued. "Well, you don't know me very well, now do you?"

Ambrosia managed to get to her feet though she didn't make another move—not yet.

At once, Bridget stepped onto Regis's balcony, her face sweaty, her body clothed in a two-piece silk sleeping set. She gripped a silver sword. A few seconds later, Regis entered behind her. He bent over the railing of his balcony to catch his breath.

"Your Majesty, it's been a while," Ambrosia said, walking to the edge of the balcony—as close as she could get to Bridget whilst remaining on Basil's platform. Ambrosia's face fell flat before spreading again into a wide and sly grin. She reached out her hand for Bridget to shake, but the queen didn't take it.

"I wouldn't forget your hideous face—not even in another life." Bridget's curls were tangled around her neck. The sword was in her right hand. "I told you never to set foot in this castle again!"

"When was that? Twelve . . . thirteen years ago?"

"You know her? Mother?" Regis shook his mother's shoulder, desperate for answers. But Bridget shimmied until Regis's grip loosened.

"Thirteen, and I've not forgotten it."

"I'm sure." Ambrosia wiped the dirt from her elbows. "Shall we mourn the loss of our love together? I found it quite rude you didn't bother to invite me to his funeral."

"He didn't love you," Bridget spat. "He loved how you obeyed his every word—worshipped him like a divinity."

With that, Ambrosia produced a golden hue around her body and leapt off Basil's balcony and onto Regis's, joining Bridget and her son. The guards muttered beneath them, trying to figure a solution. But only Basil could do that.

Ambrosia sauntered about the small platform as if it were hers. She glanced through the window to find what had to be a petrified Lydia Rose. "Who's that little lady?" she asked. "Is that your princess?" And then came the first time she locked eyes with Regis.

Unable to watch from a distance, Basil charged to Regis's balcony, too. Now the small space was cluttered with four. Regis tried to protect himself and assert simultaneously, but it didn't work. The choice was bravery or cowardice, and Regis chose the first. All of them were brave, except for the docile Lydia Rose, who'd noticeably given up. Basil peeked through the window to find her face attached to it, her features smushing up against the glass. Tears dripped alongside her flattened nose and chin.

"I did bring a sword just in case the opportunity presented itself." Ambrosia's eyes darted from Bridget to Basil. "Enchantment isn't everything, after all."

And from the pocket Basil hadn't noticed until this moment, Ambrosia pulled out a sword—but not just any old blade—the kings' sword. Its jewels gleamed though there was no sun to illuminate them. Every sapphire, amethyst, emerald . . . the same sword Regis had sliced Basil's bicep with . . . that he'd held to Haldi. That day felt like ages ago though it had barely been weeks.

"How in Philip's name do you have that?" Bridget positioned herself en garde.

"You ask your son nothing, do you? Would you be able to tell me even the first detail of his quest?"

Bridget fell silent.

"No wonder the boy wants to be noticed. Hmm. It's how I felt once, too." Ambrosia positioned herself just like Bridget, her sword pointed diagonally upward. "Your husband gave me the recognition I'd always longed for, and I thank him for that."

"You will not speak of my family in such a way." And Bridget managed the first swipe. But Ambrosia leapt away just in time. Basil and Regis leaned against the front two corners of the balcony, leaving space for the sword fight.

"I imagine you'd like a fair battle, so I'll use no enchantment, yes?"

"This foolish enchantment you speak of—it does not exist."

"Careful now, Bridget. I didn't think you'd want me to prove it. But perhaps I was wrong."

"No!" Basil interjected, knowing full well what Ambrosia implied. "You don't need to prove anything."

"Do not dare to call me anything but Your Majesty or *Queen*."

"As you wish, *Bridget*."

The queen slashed her sword again in a fit of rage, and their motions continued like this. Still, neither of their blades met the other's skin.

And soon, there was another body on the balcony, another person occupying the limited space. But he brought valuable weaponry. Hadwin entered with three swords in hand. He rushed to the corners in which Basil and Regis stood, and supplied them each with a silver blade. It would be one against four. But that *one* wasn't just anybody.

Bridget was beginning to lose her breath as the aimless sword fighting went on. It seemed the same moves repeated themselves, and the match would never end. Her body and strength were weakening.

"I can assist," Hadwin said.

Bridget nodded as no words would escape her mouth. Hadwin swiftly took her spot. He caught Ambrosia off guard with swipes she wasn't used to. And Hadwin deflected each of her hits.

He thrust his sword toward her shoulder, but she pivoted away.

Hadwin followed her, his sword at long point; if she were to move an inch forward, the blade would pierce her chest. So, at last, Ambrosia skidded to a halt, cornered. Hadwin grabbed the kings' sword from her hand and pointed it at her heart—if she even had one.

All was well now that the kings' sword was in a royal's possession—or so he thought. Ambrosia wore a defeated facade as she fell to her bum, swordless. Regis's foot, forcefully remaining on Ambrosia's chest, ensured she wouldn't move. Hadwin and Bridget then ran into the chamber to comfort a distraught Lydia Rose. Though Ambrosia was pinned down, she cast a golden hue on the doors of Regis's chamber, locking up Hadwin and Bridget along with their three swords.

Too quickly to process, her claw-like nails tightly grabbed Regis's foot. He tried to shimmy from her tight grip, but it was no use, and Ambrosia pulled on it so hard that he fell to the ground, too.

Basil sprinted toward his brother and grabbed onto his shoulders. He pulled his brother backward, but he wouldn't budge.

"He's done nothing to you. *Release* your hands."

Even summoning the enchantment seemed impossible; the boy couldn't focus, and it was especially difficult when Ambrosia was using hers, too—even if it was fading. Now Regis was caught in Ambrosia's hold, while Bridget and Hadwin just began to notice that the fight wasn't over, and they couldn't seem to escape onto the balcony. The two of them pounded on the glass.

Regis still held his sword away from his chest, in line with the small space between Ambrosia's dark eyebrows.

"Let go of me," were the first words Regis muttered to her. Basil wondered what it felt like for Regis to see her for the first time.

Ambrosia chuckled. "And why would I listen to you? You have no authority, but even if you were king, I still would not obey your petty demands."

"Bastard from hell!" Regis shrieked. Ambrosia released his foot and pinned his chest to the ground. All the while, her hands enclosed Regis's, making it impossible for him to stab the blade.

Ambrosia's laughs turned deafening, and she grabbed on the hilt of Regis's sword. Her movement was too quick for him to prepare, and the silver sword was quickly in her hands.

For an instant, Basil's gaze shifted between Hadwin and Bridget inside, and Regis and Ambrosia on the balcony. The two adults pressed their hands against the door, watching helplessly. Lydia was a mess of tears and hiccups, muffled through the door. Ambrosia was about to—

Liquid splattered across Basil's cheek. It was a deep purplish-red—blood. It wasn't draining in slow motion like Scarlett's, no. Startled at finding his identical twin's innards and what had to be partially digested eggplant strewn about the golden balcony, Basil's blood froze inside his veins.

And then a piercing shriek. It came from inside the chamber—Lydia Rose.

Pure rage and terror mixed in Bridget's irises.

"You did not," Basil whispered. His sword slipped out of his shaky hands as he sprinted to his brother.

Ambrosia beamed, admiring the blade, which was jabbed through Regis's stomach. "You are correct. Your brother isn't gone." And she pulled out the blood-encrusted weapon. Basil could barely look at it without a sudden urge to puke.

"Shut your mouth, and *never* come back again!" He couldn't cry; there were no tears left.

"I'm speaking the truth. But there is only one way to save him. And with you as a brother, he might as well be dead."

"Shut up!"

"If you crave your brother's death, I will do as you wish."

She made no sense—sputtered nonsense. But if there was any hope, Basil had to try. "How do you suppose I can save him? For goodness' sake. I have lumps of his intestines smeared on my face," he said, wiping away some gray and bloody insides from his cheek.

"Unlike Scarlett, your brother is not dead. Not yet."

"Why would you—"

"But you only have moments to save him."

Basil tried focusing on his brother's body. He tried to create that golden hue that had been so easy in times before. His brother still had a heartbeat—slowing, but existent . . . just barely existent.

"It's not working," Basil whispered to himself. "Regis is dead. Regis is . . . He's . . ." Basil wouldn't admit it aloud, but it would deem his entire mission useless; if his brother were to die, Basil would become the heir anyway. Still, it was only part of the reason he didn't want his brother gone.

Glass shattered behind him. Bridget, Hadwin, and Lydia escaped from the window of Regis's chamber, fragments stabbing at them. Basil should've used the key to unlock the door, but it was too late.

"A word of advice?" Ambrosia offered when the noise from the glass stopped.

"You've ruined my life enough. I don't need to hear another word from your filthy lips." But if there was any chance at saving his brother, he needed to hear it. The hand without a sword clenched into a fist. "What do you have to say this time?"

"Only the holder of the key can protect his own life." Slowly, calmly, she spoke the words Basil didn't want to hear.

Hadwin inched toward her with the kings' sword but didn't strike—not yet; Ambrosia's words would be the only way to save Regis.

"What are you suggesting?" But he already knew. The only way to save Regis was to sacrifice everything he'd worked so hard for.

Regis, with his shaking hands, reached for his brother's fingers as he neared his death. "Please be good to Silverkeep," he managed, choking on his words. "I trust you'll do great things, brother."

It couldn't end like this. Bridget and Hadwin loomed over a dying Regis. Lydia might've been there, too, but Basil wasn't sure; everything—his whole world—was a blur in those few moments. He had to act fast. The hardest decision of his life gave him only seconds to think; Regis would be dead for good in moments. Why was Ambrosia so evil? Why did she have the desire to ruin Basil's life for sport?

If Basil saved Regis, it would make his entire journey futile. Scarlett wouldn't have had to die for him. Basil wouldn't have had to abandon the castle. He wouldn't have had to fall in love and have it ripped away from him. But key or no key, the lessons and love Golden Grove had taught him were invaluable.

He couldn't let Regis die. He couldn't live with that guilt. He couldn't let another perish because of his mistakes. And, though he would never say it, Basil loved his brother. He loved their banter, their resemblance, and most of all, he loved to hate him. Basil couldn't live with no one to infuriate him.

"Of course, I expected you to make the petty decision. I was curious, but you've proved me right as I—"

Basil took his trembling right hand and reached for his nostril.

"Picking your nose, how kingly," Ambrosia sneered.

But he yanked the gold and emerald beauty from his nose and hardly cared about the goo that surrounded it. It was his last chance to be moral. And when Basil placed the slimy key—that was all it was, a lousy piece of metal—into his brother's palm, Basil knew he'd made the right decision. He stood in front of his brother, powerless, guarding the key from Ambrosia.

"You could kill me now if you wanted to," said Basil.

She laughed. "I wouldn't just kill you for no reason."

"You killed Scarlett for no reason."

"No, I killed Scarlett to scare you into returning the key. Of course, it didn't work, but at least it hurt your feelings. What good would killing you now do?"

"You're sick."

Regis's healing was the most beautiful image, as if his body were sewn, and all his blood and entrails were stored back in their correct positions. Regis's eyes fluttered open, and he let out a cough of blood—just one cough.

Lydia's cries suddenly calmed. They'd been in the background for so long that Basil had begun to treat them as ordinary white noise.

"Brother?" Regis V whispered, his voice rich with life.

"Oh, thank goodness." And Basil, balanced on his knees, leaned over to hug his brother for the second time that day, his eyes sweaty.

"An act of loyalty. I wasn't expecting it, but I applaud you. Truth be told, I don't mind he's alive." Ambrosia's hair fell to her sides, and the flames left them. "I expect you'll give me the key now." She flattened her palm in front of Regis, but he tightened his fist and pulled it away.

"After that? You expect me to—"

But Regis's words were interrupted by a growling Bridget. "Finish her," she whispered to Hadwin.

The noble advisor nodded and lunged toward Ambrosia, who was still seated on her buttocks. But quickly, she hurried to her feet. She had Regis's blade, scrawny and silver compared to the kings' sword, which Hadwin held, but would do the job nonetheless.

Basil and Regis rested on the ground.

Still, the thunder boomed, and the lightning surged through the night sky. It all intensified when Hadwin pounced at Ambrosia. It was as if the storm was a direct reflection of her anxious heartbeat.

Hadwin and Ambrosia were in fair opposition this time, rather equal in skill; his hits no longer startled her. So when he made for her shoulder, Hadwin's female counterpart expected it.

Basil could barely track the swipes . . . strikes . . . slashes . . . as each was over before it had started. And earlier than he could blink, Ambrosia had Hadwin in a headlock. The swords were on the floor, and Basil stared at the two of them, exhausted. All energy had left him when the key had. Bridget watched, too, her eyes bulging in terror.

Hadwin couldn't die—not tonight; who else would advise the king? Nobody had better judgment or more intelligence than Hadwin Timbers.

"I kicked you out of the castle once, and I'll do it again." Basil could just make out Bridget's whispers. "This time, though, I'll make sure you never return."

Ambrosia, her hand enclosing Hadwin's nape, was too distracted to consider that anyone else might have dared to cross her. But Bridget did just that.

The vicious queen darted toward her nemesis, jabbing her sword through Ambrosia's ribcage. The blade plunged through each bone, Ambrosia's sweet viscera decorating its edge.

And in this moment, Basil had never loved his mother more. He'd never noticed her strength . . . her courage. His mouth fell open. Bridget had done something Basil should've done ages ago, when he'd had the chance.

"You will pay. You will—this is not the end." Ambrosia choked, blood streaming from her mouth and stomach. Her hands found the crimson hole that split her body, and her palms became bloodied.

Her last few seconds on Earth were filled with deafening shrieks of pain and raucous cries of horror as she saw her trembling hands, covered in maroon—a sight thrilling yet repulsive to Basil.

Her body recoiled to the railing . . . and then over the railing. And the royals overtly watched bloody Ambrosia tumble through the black night and crash onto the cobblestone by the guards' feet.

The thunder settled.

The lightning stopped.

And that's when Basil knew—all of them knew—that contrary to Ambrosia's last words, it *was* the end. And it was marvelous.

 asil sat on the cushioned velvet chair with a direct view of the back of Regis's head . . . and the union of kingdoms, mumbling curiously amongst themselves. Days ago, Basil had thought he'd be sitting on that throne, preparing to utter an earnest speech, but things had changed in a blink.

Basil's hair had been cut the day before, and its floppy quality was lost. The brown waves parted in the middle, and his face was done up with waxy makeup. His cheeks felt stiff, imposing discomfort each time he ever-so-slightly moved or flinched his face muscles.

The echoing applause fell to a gradual halt as Bridget cleared her throat in the front of the stage-like platform. "It is with great honor and pride that I gather us here today," the queen announced, "to celebrate the commencement of my dear son's reign."

Bridget bowed her head of brown curls just enough to signal to the crowd, but the right amount to keep her sparkling tiara intact, and spread her arms side-to-side. Howling and claps spread throughout the auditorium. Subjects of Silverkeep along with authorities of the union filled up the vast space.

Basil was still in denial.

"Before the fifth Regis is crowned, he'd like to share a few words with his kind audience on this special day. He is aware that his coronation speech met the ears of most of you just last week, but he insisted he has some new knowledge."

It would've been Basil's introduction.

A rouge tunic gathered by Regis's nape—it was the same outfit Regis IV wore on his coronation day, and the king who preceded him, and so on. Some went so far as to say the blessed shawl of silk had met King Philip's shoulders, but it wasn't fact. In all his visions, Basil had expected the tunic to embrace his body, not the back of his brother.

Basil couldn't see Regis's face from his angle, for which he was glad; Basil didn't wish to see his sly eyes or triumphant grin. He hadn't come to terms with the twist of fate, and he wasn't sure he ever would. But still, a part of him was at ease.

On the throne beside Regis V—where Scarlett should've sat—was Lydia Rose, dressed in a white mantua gown with silver detailing. She sat like any other queen: regal, patient, and charming. Scarlett would've been more than a token of beauty. But she was dead.

All because of me.

"Thank you! Thank you, my loyal subjects and my virtuous equals from Silverkeep's allied kingdoms."

Damn it, his public speaking was perfect; he must've practiced enunciating thousands of times.

Regis embraced Bridget behind the podium and wiped the single tear that slid down his mother's face.

Basil should've been hugging her—*would've* been hugging her—instead.

"But the person that deserves my utmost gratitude," Regis said.

Oh, who will it be? Lydia Rose?

"Is my brother."

Basil froze. He knew full well how much he deserved it but, nonetheless, would never have expected his brother to acknowledge him, especially in front of the large audience.

"My reign will be unmatchable, all because of him. I will be ruling with King Philip's key."

Gasps spread through the crowd. All of them knew of the coveted, famous object, but nobody had believed it would be found—not after finding it had been deemed impossible for centuries to the point where it was believed to be myth.

"Yes, you've heard me correctly. I'm sure many of you know of Basil's unsuspected absence?" he asked rhetorically. "Well, he was on a grave mission. Basil is the last believer—a heroic, genius man. And it is thanks to him and his feat that I will rule so perfectly."

Regis had never spoken about Basil in such fashion.

"He shall go down in the storybooks . . . the history books that students will study in ages to come. This man restored the magic of Silverkeep. You all may be skeptical of enchantment, but listen well, for I had my doubts, too.

"Basil is the reason that I almost died a few nights ago but also the reason that I stand here today, minutes from becoming King of Silverkeep. But truth be told, he deserves this more than I do."

Yes, Regis's words were good natured, but they didn't compensate for making Basil's entire journey useless. Still, it was the first bit of kindness Regis had shown him recently.

The days since Ambrosia's death had drifted by, feelings of sourness and decency alternating in Basil's mind. Regis had pestered him to teach the inner workings of the key, but Basil had barely had time to learn for himself. The only knowledge Basil had shared with Regis was of his journey. He needed to confide in somebody, and his brother was more than willing to listen. So Basil told him about Scarlett . . . Ambrosia . . . the nymphs and satyrs . . . the clothes they wore and the ears they had.

The only good thing about that thunder-filled night was Ambrosia's death . . . and, well, Regis being saved. Ambrosia couldn't kill anyone else. There wouldn't be the voice screaming in the back of Basil's mind, worrying about the nymphs and satyrs; all of Golden Grove's inhabitants were finally safe from Ambrosia's rule. Still, it didn't make up for Scarlett's death, which replayed in Basil's mind several times a day.

"Though we are royals, our maturity, contrary to your potential assumptions, is not much better than any of yours— worse, I might add."

Bridget shot Regis a dim glare, but he chuckled. Both of the brothers did—a bit of light in the dark.

"Basil and I haven't been getting along recently." Not a hint of shame existed in his voice, and Basil loved it. "Even before my father's sudden death, our relationship was not what it could've been.

"Around a year ago, I did something terrible. Basil was in love with the princess of Lundbridge, the woman you all know as the new queen."

New queen? They must have gotten married while I was gone.

"I snatched her from my brother and never looked back, but now I do look back and wonder what life would be like if I hadn't taken her . . . if I hadn't ruined our bond."

Basil felt his cheeks blush a pinky hue, and Regis tilted his head for a moment to make eye contact with his brother. Regis wasn't at fault for being with Lydia Rose; Derek Searle had made the choice, but he was finally owning up to it, anyway.

Basil knew now that he'd never been in love with Lydia Rose. They'd shared a brief infatuation but nothing more. What she had with Regis might be different. But love or not, Lydia Rose and Regis's romance no longer mattered to Basil.

"I'm not saying I have regrets—I don't." Regis's gaze turned to Lydia Rose for a brief moment. "Because I would give anything for this princess . . . this queen. But I do wish it didn't take a near-death experience to mend our brotherhood."

Regis was certainly oversharing with his audience, but they seemed intrigued. And so was Basil. Perhaps, Regis was always meant to be king. Perhaps, Basil was simply not the heir. And perhaps, everything did happen for a reason—though Basil would never find Scarlett's death anything but brutal. Still, even if it took Basil all he went through just to understand that his brother was meant to be king, it wasn't for nothing. The royals had the key; Ambrosia could do no more harm, and above all, Basil had undeniably learned love—of Scarlett and of his brother.

But still, changing for the better isn't worth a dead body.

"Ambrosia Cromwell, my father's mis—an evil woman." Regis caught himself before revealing a secret Bridget would not have wanted him to share. "She tried to kill me. In fact, I was sure, just like everyone surrounding my bloody body, that I was moments from death. Everything became blurry. And I said to my brother something along the lines of, 'Be a great king for Silverkeep.' The next thing I knew—"

"Please be good to Silverkeep. I trust you'll do great things, brother," Basil muttered from his seat. He hadn't forgotten his brother's words. Of course he hadn't . . . couldn't.

"What was that?"

"Please be good to Silverkeep. I trust you'll do great things, brother." Basil announced his recollections louder this time. It was an unconventional interruption, but nothing about Regis's speech was standard.

"Yes, that was it," Regis stuck up his index finger. "Well, I suspect I'm boring the lot of you, but let me leave you all with this: I've come so very far. We all have. But there's a great distance I'm yet to go. So, let us get on with the coronation, shall we?"

Bridget slapped her forehead, incredibly bothered by her

son's unprofessionalism. The speech should've been more formally concluded, and more formal in general. Perhaps it had been his intention to piss off Bridget.

Regis turned around and sauntered to his royal seat. It wasn't the official throne—that one was in the throne room, not the auditorium—but it was a throne nonetheless, portable but still exquisite.

Bridget swallowed her pride and remained seated while Hadwin emerged from his chair. In his hands was the crown, sitting atop the soft velvet cushion. Its chip had been easily fixed by the metalsmiths, who had repaired the diadem the night they discovered the crack. The castle servants were always on top of things.

"Blessed be our new king, Regis Avington the fifth," Hadwin said, as he'd practiced over and over, careful not to mess up the nine words.

"Blessed be our new king, Regis Avington the fifth," the crowd repeated in unison. This was it—the words Basil had had nightmares about. But they weren't as intimidating as he'd suspected. In fact, Basil found himself mumbling along with the audience. And Regis, noticing his brother's sincerity, turned around and managed a soft smile. It was the purest, most genuine expression Basil had ever seen on his brother's face.

The bejeweled crown was placed neatly on Regis's head, and heavy applause reverberated through the auditorium. It was so surreal, yet the realest moment of Basil's life.

That darned happy grin wouldn't leave Regis's face, but it barely bothered Basil.

Only the authorities of the union of kingdoms were invited

to the post-coronation celebratory dinner. Basil was seated at a circular marble table, Regis on one side and Derek Searle on the other.

Roasted pheasant sat on all of their plates, decorated with some type of tawny brown sauce. Most of the dishes were finished with only drips of sauce remaining. But Basil couldn't bear to eat a bird, not after seeing Golden Grove . . . not after Zena. And each time he looked at the pheasant, for some reason Scarlett's death replayed in his head. Not her death, but finding her pale and bloodied, rather—the empty look in her eyes, the asymmetrical braids in her hair.

Stop it, Basil. Celebrate.

"For goodness' sake, eat already," Bridget said, glaring at Basil's untouched plate. They were the same words Bridget had uttered the night of Regis's death, the same words that had started it all. And now, it was the end of all that—Basil's quest, his spite toward his brother, his sourness, almost completely gone.

"I'm sorry, Mother, I'm not hungry." Quite literally, he couldn't stomach a bird.

Bridget rolled her eyes but did nothing more.

Derek was still chewing on the pheasant but cut through the silence. The Lundbridge king glanced at Lydia Rose and Regis, their fingers interlaced. Basil wasn't jealous, but happy for his brother.

"You two will have a charmed reign, now won't you?" Bird parts swarmed around Derek's mouth as he spoke.

And it was the first time Basil agreed with Derek. Regis and Lydia giggled, on the threshold of their fabulous rule. The prince Basil would not be forgotten—not after succeeding in the single greatest achievement Silverkeep had ever seen. And from then on, Regis was no longer his enemy but truly his brother, not only biologically, but at heart. The skilled carpenters soon built Basil a luxurious velvet throne to sit beside Regis, almost like a king.

Hadwin, Basil, and Bridget assisted his reign.

A reign that would be difficult to match.

THE END

ACKNOWLEDGEMENTS

There's not enough gratitude in my heart to thank you for reading Basil's story. It's still crazy to think that you spent your time and energy reading my words. You made my dream come true. It's scary to put my work out there for anyone to read, but I hope you enjoyed it! I've put months of hard work into many drafts—and I couldn't have done it alone.

First of all, thank you to my family. Mom, you always believe in me, even when I don't. You've taught me to shoot for the stars, and I'm so thankful for your constant support. Dad, you were the first (besides me) to read Not the Heir, and your input meant the world to me. You always seem to have the best ideas, and you push me to keep going. Sasha, my favorite (and only) sister, you make me laugh until I cry. Throughout this process, you've been my personal cheerleader. I love all of you infinitely.

Rachel Dean and Léna Roy, thank you for helping me craft Not the Heir. You pointed out plot holes and provided great ideas to make the story more compelling.

To my editor, Maggie Morris, no words can thank you enough. You polished this story into what it is today. You're truly an amazing editor!

Thank you, Stefanie Saw, for creating a cover more beautiful than I ever could've imagined. Thank you, Enchanted Ink Publishing, for transforming my words into a comprehensible novel.

I wouldn't have been able to write this without AuthorTube. I'm so thankful that I've discovered an amazing online community of writers. Your live write-ins motivated me to keep going. My author friends are the greatest role-models.

I also want to thank all of my friends that supported me every step of the way. You guys deserve the world. Thank you!

ABOUT THE AUTHOR

If you enjoyed this book, please take a moment to leave a review on Amazon and Goodreads.

You can learn more about Hudson Warm at www.hudsonwarm.com

or find her @hudsonwarmbooks on Instagram

Printed in the USA
CPSIA information can be obtained
at www.ICGtesting.com
LVHW092254191023
761630LV00023B/387